I dedicate *this book to my daughter Kerri-Ann.*

Also to the Turbosisters, Sandra & Marlene.

This book is written in memory of one of the finest Gentlemen I have ever had the pleasure to know.

Billy Kerr.

PREFACE

Due to the increase of violence in Northern Ireland the upper echelons of the British Intelligence MI5 and Army Intelligence (14 Intelligence group), had a meeting to discuss what action could be taken to stop the murders and quell the violence being orchestrated by the paramilitary organisations.

All of the recent murders were discussed and it became apparent that the majority of them were being carried out in the County of Armagh, mainly South Armagh, more commonly known as **BANDIT COUNTRY.**

A member of British Intelligence asked for the latest reports on the area.

The reply to his request shocked him, for it was found that there were no up to date reports on the movement of the local terrorists, their weapons, or supplies.

It was suggested that a member of the British Army Elite Special Air Service (SAS) could be covertly placed in the Armagh area to gather such desperately needed information.

This would mean that the soldier would probably have to spend the rest of his Army career in Northern Ireland.

He would have to take up residence in the Province; also he would not be living in an Army camp but out in a town or village and become a part of the community.

After the meeting had ended one of the Intelligence members made contact with the Commanding Officer of the 22nd SAS Regiment based in Hereford, who on hearing what had been decided at the meeting, though very sceptical, agreed to put the idea to his men.

He put out a request for any volunteers for the job on the Regiments part one orders; one of his men called Ray Rutherford jumped at the chance to do something more challenging, he felt he was cut out for this type of work and would be glad to get away from Hereford to do more than just training.

Rather than have a man go over to the Province and just appear in the area, it was decided that he would go over as a member of a Regiment that carried out a long tour of duty.

Ray Rutherford was from a Corps that trained Army dogs to work in Northern Ireland, so he wouldn't stand out, as everyone knew that the dog handlers spent more time over there than any other soldier did.

A plan was devised in which he would return to his parent Corps where he would on his arrival request a posting to Northern Ireland to work as a search dog handler.

This would give him plenty of time to build up his cover. When he first arrived in the province he became the Non Commissioned Officer (NCO) in charge of the dog section based in Drumadd Barracks on the outskirts of Armagh City, the Barracks were the home of the 2nd Battalion of the Ulster Defence Regiment (UDR).

Ray's working day was from eight o'clock in the morning until four o'clock in the afternoon, which meant that providing there weren't many call outs he would be free most nights.

It is left to the reader to discern as to whether this book is fact or fiction?

CHAPTER – 1 – SETTLING IN

After about a week in Drumadd Barracks Ray learned that there was a bar in the UDR part of the camp.
One of his dog handlers a man called Sid, was a member of the Regiment, Ray asked him if the bar was open to non-members of the UDR and if he would also be allowed to drink in the place.

"Yeah no problem, I was thinking of going there myself for a pint tonight, I'd be pleased to take you along, if you want?" Sid says.

"What time shall we meet? and where?" Ray enquired.
"I'll meet you here at about eight, or is that too early?"
"No, that's fine by me, it'll give me plenty of time for the three S's you know, a shit, shower, and shave," Ray mused.

"By the way put on some nice smelly after shave, 'cause there'll be a few bits of skirt in there tonight, you never know you might be able to chat one up?" Sid informed him.

"We'll have to see about that?"

"Why? Are you married or something?"

"No, but knowing my luck I'd probably try and chat one up that has a husband or boyfriend that's built like the proverbial brick shithouse," Ray smiled.

Having said goodbye to Sid with the agreement that they would both meet later that night Ray went back to his room to get his knife fork and spoon and his cup to go for his evening meal in the cookhouse.

As he sat eating his meal it occurred to him that if he did actually manage to chat up one of the girls in the bar and she took a fancy to him it would be a good start to his cover build up.

He would obviously have to try and get a woman that didn't look like the back end of a bus or was a real monster to look at, after all even though he was a soldier he did have some pride and he would only want a good looking woman.

At roughly a quarter to eight he went to the dog section office, which was down a hill from his room, it was a dry sunlit evening, on arriving at the kennels he found Sid already there waiting for him.

"Are you ready?" Sid asked sounding keen to get going.

"Yep, let's go, I'm dying for a Bacardi and coke," Ray answered.

"I hope it's more than just one?"

"I think I could squeeze in more than one, but it just depends on how things go?" Ray told him.

"That's good come on let's go, I can hear those beer pumps calling me," Sid says leading the way.

As they entered the bar it seemed to Ray that everybody's eyes were turned in their direction, Sid walked up to the bar and ordered the drinks, while they were waiting for them Sid started to talk to some of the people nearby.

"This is Ray he's my new boss," he introduced Ray to some of them.

The group of people that Sid had introduced Ray to was made up of a mixture of men and women, they all shook his hand in welcome, one of the women that shook his hand seemed to hold onto his for a little longer than the rest of the group.

"Are you a member of the Regiment? or a wife?" Ray asked her.

"I'm a full time member, I work in the Intelligence section, to save you any more trouble, my name's Pauline, I'm twenty five years old, I'm not married, or engaged, and I'm definitely not a lesbian, is there anything else you'd like to know?" she replied.

"As a matter of fact there is, what does your boyfriend do?"

"I haven't got one, why?" she wanted to know.

"I was just curious as to why a good looking girl like you

isn't married," Ray answered.

"I suppose you're one of these men who think a woman of my age should be at home with a load of screaming kids around her feet?"

"I hope you two aren't going to fight?" Sid says joining them.

"If you'll excuse me, I have to go back over and join my friends," Pauline says turning away from them.

"What do you think of her then?" Sid asked Ray.

"She's a bit stuck up, but apart from that I think she's lovely, where has she been all my life?"

"Probably hiding," Sid laughed.

Pauline was just what Ray had been looking for, not only was she good looking but she also worked in the Intelligence section, this would be very handy because the information he could glean from her would be first class.

It was well known that the Intelligence gathered by the UDR was always first class, this was because the men in the UDR were always from the town or area that they worked in, they knew nearly everything that happened, or every person in their patch.

"Come over here and let us have a little chat Sid," Ray says moving over to a table and sitting down.

"I bet I know what this conversation is going to be about?" came from Sid as he sat down opposite Ray.

"If you don't then you're thicker than I thought," Ray smiled.

"Before you start Ray, she isn't married, she's not divorced, she's got no kids, she hasn't got any boyfriend that I know of, she's probably never been screwed," Sid joked.

"What do you think are my chances of getting off with her," Ray quizzed him.

"As far as I know she's not interested in anybody on the camp, so all I can suggest is go for it my man."

"I'll leave it for now, if she's in anyway interested in me she'll be back for a little bit more of a chat."

"She must be a bit interested, because since we've been sat here she keeps glancing over," Sid informed him.

Just then the door of the bar opened and another man walked in, after a quick look around the bar he saw Pauline and waved over to her, she returned his wave then got up from her seat and walked over to talk to him.

"The guy who's just walked in must be in with a chance?" Ray pointed out to Sid.

"If he does then he's into incest, because that's her brother Mervyn, he's a good friend of mine, we used to work together until I became a dog handler."

When Mervyn had received the drink he had ordered he walked over to where Ray and Sid were sitting.

"Well what about ya?" he asked Sid.

"Not too bad, what about you?" Sid replied.

"You know me I'm still ticking along, who's your mate?" Mervyn asked pointing at Ray.

"Ray this is Mervyn, Mervyn this is Ray, now that the introductions are over who wants another drink?" Sid says getting up from his seat.

"I'll have one more then I'll have to go," Ray told him holding out his empty glass.

"None for me I'm only having the one then I'm off down town," Mervyn declined the offer.

While Sid was at the bar Mervyn started to talk to Ray.

"How long have you been over here?" he enquired.

"I only came last week."

"Is this your first tour?"

"No I was over here before in Londonderry three weeks after Bloody Sunday."

"I wouldn't have liked to have been up in Londonderry then," Mervyn sympathised.

"Let's just say it wasn't a pleasant place to be," Ray

agreed.

At this point Sid returned to their table with the drinks.

"I hope you two are getting on OK?" he says sitting back down.

"We're getting on great, aren't we Ray?

"Yep, no problems," Ray confirmed.

"So what do you do on the camp?" Mervyn continued to quiz Ray.

"I'm working with the dog section."

"Yeah he's my new boss," Sid put in.

Before anyone could say another word a female voice came from behind Ray.

"Can we join you Mervyn?"

When Ray turned to see who it might be, he saw Pauline with two of her friends.

"Yes by all means join us," Mervyn replied, when they had sat down he went on to introduce Ray to them.

"This is---?" was as far as he got before Pauline said.

"We've already been introduced, nice to meet you again Ray." Pauline interrupted him.

"I seem to be wasting my time so I'd better keep my mouth shut," Mervyn said sounding a little bit put out.

"It's not often we see you in here, to what do we owe this pleasure?" Pauline said to her brother.

"I was at a loose end so I thought that I'd come in here to see who's about and get a quick pint in the process, before I went down town," he told her.

"It's fairly boring in here tonight," one of the other girls whose name was Barbara says.

"Tell you what why don't we all go down town with Mervyn? It might be a bit livelier than it is here," Sid suggested.

"Do you fancy coming with us?" Pauline asked Ray.

"I don't think I'd be able to get permission to go off camp at this time of the night. It's all right for you lot you can go off camp anytime you like, but never mind the next time you decide to have a night on the town give me plenty of notice, thanks for the offer though," he told her.

"If that's the case then I'll stay here with you, you can't sit drinking on your own, we'll all go out on the town some other night," Sid says.

"I was going back to my room anyway, like I said I'm only having this drink then I'm off, you go with Mervyn and the girls I'll see you in the morning," Ray said.

After they had left Ray finished his drink and went back to his room.

On his arrival at the kennels office the next morning Sid was already there waiting for him.

"Hi Ray you missed a good night, I didn't get in till two o'clock this morning, it's a pity you couldn't have come with us," he says.

"If I'd have known earlier I would have seen about getting clearance, but trying to get it at ten o'clock at night it's a bit hard to do."

"We'll have to arrange another night soon, I'll tell you all about what happened last night when I come back from walking my dog, see you shortly," Sid says walking away with his dog.

Ray went into the kennels office picked up the telephone and rang the camps Intelligence Officer (I.O.) to get permission to be able to leave the camp at any time.

"Good morning I.O. speaking?"

"Good morning Sir, it's Corporal Rutherford here from the dog section."

"Yes what can I do for you?" the I.O. asks.

"I would like to ask for permission to be able to go off camp in my free time, because I have made some friends in the local UDR," Ray explained.

"It's completely unnecessary for you to ask permission, I know why you have been sent here and to be honest with you if you want to go off camp no-one can stop you."

"I was only checking to be on the safe side," Ray told him.

"Well that's it in a nutshell, all I can say is that you don't go off camp unless you're armed," the I.O. advised.

"You've no need to worry about that, thanks a lot Sir, goodbye," Ray said as he replaced the receiver.

A couple of minutes after this Sid came into the office whistling like a Canary, he took off his Combat jacket, folded it, placed it on a desk then sat down in one of the easy chairs, with a poor imitation of a British Comedians voice Max Bygraves said.

"Lemme tell you a story Ray, after we left here we all went down to the Wagon Wheel pub, boy did we have quite a few drinks and a good sing song, Pauline must be quite interested in you because she done nothing but give me ear ache all bloody night asking questions about you."

"What sort of questions?"

"Things like were you married, engaged, courting, or divorced, how old were you, how long had you been in the Army, you know all that sort of crap."

"What did you tell her?"

"I told her that it's best if she asked you all these questions herself, then I wouldn't end up in the shit if I told her something wrong."

"That's good, so no doubt it looks as though I'm in with a chance," Ray said feeling pleased.

"Honest to God she never shut up about you," Sid moaned.

"When do you think I might get to see her again?"

"You might get to see her in the NAAFI (Navy, Army, Air Force, Institute) Canteen when she goes there for her coffee break at ten thirty," Sid informed him.

"That's nice to know, what's the time now?"

"It's a quarter past ten now, if you keep your eye on that

brown coloured door over there you'll see her coming out through it very shortly," Sid says pointing at the door that he had just mentioned.

Ray sat in a position so that he could keep an eye on the door, a few minutes before ten thirty he saw Pauline coming through it with a friend.

The route that they would have to take to the NAAFI would mean that they would have to pass the dog section office, so he waited for them.

When he felt that they were near enough he told Sid to accompany him then stepped out of the office and started to walk in the direction of the NAAFI, making out that he hadn't seen Pauline and her friend.

"Good morning and how are you today?" he heard Pauline ask.

Ray stopped and turned to look in her direction.

"Oh! Hi there, I'm fine and how are you?" he said trying to sound surprised.

"I'm Okay, where are you going?"

"We're off to the NAAFI for a cuppa," he told her.

"Would you mind if we went with you?"

"As a matter of fact I'd be quite pleased, it would brighten my day," Ray said.

When they reached the NAAFI Ray went to the counter and ordered a cup of coffee for all of them, when they had been made he carried them on a tray to the table that the others were sitting at.

"You missed a good night, last night," Pauline told Ray.

"So I have been told by Sid it would appear that I did, but never mind I made a telephone call this morning to get clearance to leave camp and was told that I could leave camp anytime I wished," he informed her.

"What else was Sid telling you?" she asked looking Sid straight in the eye.

"Now that is for me to know and for you to try and find out," Ray smiled.

"If he opened his mouth about any of our conversation last night I'll kill him," she glared at Sid.

After a little thought Ray plucked up the courage and asked Pauline,

"Is there any chance of you and I going out together for a drink sometime?"

"I thought you'd never ask, if you want we could go for a drink tonight," she said looking very pleased.

"Where shall we go?" he asked.

"We can go to a little pub in a village near here called Hamiltonsbawn."

"I have a bit of a problem though," Ray said.

"What's that? No don't tell me you've got your hair to wash." Pauline chuckled.

"The thing is, I haven't got a car here."

"That's no problem, I've got one, what time shall I meet you?" Pauline offers.

"How does eight o'clock sound?"

"Yeah that's okay with me."

"I'll be counting the minutes," Ray told her feeling over the moon.

"Where shall I pick you up?"

"At the kennels office would be fine," Ray says.

With their break over they both went their separate ways, later that evening Ray was so keen that he was at the kennels office fifteen minutes before Pauline was due, this gave him a chance to sit and think about the relationship that he was about to embark on.

He came to the decision that he would wait for a few weeks to get to really know Pauline and then unbeknown to her he would try and get her to show him around the area that he would be operating in.

At approximately five minutes past eight he saw Pauline's car drive in through the camp gates and proceed down towards the kennels office, when she reached it she sounded her car horn and Ray went out to the car, as he opened the cars door Pauline said.

"I'm sorry that I'm a little late, have you been waiting long?"

"No I've only just arrived myself," Ray lied.

"That's good, come on let's get going," she said putting the car into gear.

They drove out through the camp gates and headed for the pub that Pauline was taking him to, as they travelled she told Ray.

"We might see my brother Mervyn where we are going tonight, while we were having our evening meal at home he asked me what I was going to be doing when I told him that I had a date he wanted to know who with, all I told him was where we were going."

"He probably won't bother coming to the pub, I would imagine that the last thing on his mind would be to see who his sister is going out with," Ray said secretly hoping that Mervyn wouldn't show up.

When they reached the pub Pauline led the way into the bar, Ray felt a little uneasy and his eyes flicked around the premises to take in all of the faces of the people in the place.

Pauline noticing Ray's uneasiness stood beside him and took hold of his hand.

"Relax Ray, I've already scanned the bar, there's no one in here that'll do us any harm," She told him.

When they had gotten the drinks that they had ordered they went to sit in a cosy corner of the bar where they could keep an eye on the entrance door, this was so that they would be able to see who was coming in and out.

They had a nice night and Ray told her all about himself, except of course that he was a member of the SAS and the real reason for his being in the province, things went quite well and the relationship blossomed.

Nearly six weeks after they had started to see each other Pauline told Ray that her mother and father wanted to meet him and that he was invited for Sunday dinner, when that day came Ray met her at the kennels office, he had in his hand a big bouquet of flowers and a box of chocolates.

"Oh! Darling they're lovely, are they for me?" she asked jokingly.

"You know they're not, I got them for your mum."

"Why? Are you after my mum?" she still joked.

"Only if she's better than you," Ray retorted.

"I must tell her that."

"You'd better not," he says taking hold of her arm and giving it a light squeeze.

"If you give me a kiss I'll let you off," she blackmailed. Ray leaned across to give her just a peck but it turned into a full-blown necking session, just as things were starting to get really hot a soldier who was walking past the car let out a loud whistle; this brought the matter to an abrupt end.

After sorting herself out Pauline started up the car and they drove out of camp, when they arrived at her home, her father and mother met them both at the house front door.

Ray had seen her father before on the camp and as far as he could remember he had been wearing a uniform.

"Ray this is my father Billy, and my mother Elizabeth," she introduced them.

"You can call me Bet," her mother told him.

"How do you do?" Ray said shaking their hands.

"Don't just stand there come on in," Billy said putting his hand on Ray's shoulder and ushering him into the house. When they entered the living room Ray offered over the chocolates and flowers to Bet.

"I would like you to accept these as appreciation for inviting me to dinner," he said.

"Why thank you very much, you're a real gentleman," she replied holding the flowers to her nose to smell them.

"Watch out I think he's after you mum," Pauline laughed.

"Don't embarrass the poor fellow, you can come and help me in the kitchen while your father and Ray have a drink and a chat," Bet told her.

When they had both left the room Billy pointed to an arm chair saying, "Sit down Ray, what will you have to drink?"

"I don't really drink a lot, but if you had a glass of Coke I wouldn't say no."

"I think we can manage that," Billy says opening a drinks cabinet.

"Tell me something Billy, haven't I seen you on the camp in uniform?" Ray queried.

"Yes you have, I've also seen you a couple of times as well," Billy replied.

"I wasn't exactly sure whether it was you or not?" Ray says.

"I'm only a part time member of the Regiment, more commonly known as weekend warriors, I hold the rank of Captain, Mervyn is a full time member as is Pauline I became a part time member after they disbanded the 'B' Specials, I used to be a Sub-District Commandant in them."

This was good for Ray to hear, all he had to do now was to keep his relationship with Pauline going because then not only was his cover good, but he would also have people whom he could tap for information.

Ray spent nearly all of his free time at Pauline's house and in the course of a few of his conversations he would drop the occasional hint that he was thinking of leaving the Army.

Pauline was so much in love with him that she told him how much it would please her if he did leave the Army as it would break her heart when it came time for his tour of duty to end.

"What would I do if I did leave the Army?" he asked her.

"You could always transfer across to the UDR."

Ray didn't like this idea, as it would mean that his records would be sent to the UDR and this wouldn't do his cover much good.

"I wouldn't like to leave the Army just to have to start all over again," he told her hoping that it would put the subject out of her mind.

"What about joining the Police or Prison Service?" she suggested.

"I don't think I would be brainy enough for them," he said, however he knew that getting into either of the jobs would be no problem with the backup of Army Intelligence.

"You never know till you've tried, we could go down to the Police Station and make a few enquiries."

"I suppose I could give it a try, shall we go there now?" Ray said getting up from his chair.

At the Police Station they spoke to the Station Sergeant who told Ray how to go about joining the Police, the Royal Ulster Constabulary, prior to leaving the Station the Sergeant handed Ray an application form.

Pauline was over the moon she couldn't wait to get back home to help Ray fill it in, while they were doing this Bet came home from work.

"Hello what are you two doing?" she enquired.

"You'll never guess what? Ray's going to leave the Army and live over here," Pauline told her excitedly.

"If you do what'll you do for a living?" Bet asked.

"At the moment I'm thinking of applying to join the RUC," Ray answered.

"That would be a good job, that's if they take you in," Bet said sounding sceptical.

"Well if you're not in you can't win, we can but try," Pauline says.

"Like Pauline says all I can do is try," Ray told her

continuing to fill the form in.

Roughly three weeks after sending the application form off to the RUC recruiting branch Ray received word that he had to attend an interview with a Police recruiting Sergeant in Portadown Police Station and sit a Police entrance exam.

During the course of the interview he told the Sergeant that his tour of duty with the Army was to shortly terminate and he would be sent back to England, the Sergeant assured him that he would be sent notification as to which way his application went anyway.

Two weeks after his interview Ray returned to England, he didn't go back to the SAS in Hereford, instead he went back to his old Corps Headquarters (HQ) where he let it become known that he was leaving the Army and joining the RUC.

The reason for this was that just in case anybody from his Corps was to come across him in Northern Ireland they wouldn't become suspicious.

A month following his return to his Corps HQ Ray was notified that he was to attend another Interview at RUC headquarters in Lisnasharagh in Belfast, this was to be his final Interview.

Two weeks after this interview he was sent a letter telling him that he was to start his Police training three weeks later, he immediately let SAS headquarters know of this and his discharge procedure was speeded up.

When his final day came he drove from his Corps headquarters in Melton Mowbray, Leicestershire, to Stranraer in Scotland where he caught a ferry across to the port of Larne in Northern Ireland.

The ferry would make the crossing at two o'clock in the morning and would take four hours.

The reason for going from Stranraer was that if he went from Liverpool it would mean an all night crossing which to Ray was far too long, he wanted to get back to the

Province as soon as possible.

When he drove his car off the ferry he loved the feeling that he got, this was partly because he couldn't wait to be back with Pauline and also because this was a new adventure in his life.

He knew that Pauline would be waiting up for him to arrive as he had telephoned her earlier in the evening to tell her when he would roughly be arriving at the house. Three quarters of an hour after leaving the ferry Ray pulled up outside of the house,

Pauline came running out of the front door threw her arms around him and showered him with kisses.

"I'm so happy to see you again, every day seemed like a year, I've really missed you, I hope you never have to be away from me again," she said with a tear of happiness in her eye.

"I feel the same way," Ray says holding her tightly.

"Now we can make plans for our future together," she said.

Warning bells started to ring in Ray's ears, yes it was great to be missed but at the end of the day he had no intention of staying in the Province when his time in the Army was up.

That was IF he wanted to move on, it had been agreed that when he had finished serving with the Army he would be able to stay as a Policeman, however at this point in time he had only fourteen years left to serve as a soldier

Being as he was not going to start his Police training for another three weeks Pauline had asked to get some leave from the UDR, the three weeks were mostly spent driving around Armagh and visiting her relations.

On one of these days as they were driving through Armagh they were stopped at an Army vehicle checkpoint (VCP).

"Good morning, how are you?" the soldier who had

stopped them asked.

"We're fine thank you," Pauline replied.

"Do you have any form of identification (ID) on you please?" asks the soldier.

"I have my Army ID card with me, and this is my boyfriend he's just left the Army and is about to start training with the Police," she says handing the soldier her ID card.

"Do you have any ID on you please Sir?" the soldier says as he hands Pauline her ID card back.

"I only have my English driving licence on me, is that any good?" Ray says handing him his licence.

"Just a moment Sir," the soldier says as he took Ray's licence to show to another soldier who appeared to be in charge of the VCP.

"Could you get out of the car please Sir? I'd like to see you over here please," this other soldier asks Ray.

Ray started to get out of the car and at the same time so did Pauline.

"No you can stay where you are Miss, I only want to speak to Mister Rutherford," the soldier told Pauline as he and Ray moved to the back of the car out of earshot of her.

"Sorry to hassle you Ray, but I'm from 14 Int. Lisburn, I've been told to tell you that the new Intelligence Commanding Officer wants to see you, we've been doing VCP's around here for three days trying to catch you, now we can pack it all in," he smiled.

"When does the boss want to see me?" Ray enquired.

"He would like it as soon as possible (ASAP).

"It'll be difficult, Pauline's with me nearly all the time."

"I'll let him know when we get back, you'd better get back in the car before she becomes suspicious, good luck," the soldier says as Ray went back to the car.

"What did he want to speak to you about?" Pauline asked him as he closed the car door.

"He wanted to know how long I've been out of the Army and living over here," Ray lied.

"Did he tell you why he wanted to know?"

"Yes, to make sure that I wasn't still a serving soldier and wasn't over here without Authorisation or clearance," he spoofed her.

"I'll be glad when you get in the Police then you'll be able to show them your warrant card," Pauline said sounding annoyed.

Two days later Pauline was called into work as one of the other people in her office had gone off duty sick, this was the chance that Ray had been hoping for, no sooner had she left for work than Ray got into his car and drove to Lisburn.

Having knocked on his new Commanding Officers door he walked in.

"Good morning Sir, I believe you wanted to see me?" Ray says.

"Who are you?" the CO asks looking puzzled.

"I'm your sneaky beaky from South Armagh, Ray Rutherford."

"Ah! Yes, how do you do, we've never met before, I'm sorry to have to ask you to come here, it's just that I like to meet who is working for me," the CO says shaking Ray's hand.

"I'm sorry that I haven't been in to see you earlier but I've been a little bit tied up Sir."

"Why? is she into bondage?" the CO says laughing at his own joke.

"I don't know I've never asked her," Ray replied coldly.

"How is the relationship going? Any sound of wedding bells yet?"

"You've got to be joking Sir they're the last thing I want to hear."

"Good, just you remember what your job is over here, don't go falling hook line and aisle," the CO warned.

"What if I did Sir?" Ray asked curious.

"I wouldn't like to think that you were that stupid."

"She's a lovely woman, you couldn't blame a man for wanting to marry her," Ray said in defence.

"As a matter of fact that might be a good idea, your cover would be very complete if you did marry her," came from the CO.

"And what about when my Army service is up, it might mean that I'd have to stay in this God forsaken hole for the rest of my life."

"You could always divorce her, I'm sure the Army would help you pay for it being as they got you into it for the name of National Security," the CO says.

"I never thought of that, it would help wouldn't it?" Ray said ponderously.

"Just don't let it interfere with your task, because as soon as it does you're out of here, so I shall look forward to getting some good Intelligence reports from you then."

"You'll get plenty of them Sir I can assure you," Ray promised.

"Where's the little lady now?" the CO asked.

"She had to go into work today because someone in the office went off on the sick."

"That'll do for now, when you leave here go and find the IO I think he's wanting a word," the CO says ending the meeting.

Ray left the office and went in search of the IO, when he managed to track him down they went through the procedure that they would use for Ray to pass on the bits of intelligence that he had managed to gather.

The IO also informed him that the only people in the Police who would know of his true reason for being a cop would be the Chief Constable and his two assistant Chief Constables.

"The least amount of people who know about you the

better, your security is of the utmost importance," the IO told him."

"If anyone in authority takes a dislike to me and starts to make my life a misery, what then?" Ray wanted to know just in case he might happen to fall out with any senior ranks in the Police as he already knew that quite a few of them didn't like Englishmen being in the job.

"Then all you do is phone here and we'll get them sorted out, that's if you can't deal with it yourself."

"I suppose that you've already got it seen to what Station I'll be in?"

"You'll be stationed in Newry, it's all been arranged."

"Well that's it then, I'll see you when I've finished my training," Ray says getting up to leave.

"Have a nice time, see you soon good luck," the IO says raising his hand in a wave.

CHAPTER – 2 – SOUTH ARMAGH

When he had finished his Police training Ray started work as a Probation Police Constable in the town of Newry, being as Newry was a rather large shopping town near South Armagh a lot of the known terrorists from the area frequented the place.

Also a lot of terrorists from the town of Dundalk an IRA stronghold in the South of Ireland shopped there as well. Dundalk was always considered the main staging base for IRA attacks in the North; it is a well-known fact that the majority of the population of Dundalk were either IRA members, or sympathisers.

As his probation progressed Ray got to acquire a lot of knowledge on the terrorists in the area, and also on the terrorists that came up from the South of Ireland. Because at one point he felt that his knowledge on the terrorists from rural South Armagh was not very good he applied for a transfer to the little village of Crossmaglen. His relationship with Pauline was going strong and he would be at her house nearly every day that he was off duty, on one of these days her mother suggested that being as they were getting on so well they should maybe think about getting married.

Ray nearly shit himself at the idea of making such a commitment, as this was a little bit further than he wanted the relationship to go at this time, however he knew that if he didn't appear enthusiastic about it both of them might become suspicious of him.

He tried to get them to choose a date for the wedding, to take place sometime in the month of August, this was so that hopefully his transfer to Crossmaglen might be through by then, if it was, this would give him a chance to try and stall things.

He tried his best to get his transfer moved along quickly but alas it never happened and the wedding took place, it wasn't until he came back from his honeymoon that his transfer came into effect.

His working hours were different from other stations in the way that he would drive to the little village of Bessbrook where he would board a helicopter to be flown into Crossmaglen Police\Army camp.

He would have to work for three days before he was picked up again by helicopter to be flown back to Bessbrook, then after the one night out, the cycle would start again, after seven days he was allowed one full day and night at home.

After working for nearly six months in Crossmaglen, (during which time he had gathered a lot of Intelligence and information, which he had passed on to HQNI) he had also befriended a number of people in the village. As he was patrolling the village square one morning one of these people (who occasionally gave Ray bits of information for money) gave a pre-determined signal alerting Ray that he had information to pass on.

Ray met the man at a place, which had also been pre-determined, later that night when he was back on patrol.

"What do you have to tell me?" he asked the man.

"The boys are going to do a job very shortly."

"Where and what?"

"What are you going to pay me?" the man said holding out his hand.

"It depends on how good the info. is."

"They're going to have a go at bombing Newtownhamilton cop shop," the informant says.

"How many are going to be involved in planting it?"

"There'll be nine in all, six in two car's, and three in a Red Hi-ace van with the bomb in it."

"This had better not be a load of crap," Ray said to the man.

"It's all good info, so how much is it worth?" the man said again holding out his hand.

"Where's the bomb being kept at this moment," Ray

went on ignoring him.

"It's being kept at a farm just over the border, between here and Forkhill."

"When are they going to do this job?" Ray wanted to know.

"This Friday," came the reply.

"Why didn't you tell me this earlier," Ray said sounding angry, as the day was now Monday.

"I only just got to hear about it myself yesterday."

"That doesn't give me much time to organise anything to try and ambush the bastards on their way to the job," he told his informer.

"That's your problem not mine."

"Like I said earlier I hope this is not a load of crap you're giving me."

"It ain't honest to God," the informant replied worriedly.

"If it is then I would have to think about dropping your name in a few unsavoury places," Ray warned.

"Please don't do that, I've a wife and two kids."

"You should have thought of that before you joined the Provies," (slang for IRA) Ray sneered.

"I suppose that because I've given you a bit of info you'll hold me to your threat from now on?" the informer moaned.

"You could say that, yes."

"Boy, but you're one evil bastard,"

"We're in a bloody war here, nice guys don't get to go home," Ray tells the man.

"Have you finished with me?"

"No, just one more thing, why haven't they asked your ASU (Active Service Unit) to carry out this bombing?"

"Because this job is going to be done in the next village as soon as the bomb goes off there's no doubt that your lot will round us all up for questioning, so the plan is that we will all be in the village square here so that you will be able to see that we were nowhere near

Newtownhamilton, great alibi eh!"

Just then another man happened to walk past them, so as not to arouse his suspicion Ray took out his notebook and began treating the informer in the usual stop and check manner that was always carried out by any of the security forces whenever they stopped a suspect or known terrorist.

When he had disappeared from sight Ray asked his informer, "How is your cover? Do they suspect that they've an informer in the ASU?"

"No and I hope to God they never find out, if they do I'll have a very long slow death,"

"Well providing you haven't given me a bum steer here, they'll never know," Ray said.

With that the meeting was ended and the informer walked off muttering to himself, Ray knew the farm that his informer had mentioned and now he had the problem of trying to stop the bombing.

On his return to the Police Station he went to his room and took out a radio that he had hidden in the bottom of his wardrobe, this radio was unknown to the Police that he worked with, it was for his use to be able to contact Army Intelligence.

After making sure that there was nobody within earshot he began to try and make contact.

"Bravo India zero, Bravo India zero, this is Charlie Golf 1, message over."

Charlie Golf 1, this is Bravo India zero, send your message over," came the reply.

"Roger, could you tell India Oscar (IO) to meet me at usual place at approximately 1700hrs tomorrow evening, over."

Ray and Pauline had taken up residence in the little village of Richhill which was approximately 5 miles outside of the city of Armagh, nearly 75% of the population in it were Security Force personnel.

The following day at 1530hrs Ray was flown out of Crossmaglen for his weekly day off, he met the IO just outside of the little village of Markethill and told him of the information that he had been given.

The IO informed him that being as the bombing was going to be taking place very shortly Ray would have to go to give a briefing to a SAS ASU that was working out of Londonderry.

When he finally got home that night Pauline was sitting worried, waiting for him.

"Where have you been darling? I was just about to phone the Police Station to see if anything had happened to you," she said.

"The chopper was late picking us up," Ray lied, kicking himself for not calling her to tell her that he might be a little late getting home.

"I've got some bad news for you, I've got to do a twenty four hour duty tomorrow, I hope you had nothing planned?" she says.

"Why didn't you tell me on the phone last night when I called you?" Ray said, making out to be unhappy about what she had just told him.

"I only found out myself this morning when I went in for work," she said in defence.

"Never mind if you have to work, you have to work, I suppose it's all part of the course," Ray said trying to sound pissed off, although really he was quite pleased because this would mean that he wouldn't have her with him all day, it would make it easier for him to be able to get away up to Londonderry to give his briefing.

"I'm sorry," she said moving over to him and giving him a kiss.

"If you're working tomorrow rather than sit here on my lonesome I think I'll take a trip up to Londonderry in the morning, I'll go and see a few of my old Army mates, they're always asking me to call up and see them," Ray says.

"That sounds a good idea, you should do that."

"What have you cooked for tea? I'm famished," he asked changing the subject just in case she asked him exactly whom he was going to see.

"I've made you a lovely peppered sirloin steak, chips and peas with onion rings," she replied.

"And what's for afters?"

"Me," Pauline giggled.

While Ray ate his meal Pauline went upstairs for a shower then waited in the bedroom for him.

After a night of love making, the following morning when he had finished checking his car for booby trap bombs just in case someone had planted one on his car during the night.

Ray got into his car, (an old looking Vauxhall Cavalier) put his Police issue Ruger .357 magnum revolver on the passenger seat and commenced his journey to Londonderry.

The journey was ninety miles long and would take him nearly two and a half hours, when he reached the camp that the SAS were in he drove to their compound which was miles from anywhere else on the camp, and was surrounded by a high wall of corrugated metal sheeting to stop prying eyes.

On getting out of his car he made his way to the troop Commanders (TC) office, who on seeing Ray says,

"Ah! Ray long time no see, how the devil are you?"

"Not too bad Sir, and you?"

"I'm just cruising along, now then what can I do for you?"

"I don't know if Lisburn have been in touch but I have a bit of a problem, I need the use of the ASU to help ambush a bunch of IRA terrorists who are planning to blow up the Police station in a little village called Newtownhamilton in South Armagh."

"And when is this likely to be taking place?" asked the TC.

"It's supposed to be happening this Friday."

"Crikey that's a bit of a problem, the ASU here is on an operation in Strabane up in this neck of the woods, from what I've been led to believe things are getting really close to a little shootout with the local IRA.

So I can't risk calling them in now, can't you use some of the 14 Intelligence men from Lisburn? I'm sure that they would jump at the chance for a bit of action."

"I wouldn't risk it Sir, they're all a bundle of bloody cowboys, this needs a crack unit to make sure the job is done properly," Ray said not very pleased with the Commanders suggestion.

"Well that is all I can suggest, or you could speak to the boss and have a Unit sent over from Hereford if it's that important to save this piddling little Police station, how about that?"

"I'll have to do that then Sir because this station is quite important for the Policing in that part of South Armagh," Ray told him.

"If you want I'll phone the boss and tell him of your plight?" the TC offered.

"I'd be most appreciative if you would Sir."

The Troop Commander picked up his phone that was a direct line to the SAS overall Commander in Lisburn, the phone was attached to a device known as Goliath, this device is used to scramble any secret telephone messages.

When he had finished making the call the TC turned to Ray saying, "That's it then Ray, there will be an ASU sent over from Hereford straight away, they should be here by lunchtime at the latest."

"Which team is coming?" Ray enquired.

"I think he said it would be the Halo's."

"That's all I need, they're my old unit, I'll get some shit

of this lot, it'll be like a reunion," Ray said pleased now that he knew there was a good team coming.

"Meanwhile we'll go and get a cup of tea and something to eat while we wait for their arrival, shall we?" the TC, says making his way through the office door.

"Good idea Sir, lead on," Ray says agreeing and following him.

They made their way to the canteen where they both sat down to sausage chips and beans, this was the normal sort of food the Army slop jockey's (cooks) turned out.

At approximately 1330hrs the sounds of a helicopter (chopper) could be heard slowing down above the compound, Ray went out of the canteen to watch it land, as it circled before starting its decent he saw sitting in the doorway his old ASU Commander a man called Vic.

Ray gave a little sarcastic wave to him, to which Vic started to shake his clenched fist in Ray's direction, the other members of the ASU must have seen this happening as they all moved forward to take a look through the choppers doorway at whom Vic was threatening.

These other men were called Steve, Alex, Benny, and another man whom Ray hadn't seen before.

As the chopper touched the ground the ASU quickly jumped out of it and began walking towards Ray.

"Hello Vic how the devil are you?" Ray asked putting his hand out for Vic to shake.

"I'd be a lot sodding happier if I wasn't here," he moaned in reply as he took hold of Ray's hand and shook it.

"I'm sorry but I was missing you," Ray laughed.

"Was it you who sent for us?" Steve wanted to know.

"I'm afraid so, but look at it this way it beats sitting around Hereford training all day doesn't it?" Ray replied.

"Me and Alex were just getting a bit of a sleep," Benny said as both he and Alex reached Ray and the others.

"Sorry mate but what we have to do is rather important, come on with me to the briefing room and I'll tell you all about it," Ray says as he walked towards the buildings. Once they were all seated Ray began his briefing. "Right guys there is to be an IRA hit on a Police station in the village of Newtownhamilton in South Armagh, I have very good info. that a bloody big bomb which will be in a red coloured HI-ace van, will be driven across the border from the South and placed outside of the cop shop, this is supposed to be taking place on Friday at around ten thirty in the morning."

"Which terrorists are going to be involved?" Vic asked.

"It's not going to be the ones in Crossmaglen, or Forkhill, but a bunch from Dundalk in the South."

"So where are we going to ambush them?" Steve asked.

"Why ambush them? if we know where the bomb is, why don't we booby trap their own bomb for them, you know what I mean? tinker with the wiring system then instead of blowing up the cop shop they'll do themselves in," Benny says leaning back in his chair with an evil smile on his face.

"That's a great idea," the new guy whose name was Jerry said agreeing with the suggestion.

Ray had given this some thought previously, however he had changed his mind because to do this would mean that they would have to take a little trip over the border. "Well we do know where the bomb is, at this present moment it's being kept in a barn on a farm just over the border in the South," he told him.

"How far over the border?" Steve queried.

"About three miles," Ray informed him.

"That's not far, we could easily do it," Vic says.

"If you want to you can, so who's the explosives man who can do the job?" Ray quizzed them.

"Since you left us we've had to rely on Alex, but being as you are here we can use you, after all you used to be the main explosives man in our ASU didn't you?" Steve laughed.

"You've no chance of me going on this little expedition, I have to return to duty tomorrow." Ray smiled.

"You could always ring up the station and tell them you're sick and can't go in for duty," the TC puts in.

"That's a good idea Sir," Vic agrees with him.

"It would also be ideal for us to have a man, who knows the lay of the land in South Armagh," Benny puts in.

"I think it has been decided for you Ray, it looks like you're going with them, after all you are an explosive's man," the TC tells him with a smile.

This really pissed Ray off because he didn't relish the thought of going on any missions across the border, however on the other hand, the thought of being able to get his own back on the IRA appealed to him.

"Alright Sir, I'll go with them, I like the occasional bit of blood sport, it would also help me to keep my hand in," Ray relented.

"I knew you'd want to go, you couldn't resist doing a little bit of legal murder, could you?" Steve said laughing.

"Yeah you always were an evil bastard," Alex says supporting Steve.

"If I've to go out with you lot tonight I'd better get back home and get my kit ready, the TC knows the rest of the briefing about how we're going to get there and what to do if we're caught by the Southern Army or Garda, so I'll leave it all in his hands, I'll meet you all tonight at about 2300hrs at Bessbrook Mill," Ray told them as he left the room.

When he finally got to his home in Richhill he went up into the loft of his house and retrieved the army equipment that he had up there, Pauline knew that the equipment was in the loft and had asked him when she first saw it why he had it.

Ray had fobbed her off with a story that it was equipment that he had managed to keep when he left the army.

It was lucky for him that she was doing a twenty four hour duty otherwise he would have quite a bit of explaining to do, he mentally made a note that he must make sure that in the future he couldn't be used for any incidents.

After checking all of his kit he telephoned the Police station and reported in sick, he told the Sergeant that he had a migraine headache and stomach upset.

Later that night he drove to Bessbrook Mill camp where he awaited the arrival of the rest of the team, he stayed in his car so as not to be seen by any of the soldiers in the camp.

This was because he didn't want to be recognised by any of them just in case one of them should recognise him as one of the Policemen that flew to Crossmaglen regularly. It wasn't long before he heard the sound of a Lynx helicopter coming in to land, he got out of his car and took his army ammunition pouches and belt from the back seat, he checked his explosives pouch it contained different fuses, bomb timing devices, masking tape, and pieces of wire.

He didn't need to have any explosives with him; there would be enough in the van.

Ray made his way to the flight control room where he met up with the others, with them was the flight controller who was an army Sergeant Major and two other men who Ray knew from 14 Int. Group, the flight controller got a shock when he saw Ray.

"Are you with this lot?" he asked.

"Yes I am, so I would be most thankful if you'd keep it to yourself," he told him noticing that the other men were looking at him.

"Oh he'll do that, won't you Sergeant Major? Or your

pension will be a long time coming," one of the Int. men said.

"I certainly will Sir, my lips are sealed," the Sergeant Major assured him.

"We'll be leaving here at 2345hrs Sir, the chopper will drop us at this point," Vic said to the Int. men while pointing at a map.

"How long do you think it will take?" they asked.

"Can't say Sir, we don't know what sort of things might go on," Vic answered.

"The best thing you can do Sir's is go home and have a good night's sleep," Steve told them.

With this the ASU all picked up their kit and started to leave the control room and made their way out to the chopper landing pad to wait for their pick up.

It wasn't long before they were in the air flying to their drop off point, it would only take them a few minutes as this was about three miles from their objective, then they would have to walk across country to the farm.

As they started out for their objective it started to rain, "I hope this fucking rain isn't on for the night," Benny moaned.

"That is the one thing about this bloody hole that I hate, it never stops raining," Ray said rather annoyed.

"I'd have thought you would be used to it by now," Vic laughed.

The going across country was rough, at one time they had to cut through a bit of marshland, this made Alex and Jerry get really hacked off.

"I could kill you Ray, I would have been home tonight having a nice cool beer in my local, but thanks to you I'm here getting piss wet through," Alex said grumpily.

"Yeah and I was supposed to be meeting my girl tonight," Jerry whined.

"Right we're getting near to the farm keep quiet," Vic told them.

They got within 200 yards of the farm and took up cover at the side of a field, Vic and Ray both took out their infrared binoculars and scanned the field and farmyard, as Ray scanned the yard he saw an Alsatian dog wandering around.

"Shit there's a dog running about, that's all we need," he told Vic.

"Where is it?" Vic said trying to catch sight of the dog in his binoculars.

"It's over by the barn."

"I see it, I think we'll have our work cut out now," Vic said as he lowered his binoculars from his eyes.

They both turned to talk to the rest of the team.

"There's an FBA in the yard, this could give us a bit of a problem," Vic told them.

"What's an FBA?" the new boy Jerry asked.

"A Fucking Big Alsatian," Steve told him.

"How are we gonna get round this little problem?" Alex wanted to know.

"As far as I can remember, weren't you a dog trainer before you came to us Ray? surely you could deal with it?" Steve suggested nonchalantly.

"Yeah you would be the best man for this," Alex says.

"You've got no chance, I'm not here to be eaten by some farmyard mutt," Ray snapped back.

"You're our only hope Ray, so go to it," Vic said patting him on the shoulder.

This caused Ray some concern as he realised that he was the only hope for the task to be successful, it was either booby trap the bomb here or ambush the vehicles in the morning, if it came to an ambush innocent people might end up getting hurt or maybe killed.

It suddenly came to him that he had some tablets in one of his pouches that would drug the dog; these tablets were called Acepromazine more commonly known as ACP. an animal sedative, these would make the dog sleep.

His only problem now would be to make sure that the dog ate them,

"Benny have you got any of your Mars bars left?" he asked.

"I've only got one and I'm keeping it for later on," came the reply.

A bit disappointed with this refusal Ray turned to Vic.

"Look I've got some tablets here that would drug the dog, if Benny would give me the mars bar to put the tablets in I could creep nearer the yard and throw it to the dog, then in about an hour the bloody thing would be sleeping,"

"Good idea, Benny give Ray the Mars bar, I'll get you another when we get back, that's if you can wait that long?" Vic told him.

The mars bar was quickly thrown over to Ray, who opened the tablet container and took out some pills, Steve sat watching him, and Ray counted out nine of them and began putting them into the Mars bar.

"With that amount of pills you'll end up killing the thing," Steve said to him.

"Not at all, you have to give the dog one pill for every ten pounds of bodyweight, and I estimate that the dog weighs about ninety pounds," Ray assured him.

"I hope you're right, I might be a ruthless bastard but that's only towards humans, not dumb animals," Steve says.

When Ray had finished putting the pills in the bar he and Steve began to make their way towards the farmyard, when they were approximately fifty yards from it the dog suddenly pricked up its ears and looked in their direction.

They both stopped where they were and Ray began to make a very slight noise, this had the desired effect and the dog started to walk over towards them, when Ray felt the dog was near enough he threw the Mars bar in its direction.

The dog soon gulped the chocolate down then it began to make its way over to Ray and Steve who by this time had both laid down in the field.

"What are we going to do if this mutt wants more chocolate?" Steve asked nervously.

"Let's just hope that he only wants to be friendly, otherwise we've shit it," Ray told him.

Shortly after the dog reached them and after a bit of sniffing it started to wag its tail, Ray encouraged the dog to follow them as they both made their way back to the others, when they reached them Ray put a length of army green nylon parachute cord around the dogs neck and held it out to the new boy Jerry.

"Here you are Jerry a little present for you, keep hold of him until he falls asleep,"

"What if he turns funny and bites me?" Jerry whined.

"If he bites you, don't cry out, just bleed all over him," Ray said as he moved away to speak with the others to discern the best way to get into the barn.

"Right Alex, you and Benny go around the back of it to see if there's anyway loose panels or other doors, Ray you and Steve try to see if you can get into the farmyard, with a bit of luck there won't be a lock on the door," Vic detailed them.

Both teams set off in different directions heading for their allotted areas, they still stayed as close to the ground as they could, this was just in case anybody should come out of the house and see them.

It took Ray and Steve nearly twenty minutes to get into a good position to get a close look at the barn door.

"Fuck it the bloody things got a naffing big lock on it," Steve said looking through a small pair of binoculars.

"That's all we bloody need, I hope Alex and Benny have better luck than we have, we've got to get into it without making too much noise, and make sure that no one notices that we've been."

No sooner had Ray said this than they heard Alex's voice come over their radios saying that he and Benny had found a loose panel at the back of the barn.

"We'll be with you in a couple of minutes," Ray replied into his throat microphone.

When he and Steve reached Benny and Alex, Ray told them both to get into cover and keep an eye open for any movement while he and Steve went into the barn. It wasn't long before they managed to get inside of the building where they both tried to open one of the van doors, however all of them were locked.

"Now what'll we do?" Steve said exasperated.

"Don't worry I can get into one of these with no problems," Ray assured him.

"How can you do that all of the doors and windows on the fucking thing are locked?"

"Watch and learn," Ray said as he started to look in his pouches.

"What're you doing?" Steve asked.

"I'm looking for a piece of packing tape that I usually carry, Ah! here it is," he said holding it up.

He moved over too one of the van doors took out his combat knife and put the point of it in the gap between the door and the body of the van.

Gently he pushed the handle of the knife against the doorframe causing the door to be prised away from the van body.

"Here hold this," he told Steve.

When Steve had done this Ray put the two ends of the Packing tape together and folded it in the middle; he then began to feed it through the gap.

When he felt he had enough of it on the inside of the van he gently worked it down until the tape was level with the door locking button.

With another slight pull on the tape he caused it to bow then slid the tape down over the button, pulled it back and up all in the same movement and the door-locking button popped up unlocking the door.

"You should have been a bloody car thief not a cop," Steve said smiling and sounding relieved.

"All I can say is thank god there wasn't an alarm on it," Ray replied.

On peering into the back of the van they could see eight milk churns, looking more closely they found that they had been packed with Home Made Explosive (HME) with an arming Device down by the front passengers seat.

"I hope this thing doesn't go off while you're playing with it," Steve said worriedly.

"If it does we'll never know, but don't worry I'll meet you in hell," Ray laughed.

Ray began to look at the arming device, which was an ordinary light switch connected to a car battery and a timing mechanism.

This was so that all the person who was going to arm the bomb had to do was flick the switch and walk away when the hands on the timer, which had solder on them, met the power connection from the battery, then bang.

After a bit of fiddling around he removed the timer from the box that it was in, he turned the timer upside down and then removed a pencil type gas soldering iron from his pouch.

He melted a piece of solder and a very light length of fuse wire onto the back of the timing Mechanism, knowing that the bomb would go off prematurely, with this done he replaced the whole system.

"Whoever flicks the switch now, it'll be the last thing he ever does," Ray whispered to Steve as they both got back out of the vehicle.

Suddenly Benny's voice came over the radio telling them that someone had come out of the farmhouse and was walking towards the barn.

Quickly Ray and Steve looked around for somewhere to get into hiding, Ray managed to get behind some big forty gallon oil drums but there was nowhere for Steve to hide, realising this Steve got down on the ground and pulled himself under the van.

He had no sooner got out of sight than the barn door opened and two men walked in,

Luckily for Ray when they switched on the barn light he was covered by the shadow from the oil drums.

The men walked over to the van and opened the passengers door and discussed the bomb, roughly five minutes later they left, when Steve and Ray felt that the men were not going to return they both came out of their hiding places.

"Christ! that was close," Steve said brushing himself down.

 "Tell me about it, the last thing we want is to get caught at this stage of the game, thank god neither of them decided to move the van," Ray said.

"Come on let's go whilst the goings good," Steve said making his way towards where they entered.

It wasn't long before they were back with the others, after making sure that the drugged dog was comfortable they all started to make their way back to the pickup point approximately five miles away.

On landing back at Bessbrook they reported to the Int. cell that the job had gone smoothly, then Ray bid them all farewell got into his car and started his journey home. Due to it being the early hours of the morning he knew that he would be home and in bed long before Pauline had finished her duty.

CHAPTER – 3 – NEWS REPORT

Ray had not been home long and had only just got into bed when he heard a car pull up outside of his house; this was followed shortly after by the sound of a key being turned in the lock of his front door.

He picked up his Police revolver, which was on his bedside table and made his way to the top of the stairs so that he could see who was coming in.

As the door opened he raised his revolver into a firing position and took a bead on the shape of the person coming through the door, he watched the person reach out a hand and switch on the downstairs hall light.

When the light came on he could see that it was Pauline. "What the heck are you doing home this early?" he said to her from where he was. Pauline startled looked up towards him, "I managed to get off early, I hope I didn't scare you," she apologised.

"You nearly got a bullet in the head, you should have telephoned to let me know you were finishing early,"

"I didn't want to waken you, I was hoping you'd be asleep then I could just cuddle up nice and warm," she smiled.

"Well no harm to you, but you were nearly cuddling into a coffin," he scalded her.

"I'll definitely make sure and phone the next time," she says.

"Would you like a cup of tea and some breakfast before you go to work?" she asked.

"I'm not going in today I phoned in sick, I told them that I had a bad migraine and as you know I don't suffer from that, I just fancied spending a little more time with you, as it is with your duties and mine we hardly see each other," Ray told her.

"That's good so now we can spend the day in bed and catch up on some serious love making."

"Seems like a good idea to me," Ray agreed smiling from

ear to ear.

"Good I'll just make those cups of tea then, you go back to bed," Pauline says making her way to the kitchen.

Ray turned and went to the bathroom for a shower, when he had finished he returned to the bedroom with only a towel wrapped around him, Pauline was sitting naked on the bed waiting to get a shower as well.

"Okay It's your turn," he told her.

"I shan't be long," she said getting up from the bed and walking towards him she stopped to kiss him, as she did so she took a quick feel of his groin before moving on.

Ray pulled the continental quilt back on the bed and lay on it then removed the towel, he took hold of the television remote control, turned the television on at the Sky twenty four-hour news channel.

This was mainly for curiosity as he knew that there would be no reports yet of the bombing at this time of the day, as the terrorists wouldn't be moving it into position till later that morning.

Shortly after this Pauline returned naked, "That's a pleasant sight as you walk through the door," she said pointing at Ray.

"It's nice to see you coming in like that as well," he replied.

It wasn't long before they were making love, when they had finished both of them stayed in the bed watching the television.

"How did your duty go?" Ray asked.

"It was long and boring I was the only woman there amongst twelve men,"

"I bet you enjoyed that?"

"Not really they had me making tea and coffee nearly all day."

"Did you not get chance to have a kip?"

"I wouldn't there, just in case I should start snoring or talking in my sleep."

"You don't do that here so I shouldn't worry if I was you."

"I wouldn't go to sleep in their company anyway, you never know what they might try to get up to."

"Providing you don't wake up pregnant it shouldn't really matter," Ray laughed.

"If I ever do it's your fault," Pauline said smiling but with a worried look on her face.

"You're looking worried, what's wrong? You're not pregnant are you?"

"I don't think so, but I am a little late with my period this month," she replied.

"Well maybe you are, it would be good if you are because it could mean another one of me running around in years to come," Ray joked.

"I've got an appointment with the doctor this afternoon just to check anyway."

"What time?"

"It's at three o'clock, do you want to come with me?"

"No I've plenty of things to do around here," Ray told her not really wanting to go into Armagh as he knew that Pauline would probably want to leave early so that she could call in with her mother.

Just shortly before twenty-five minutes to eleven o'clock the sign of a news flash came up on the television screen.

This was shortly followed by one of the local newscasters reporting that a bomb had gone off near the border village of Newtownhamilton and that a further report would be given out later when the Police released more details.

"I wonder who has been murdered this time?" Pauline remarked.

"I don't know but I hope it was some of their own," Ray answered knowingly.

"I wish they would bring the SAS in over here," she

moaned.

"You never know they might already be here." Ray replied.

"Well they can't be doing much, what with all the bloody murders going on," she said angrily.

"That's the trouble with the SAS you never know what they're doing," Ray said inwardly smiling.

"If the Government pulled out the soldiers and left the UDR to clean it up we could settle things once and for all," Pauline told him.

"We'll just have to wait to hear what or who was killed,"

"I can't be bothered waiting I'm off to my mums, I'll see you later darling," Pauline said leaning over to give Ray a light kiss on the lips.

"While you're away I'll go and tidy the garage, I can hardly see the floor because of the wood shavings."

Ray followed her to the front door where he stood in the doorway while she got into her car, when she was ready she started the engine and backed the car onto the road, then before pulling away she turned and waved goodbye.

Ray went back in the house and changed the television on to the Sky news channel, a few minutes after this a bulletin about the bombing came on.

"At approximately ten thirty this morning a van bomb exploded near to the village of Newtownhamilton in the South Armagh area of Northern Ireland. It is believed that the bomb was destined for the Police station in the village, the van was a Red Hi-ace, which had been stolen from a car park in Dublin. Early reports say that three bodies have been recovered at the scene, these bodies are believed to those of the men who were transporting the bomb, further updates will be forthcoming throughout the day."

Ray very nearly let out a whoop of joy, he loved it when things came together and he knew that he had done his job properly.

"That's three less to deal with," he said to himself.

He went into the kitchen and started to make himself a cup of tea to take out to the garage, when he had made it he went into the utility room part of the garage where he switched on a radio, which was tuned to Downtown radio.

He placed his cup on the sideboard and went into the garage and set about cleaning it up, he made sure to keep an ear open for any further news flashes.

Cleaning the garage took a little bit longer than he thought and it wasn't long before Pauline returned, Ray heard her car pull up outside in the driveway and then the car door slam shut and her footsteps walk up to the house front door.

A few minutes later she entered the garage, "I'm home darling," she said.

"So I heard," he replied continuing to put some of his tools away.

"Aren't you going to ask me how I got on?" She queried.

"I'm sorry love, how did things go?"

"Great, you're going to be a daddy," she said grinning like a Cheshire cat.

"That's fantastic, I'm really happy," Ray replied with a big grin on his face throwing his arms around her and kissing her.

This news to him however gave him some concern, he didn't mind the fact that his job was risky for he knew that before you took it on, but the last thing he ever wanted to do was to put the innocent lives of Pauline and his unborn child at risk.

His main worry was that should the IRA ever discover that he was Special Forces they would have a price on his head, also should they ever manage to catch him his death would be long and slow.

Ray and Pauline both sat up nearly half the night talking

about the future.

"Well now, we will have the fun of shopping for baby clothes wont we?" Pauline said giggling with happiness.

"We sure will, and we'll also have to think of some names, mind you that can wait until we know if we are going to have a boy or a girl," Ray replied.

"Ooooh but I am so excited, I can't wait to tell my mum," Pauline laughed.

"I thought you might have told her on your way home?"

"I was too excited and I wanted to get home and tell you first, after all it wouldn't be right for me to tell my parents before telling you, would it?"

"I suppose you're right there, I think I would have felt a little put out if you had," Ray told her.

"Tell you what, how about we arrange for Mum and Dad to come over here for Sunday dinner, that's if you can get Sunday off work?" Pauline suggested.

"I'll see what I can do tomorrow, meanwhile we had better get off to bed, otherwise I will never get up in the morning," Ray told her.

The following morning he went into work he was on cloud nine and really pleased that he was going to be a father.

He had not been in the station long when he got a telephone call.

"Police Crossmaglen," he answered the caller.

"Ah! Good morning could I speak to a Constable Rutherford please?" came the reply.

"You are speaking to him." Ray immediately noticed the voice of his SAS Commanding Officer.

"Jolly good, Ray that was a very good piece of work, I thought that I would let you know because the G.O.C (General Officer Commanding) land forces telephoned me to congratulate me on a job well done, so I'm passing on his thanks."

"I'm pleased to hear that we are doing the job properly

and that the upper crusts are noticing it Sir."

"Oh they are my boy, they are, now tell me what else have you in the pipeline?"

"I'm sorry Sir but I can't tell you that at this moment in time because we are not on a secure phone line, however next time when I'm back in civilisation I'll drop in and let you know personally."

"Yah fine, make sure you keep up the good work I'll speak to you in a couple of day's time then, so bye for now."

"Goodbye Sir," Ray said as he heard the telephone at the other end being replaced.

Shortly after this the station door opened and the Sergeant walked in.

"Glad to see you're back, I've just done an early morning foot patrol in Cullyhanna, and I was bloody freezing," the Sergeant said.

"Sorry Skipper but I wasn't too good yesterday, the old migraine was playing me up I also had a dose of the trots,"

"I'm not surprised with the shit they serve up in that Army cookhouse, those cooks must do a special course on how to ruin good food," He says laughing at his own wit.

"Yes they do have a wonderful knack at cocking it up don't they?" Ray agreed.

"Do me a favour Ray, make me a cup of steaming hot coffee, would you please? while I get all this kit off," the Sergeant asked as he began taking off his patrol equipment.

"When I have made it I'd like to have a chat with you, if you don't mind Skipper, it is important," Ray told him.

"Well when you've made it bring it along to my office, and bring your cigarettes with you, I haven't got many left."

"Okay I won't be long," Ray says leaving the enquiry

office and heading for the station kitchen to make the coffee.

There was no problem leaving the enquiry office because unlike most police stations where the public could come in at any time, in Crossmaglen nobody ever came to the station to report anything, this was because the Police are hated so much there.

About ten minutes later Ray went to the Sergeants Office with the coffee,

"Here you are Skipper," he said placing the cup on the Sergeants desk in front of him.

"Did you bring your cigarettes?"

"I sure did because we could be in here for a while, the Army gate sentry will give us a shout if anybody wants into the station."

"Right what's the problem Ray?" the Sergeant asked as Ray sat down in one of the office easy chairs, "It's nothing serious I hope?"

"It all depends on what you call serious."

"Well tell me and we'll see."

"Well my wife found out yesterday that she's pregnant," Ray told him.

"So you're gonna be a daddy, congratulations, I don't see that being a problem, I've got two kids myself."

"It isn't a problem Skipper, as a matter of fact I am over the moon, however being as I am now Stationed here, it's going to be very awkward to be able to go to all of the Hospital visits and Doctor's appointments, as I would like to be there for them, and so I would very much appreciate it if you would be able to pull a few strings to get me moved out of here?"

"I see, I'll be sorry to see you go, you've really done well here and the others like having you about, but I have a few contacts and will see what I can do, ok?"

"Thanks Skipper if you manage it I'll owe you one," Ray told him as he left the office.

He made his way back into the enquiry office where he took out his paperwork and proceeded to catch up on a few prosecution files that he had to do.

Roughly three-quarters of an hour later the Sergeant came in to speak to him.

"Right Ray, I phoned a friend of mine in the personnel branch, he told me that if you want you can go back to Newry, you'll start there on Monday is that alright?"

"Bloody Norah that was quick," Ray answered surprised.

"Normally you wouldn't get away from here unless you had served two years, but because some other guy has shit the nest he is being transferred here for punishment, I don't think he's gonna like it because we used to work in the same station before, he and I never got on."

"He'll be chuffed with me then," Ray says smiling.

"It'll be a shame to lose you, you were doing a great job here, if you ever want to come back or want to work with me again give me a bell and I'll swing it for you."

"That would be nice Skipper I'll hold you to that one day, thanks for your help in getting me moved," Ray told him shaking the Sergeants hand.

Ray's last week went pretty quickly and he left Crossmaglen, to start back in Newry.

CHAPTER – 4 – BACK IN NEWRY

Ray was lucky when he returned to Newry because he was put back in his old duty section, so he knew most of the other guys that he would be working with, he just slotted back into section ways with no problem.

Since he had been away from Newry and in Crossmaglen for the past six months he decided to go to speak with the station Special Branch (SB) members to update himself on the local terrorist activities.

This was so that he could learn who was still on the local terrorist list and who was new to the scene; he went to their office where after knocking on the door and waiting for a short while his knock was answered by one of the men whom he knew.

"Hello Ray come on in, what brings you back here, are you lost? You'll find Crossmaglen that way," the man said pointing in the direction of Crossmaglen.

"I already know that Tom, didn't you know I've been transferred back here?"

"No, they kept that quiet."

"And you're the SB and are supposed to know everything?" Ray laughed.

"We must have been on a tea break," Tom replied.

"You've been on one since you joined the Branch," Ray retorted.

"Now that you're here what can we do for you?" Tom asked.

"I thought I would come and get an update on all the local shitheads."

"A few of the old ones like McStravick, Nolan, and Blair, are out of the North they are on the run (OTR) in the South, they're living in Dundalk, they got a whisper that we were going to arrest them for the murder of a part time UDR guy, so they legged it before we got them."

"I wonder how they got the info." Ray queried.

"We have an idea, we think it's someone in the station

who is letting things get out, if we find out who it is he won't be here for much longer he'll be in a prison cell." Tom answered.

"If you catch him tell me who he is and I'll make sure he's retired early, if there is one thing that gets up my nose it's having your enemy in the same house as you," Ray threatened.

"That's why I shouldn't really say anything to you, I know if I did he wouldn't be living for much longer," Tom said raising his eyebrows.

"Oh! well be like that then," Ray commented not really bothered.

"No you leave it, we'll deal with this one, we have our ways," Tom says winking.

Just then the SB Inspector came into the office, he knew Ray from the last time he was in Newry.

"My God look what the cats brought in, how are you Ray? It's good to have at least one cop in the station that is more interested in the terrorists than just handing out parking tickets," he said as he held his hand out to shake Ray's.

"I didn't expect to see you still here governor, I imagined that you would have been put out to grass by now," Ray replied laughing.

"There's still life in the old dog yet, I might have put on a few pounds since you last saw me, but don't be fooled by the extra tyre around my gut."

"Who is fooling who?" Ray asked.

"Now let's not fight you two," Tom put in, smiling at the fact that Ray had gotten the better of the Inspector.

This put an end to the joking and Tom handed Ray a book of mugshots of the local up and coming terrorists who were now living in the area.

"Before you get engrossed in those pictures, can I see you in my office Ray?" the Inspector said pointing at the office door.

When they had both entered the office the Inspector closed the door behind them.

"Things have changed since you were last here Ray, the IRA have a new junior wing of the organisation being built up, we have it from a good source that these new boys will be taking over a lot of the attacks on the Police and Army."

"Why are they letting the youngsters do it," Ray asked puzzled.

"Because they know that all the old hands are being watched carefully, they can't have a crap without our knowing it."

"So we can expect a lot of botched jobs to take place then?"

"Let's just hope they are all botched, then we don't have to attend any funerals, I've been to more than enough in my time in this job," the Inspector says downheartedly.

"Is there anything you particularly want me to do for you, when I'm out on patrol, or anybody you would like me to pay attention to," Ray offered.

"This new junior wing is our main problem at the moment, we are not exactly sure who all is in it, so if you want you can do some sniffing around for us."

"That's no problem I'll probably have the names for you in a couple of weeks, or maybe sooner if I can find out who just one of them might be in the unit then I can work on him a little," Ray smiled.

"Why is it I have a funny feeling that things won't be done very kosher," the Inspector asked looking worried.

"Because it ain't a kosher bloody war," Ray replied seriously.

"What section are you in?" the Inspector wanted to know.

"I'm back with 'C' Section, that is the one I used to be with before I went to Crossmaglen."

"Try not to let anyone in the section know what you are

up to for us, I don't know if Tom has told you there is someone tipping the local IRA off as to our activities, and we don't want them to get wind that we know nothing about this new unit they are building up."

"Tell me this Governor, why is it you're telling me all this?" Ray said with a puzzled look on his face, as he was really curious as to why he was being taken into the SB confidence.

"If you must know, I was at a top level meeting in the Army HQNI a couple of days ago and guess what? Your name came up, not only that I was taken to one side by the Chief Constable and told about your real purpose over here."

"I'm sorry but you've got me there, what are you talking about?" Ray put to him, seething inside as he was under the impression that his real job would only be known by the upper ranks of the Police.

"If you want to be like that, answer me this then, how long have you been SAS?"

This shocked Ray because he now knew that the Inspector must have the full run down on him.

"I've been SAS since 78, I failed the first time around, but I got it on the second, I worked bloody hard for it, the only thing is you do nothing but training all the time, this can become a pain in the arse, so when this job came up I volunteered."

"I thought you guys were on the go all over the world and never stayed anywhere for very long?"

"Let me tell you this, there are not a lot of jobs where we can be used, or where we are used except for over here, it's alright doing nothing but training but it's better putting all that training into practice," Ray told him.

"Have you any touts (informers) here in the town?"

"A policeman wouldn't ask you that sort of question," Ray replied laughing.

"I just thought you might have, after all you had one in

Crossmaglen?" the Inspector quizzed.

"Just because I had one there doesn't mean to say I've got one here, why are you asking me this anyway?" Ray wanted to know.

"Because I noticed that most of the terrorist sightings and information on their activities in this town was very good up until you left."

"Okay I'll tell you this much, I have four people in this town who tell me things they are very good with their info. and two of them are at the top of the pile," Ray reluctantly told the Inspector.

"Don't you have to pay them for their information?"

"No because they are more scared of me than their own side, and anyway I couldn't afford to pay them."

"You don't have to, we would do that for you that is providing their info. is good."

"Like I said I don't want to start having to do that."

"Who are they? Where in the town are they from?"

"That is something you will never know, and believe me no one else will either, my dealings with them will stay the way they are."

"For your own security you should let us know who they are because what if you were kidnapped or something worse when you go to meet with them? You should always take one of my men go with you just to back you up."

"That would be the last thing I'd want, I've seen the way your guys work they haven't got a bloody clue how to use or handle a tout properly."

"Now they're not that bad Ray, they do get the job done."

"Yes they are that good, so good in fact that you know all about this new IRA unit, don't you?"

"You have to give them a little time, to find out that sort of information isn't easy in this town, you should know that," the Inspector said in defence of his men.

"How long have they been at it now?"

"Well it only came to light about seven weeks ago."

"No harm to you Inspector they should have known who they are and all about them long before now," Ray replied getting a bit angry because he knew for a fact that he would probably be able to find out all about the unit within a week or two.

"We would be most appreciative if you can find anything out about them."

"I will have a chat with my touts and get back to you, now I'm going to have to go out on patrol, I'll see you later Governor," Ray said getting up from his chair.

He walked out of the Inspectors office and into the main SB office where Tom was sitting reading one of the local newspapers.

"Boy but you have a cushy life just sitting reading the papers," Ray mocked him.

"This is where we find out most of our information didn't you know?" Tom replied.

"I'll take a look at those photo's another time, I had better got out on the streets before my Sergeant starts to go daft, I'll see you later Tom," Ray said as he left.

"Yep see you mate, take care, as if I need to say that?" Tom answered as he turned one of the newspaper's pages.

Ray went down the corridor and out into the backyard of the station where the patrol cars were kept, the car that he had been detailed to work in with two other men was not there, so he got on his pocket radio and contacted it, roughly ten minutes later it turned up to collect him.

"Hi guys and how are you both?" Ray said to them as he opened one of the car rear passenger doors and got in.

"We were both thinking that you had got lost, or maybe decided to go home," the driver who was called Jimmy laughed.

"He has probably forgotten what a car looks like, after all in Crossmaglen the Police vehicles there have rotor blades don't they?" the other man who was called Bill put in with a snigger.

"Alright, alright, I wasn't in Crossmaglen that long, come on Jimmy show me about my old haunts again let me refresh my memory," Ray says.

"Tell me this Ray, what are you doing back here I thought you liked the bandit country?" Bill asked.

"I did, I really loved it there, however my wife is pregnant now and that will mean a lot of doctors and hospital visits so it's only the right thing to do getting a transfer back here."

"Well you're right there Ray I think if my wife was pregnant I would do the same thing." Jimmy agreed.

"Take a spin up and around Drumalane Park, will you Jimmy, I want to see if any of the old shitheads are still knocking about there?" Ray directed him.

They went to the Drumalane Park housing estate and drove around the place for a while, just as they were about to leave the area Ray noticed one of the known local IRA members.

"Look over there to your right, there's Phely let's go and have word with him, I would like to let him know that I'm back in town," Ray suggested.

Jimmy drove to where the man was standing obviously watching them, when the car pulled up beside him Ray got out of the car followed by Bill while Jimmy stayed in the car with the driver's door open.

"Well what about ya?" Ray said to Phely as he walked towards him.

"Worse for seeing you," he replied.

"You still don't love me do you? Why do you not like me Phely, because I think you are a great chap," Ray mocked.

"I don't think you are," came the reply.

"I stopped especially to have a chat with you, and to let you know that I'm back in town, also if I ever get the chance I'm gonna kill you," Ray threatened him.

While Ray was talking to him he noticed another member of the unit come around the corner of some garages and on seeing Ray and Bill he turned and started to walk the other way.

"Hey! Seamus, where the heck are you going, get your arse over here," Ray shouted to him.

The man done what he was told and walked over stopping beside Phely.

"Now where were you going?" Ray quizzed him.

"Just going for a walk to see what's about," Seamus answered.

"Why did you turn the other way when you saw us?"

"Because I didn't want any hassle."

"I'm not hassling you, I've just got back into town so I thought that I'd come here and see my old buddies," Ray told him smiling.

"You're no buddy of mine, I remember the time you were on foot patrol in the estate here and you took me for a walk up the alley at the back of the garages and beat me."

"It was for your own good, if I remember rightly I tried to give you some good advice about the company you were keeping."

"Like I told you at the time I don't need your advice," Seamus replied aggressively.

"We'll see, now I can't stand here chatting all day I've work to do, so you two run along and be good now, no doubt I'll see you again sometime, have a nice day now, bye," Ray says as he got back into the police car.

As they drove away Bill commented, "Did you see the way they both looked at you Ray? If looks could kill we'd be planning your funeral."

"Well one thing is for sure, they will be on the phone

ringing around letting the others know I'm back."

"I'll tell you one thing Ray, I'm bloody glad you're on our side," Jimmy laughed.

"So am I," Bill added.

"Shall we take a trip up to Derrybeg then Barcroft, to see who is about up there now, that is if they aren't all on the phone," Ray smirked.

"We'll go in for a cuppa first, you can buy, Ray."

They made their way back to the station, when Bill and Jimmy had finished putting their Flak jackets onto the rear seat of the car on top of Ray's the three of them headed for the canteen.

Inside the canteen Ray ordered the coffees while the other two got themselves seated, once the coffees were ready Ray took them to the table and joined them.

No sooner had they sat down than the Sergeant walked in, "Rutherford I want to see you in my office, now," he snarled looking rather cross.

As the Sergeant walked out of the canteen Jimmy looked at Ray saying, "Who's pissed on his bonfire, it looks like you are in for a hard time Ray."

"Well at least I know he can't make me pregnant and if he does I don't have to keep it do I." Ray smiled.

"You'll not be saying that by the time he's finished with you, by the look on his face," Bill chimed in.

Ray left the canteen and went to the office, he knocked on the door before entering, and when he got the reply to come in he entered and stood in front of the Sergeant.

"Yes Sergeant what did you want to see me for?" he asked.

"You have been out on those streets for less than two hours and I have received two complaints about you already, what the fuck do you mean by threatening people, if you carry on the way you're going I'll write you out of this job," he warned.

"Why? Who has complained about me?"

"You were in Drumalane estate this morning, and apparently you were talking with two of the residents there, they telephoned here wanting to make an official complaint, they say that you threatened to kill them, am I right?"

"Yes I was speaking to them, and no I did not threaten them, I know you haven't been in this station long Sergeant, but do you know who those particular people really are?"

"Of course I do, but you can't go around threatening people."

"No, but it's alright for them to go round terrorising people, and killing them, isn't it?"

"Don't you start getting an attitude with me Constable, if you have any sense you will cease this stupid activity of threatening people, I won't put up with it, do you understand?" the Sergeant warned.

"If you don't like the way I operate then you had better go and report me to the Superintendent," Ray offered.

"If that's the way you want it lets go," the Sergeant said putting on his hat and leading the way to the Superintendent's office.

As they reached it the Sergeant told Ray to stand outside while he knocked on the office door and went in leaving Ray alone.

The Sergeant was in the office for roughly ten minutes talking to the Superintendent before he opened the door and called Ray in, Ray marched into the office in a very military manner and slammed to attention before saluting the Superintendent.

"What's this I hear about you threatening the local terrorists Ray?" the Superintendant asked.

"I told them that if I ever get the chance, I will do to them, what they would quite happily do to me Sir."

"You are no longer a soldier, you're a police officer and

therefore you do not threaten people, this is not a war."

"I thought that killing people, and the words Irish Republican Army meant that the last word Army, was meaning an armed force Sir, surely an Army is a group of men or beings who fight and kill their enemies, in this case the forces of the Crown?"

"What is going on over here is what the politicians call civil unrest, or don't you know that?"

"I'm sorry Sir but in my books anybody trying to kill or murder any members of the Police or Army to undermine the security of a country is at war with that country, and as far as I am concerned over here it is a bloody war," Ray told him.

"I can see that I am going to get nowhere with you on this, I think its best that I inform the Chief Constable of your attitude and he can have the pleasure of dismissing you from the job, what do you think of that?"

"If you feel that you have to do it, then do it," Ray replied not really bothered.

The Superintendent then turned his attention to the Sergeant.

"Sergeant I want Constable Rutherford to get his patrol kit out of his car and stay in the station until I get further instructions from the Chief Constable," then he turned back to Ray, "You Constable are to remain in this station until told otherwise, is that clear?"

"Yes Sir, what will I do? I have no paperwork to keep me busy as I only came here today," Ray acknowledged.

"You can assist the Station Duty Officer," (SDO) came from the Sergeant who was stood behind him.

"Right you can go now, I will let you know what has been decided later," the Superintendent told him.

Ray left the office and went back to the canteen, he was pretty hacked off, mainly because he was not allowed back on the streets, and he was not looking too happy when he made his way back to Jimmy and Bill.

"Who stole the cream out of your cake?" Jimmy asked him.

"I've good news for you both, I'm not going back out with you, I've been grounded, that bastard Sergeant had me up in front of the Super. who has told me that I'm confined to the station as my attitude is wrong for the streets," Ray informed them.

"Why? What happened?" Bill enquired.

"Those two arseholes this morning reported me and made a complaint."

"So we're on our own, well I suppose we had better get back out then, come on let's get your kit from the car," Jimmy said getting up to leave.

When Ray had finished getting his kit out of the car he took it to his locker then locked it away before making his way to the station enquiry office.

As he entered the office the SDO looked up from the desk.

"Hello Ray what brings you here?" he wanted to know.

"I've been told that I am to assist you."

"I don't need any help, the place is dead quiet, unless you know something I don't."

"No I've had a little lovers tiff with the Super. He told me to come here, as he doesn't want me on the streets, he feels that my way of Policing doesn't go with the way in which it should."

"I don't understand?" the SDO said looking puzzled.

"Apparently I got two complaints against me this morning."

"Oh! Yes I heard about that, you shouldn't go terrorising the terrorists, they are such lovely peaceful murdering bastards," the SDO says with heavy sarcasm in his voice.

"It's funny you should say that, because that's what me and the Super. fell out over, I think he feels we should just leave them alone to carry on murdering us, he says that the troubles here are only civil unrest, someone should wake up all the Authorities as to what the hell is going on in this God forsaken hole."

"Now settle petal, you'll give yourself an ulcer the way you're going on, you should be like me, just sit back and let it all happen, are you here just for today or will you be here every day?"

"It all depends on what the Chief Constable decides, the Super is trying to get me either thrown out of the job or moved to where I can't do anything but sit in an office and answer phones," Ray replied.

"Tell you what hang on here for a minute and I'll go and get the tea's in," the SDO said getting up from his chair and heading towards the canteen.

Just as the SDO left the internal phone in the enquiry office rang, Ray picked up the receiver saying.

"War Office who wants a fight?"

"Is that you Constable Rutherford?" Ray instantly recognised the Superintendents voice.

"Yes Sir it is, what can I do for you?"

"When you get the chance come up to my office I want a little word with you about what went on this morning," the Super told him.

"I'm here on my own at this moment in time but when the other guy gets back I'll be right up Sir."

"Okay that's fine, I'll see you then," was the reply.

Roughly five minutes later the other man returned with two cups of hot tea, he was trying his best not to spill any.

"Shit, I manage to burn myself every time I try and bring tea back to this place, I think we should get issued special tea carrying gloves, it's a must for this job," he laughed.

This caused Ray to smile, then he told the man about the telephone call from the Superintendent.

"What did he say when you answered the phone like

that?"

"Funny enough, not a thing all he would say is that he wanted to see me," Ray said, puzzled at why the Super hadn't at least mentioned the manner in which he had answered the phone.

"You'd better get up and see him then,"

"I'm gonna finish my cuppa first, he can wait until then, I'm in no hurry," Ray said picking up his cup.

Shortly after he had finished his tea Ray went up to see the Superintendent, he straightened out his uniform before knocking on the office door.

When he heard the words 'come in' he again marched into the office and slammed to attention quickly followed by an exaggerated salute.

"You wanted to see me Sir," he said standing stiffly to attention.

"Yes I do Ray, take a seat," the Super. said pointing to a nearby chair.

When Ray was settled the Superintendent started the conversation,

"I have been on to the Chief Constable about you, and I was very surprised to hear what I was informed of, I didn't have a clue as to your real purpose of why you are a policeman, why didn't you tell me?"

"The less people who know the better for me, and I certainly wasn't going to tell you in front of the Sergeant," Ray replied.

"I see the point of that, I was told that what I now know, must stay within this office, I never had a clue as to what was going on, it would appear that I am to give you as much co-operation as I can. However let me tell you this, I don't care what you are up to, but you must remember you are still under my command, is that clear?"

"Yes Sir I will always play by the book," Ray smiled

"However I would be most appreciative if ever I have to

take the occasional day off work if no questions were asked, I promise you that if I ever have to it will be for a good reason," Ray informed him.

"Surely you would be better employed as a member of the Special Branch, would you not?"

"No Sir that would take me off the streets, the streets are my main area of operation, I can then keep an eye on the people whom I am most interested in, I can't do that from an office."

"Does anybody else in this station know about your real job?"

"Yes Sir, the SB Inspector."

"Hold on, I want him in here to explain why he hasn't told me before," the Super. says picking up the phone and dialling the SB office.

A couple of minutes later the SB Inspector came into the office.

"Yes Sir what can I do for you?" he asked the Super.

"How long have you known about Ray?" the Super. asked pointing to Ray.

"I'm sorry Sir I don't know what you mean," He replied.

"Well let me just say undercover intelligence, does that ring a bell?"

"Oh that I found out about him at a briefing which was being given at Army HQ in Lisburn the other day."

"Why didn't you let me know?"

"Because I was sworn to secrecy, anyway I thought you would have already been informed?" the Inspector says surprised that the Super. was unaware.

"Well for your information I have only just learned of his true purpose for being in the force, and I had to find out from the Chief Constable." the Super. told the Inspector non-too happily.

"I'm sorry Sir, I suppose I should have told you,"

"If ever you get to hear anything like this again I would appreciate it if you let me in on it, then I don't have to make a fool of myself with the Chief, that's if you don't mind." was the Super's sarcastic reply.

"I will Sir I can assure you," the Inspector grovelled.

"I have been told to give Ray full support in his activities, that also refers to you as well," the Superintendent said pointing at the inspector.

CHAPTER – 5 - ON THE STREETS

On leaving the Super's office Ray went into the radio
control room to have the operations controller call back
the car that he was in, about fifteen minutes later the
car pulled into the backyard of the station.

As it pulled to a stop Jimmy opened the driver's door and
put his foot against it to stop it from swinging shut.

"What are we back for?" he asked Ray.

"To pick me up, I'm allowed back out,"

"Who did you bribe," Bill wanted to know.

"No-one, they just saw things my way."

"If you are sneaking out without the Sergeant saying so
then you're not dragging me into the shit with you, I'll
have to get it from him," Jimmy says getting out of the
car walking towards the offices.

"Whilst you go and ask him me and Bill will go and get a
cuppa, see you soon, we'll be in the canteen when you're
looking for us, come on Bill," Ray told him heading
towards the canteen.

"Only if you are buying," Bill says getting out of the car
and following.

"I suppose I can stretch my bank balance to that, come
on mister skinflint, the next time you buy." Ray laughed.

"I'm not rich like you, I can't extend to all the
extravagance that you can."

"Go on into the canteen and order the coffee I'll pay for
it when I get there, I'm just off for a pee, and make sure
it's only coffee, no sticky buns," Ray told him as they
parted company.

While Ray was making his way to the toilets he came
across the SB Inspector in the corridor, the inspector
was looking a little worried.

"Ah! I'm glad I caught you Ray, I've got a bit of a
problem?"

"Tell me all your worries, let me try and help you my
son," Ray joked with him.

"The thing is that I have had a bit of info. That PJ (one of the towns known terrorists) is at his moms in the Derrybeg, he has been on the run for some time, we want him for questioning about the attempted murder of Andy, the cop from your section who is off on sick leave because of gunshot injuries."

"All you have to do is get a patrol car to drive past and see if his car is outside of the house, if it is then sit and wait for him," Ray advised.

"It's not as simple as that, what if his car isn't there and he got a lift?"

This would cause a problem because it would mean that a police car would have to keep an eye on the house and a Police car static in a very well-known Republican estate would soon be either shot at, or bombed.

Police cars never stopped in the estate unless it had good back up from other cars, the estate was a really anti Police and Army Ghetto, there had been many attacks on the security forces while in the area.

"As well as that if a car is seen too often near his moms house he will take flight again, this could be a good chance to get him, however we have to know if he is in the house or not, so you see my problem, don't you Ray?"

"That's no problem at all, I can try and find that out for you," Ray told him with confidence.

"How'll you do that? Walk up to the front door and knock?" the Inspector laughed.

"No I will go into the Violet Hill estate which as you know is opposite the Derrybeg on the other side of the valley and over looks it, then I will get out my little pair of binoculars and watch the house, I know a very good spot to watch from as I have often been in Violet Hill estate doing exactly the same thing on other occasions," Ray suggested.

"That's a great idea, but you're on mobile patrol, what'll

you tell the others in the car?"

"If you clear it with my Sergeant I'll get into plain clothes and take a trip into Violet Hill and hole up for a while."

"You're not taking your own car are you?"

"No I'll be walking, I won't go anywhere near the houses in the estate I'll go along the railway line at the bottom of the valley and work my way up the side of it, then no-one will see me, or even know I'm there."

"You seem to know that area very well Ray, there's no doubt you've done it quite a few times before?"

"Let's just say when I'm off duty it's an extra-curricular activity." Ray smiled.

"Okay I will go and get things arranged, meanwhile you go and get changed." The inspector said.

"Just one thing Inspector, I have a radio in my locker that I sometimes use to get in touch with HQNI, I believe that you have one in your office drawer for when the SAS are working this area. Before I go out I'll contact them and they will give me a channel that we can both work on, then I can keep in contact with you, is that okay?"

"That is a great idea I was wondering how we could get over the communications problem, I never knew you had a radio for that, boy you learn something new every day, don't you?" Says the Inspector, shaking his head.

"I'll see you in your office in about fifteen minutes then, is that alright Sir?" Ray said as he left to go to his locker and tell Bill that he would not after all be going back out with them.

Upon reaching his locker he got into civilian clothing, got all his equipment ready putting a small pair of binoculars in his jacket inside pocket, his pistol in the waist pocket, then put his radio earpiece in place.

He checked that the throat microphone was fitted right, and most important of all that the radio batteries were charged, then he left the locker room and made his way back to the SB office.

Once he was there he was there he telephoned HQNI to get a safe channel to use, on receiving it he asked the Inspector to switch the SB radio on and he carried out a radio check, his signal was load and clear.

"Right Inspector, I'm off, here is the route and location that I will be at," Ray told him pointing at a map of the area, the place was the waste land at the back of the Violet hill estate where the railway track passed.

The embankments to the railway track were quite high and overgrown and Ray knew that he could get into a good position that overlooked the front of the house.

"I'll get the local mobile patrols to cover the area, just in case anything goes wrong, like the local IRA men getting wind of you being there and sending a squad to take you out," the Inspector suggested.

"No thanks, that would only bring attention to something going on, if I need help I'll call you, it would be best if they kept away and only answered necessary calls there," Ray told him.

"When will you be back in Ray?" asked the Inspector.

"You'll see me when you see me, as Arnold Swarzenneger would say, I'LL BE BACK, so don't worry," Ray laughed.

"I bloody hope so, all we need is for you to get your bloody head shot off, we'd have a heck of a job trying to explain to the Chief Constable how we lost one of his men,"

"It's nice to know you care, anyway must dash got a house to watch bye," Ray says as he left the office.

He made his way to the rear of the station where the gate guard let him out into Catherine Street, where he quickly made his way up the slight hill that led him away from the station.

At the top of this hill was a break in the brick wall that

edged the road, the gap was covered by a couple of sheets of corrugated iron, after a quick look around Ray pulled one side of them away from the wall and passed through the hole.

Once he had replaced the sheet of corrugated iron he was in a grass paddock, the paddock was at the top of the embankment, rather than just walk straight across the grass area to the opposite fence he skirted around the side of it, just in case someone might see him from the upper parts of the houses that surrounded the field.

On reaching the other fence he pushed down the top length of barbed wire and got over it and stopped for a few minutes and knelt down to work out his best route through all the stinging nettles and brambles, also he wanted to check to see if anyone had seen him or was following him.

After about five minutes he proceeded to make his way along the bank, things were not that easy as he thought they would be, the brambles kept tugging at his jacket and jeans, with the stinging nettles managing to penetrate his jeans every so often and stinging him he started to wonder why he had bothered to offer his services.

Roughly twenty minutes after starting he was in a position which would enable him a clear and unobstructed view of the house which would be nearly six hundred yards away as the crow flies.

His immediate surroundings and cover was a thick clump of brambles and gorse bushes the only angle that he could possibly be seen from was head on.

Where he was hidden gave him a good view of anyone or thing moving along the railway track.

He had an arc of vision of one hundred and eighty degrees, Ray made himself comfortable took out his binoculars and focused them on the house, for once it wasn't raining which pleased him.

Around an hour and a half he had been sitting in his little hide away when he saw a car drive past the house he had been watching, the car seemed to slow down as it passed the premises.

This seemed a little suspicious to Ray so he trained his binoculars on it he could see two men in the front and a woman in the back of the car, he kept watching it and saw it start to turn around in the road and head back in the direction it had come.

He continued to observe the vehicle, as it approached the house he saw it pull in to the side of the road and stop directly in front of it.

He then saw the woman get out of it from the back seat and start to make her way to the house front door, while watching the woman walk he noticed that her walk was nothing like a woman's, her gait was very masculine, looking closer at the legs of the woman Ray came to the conclusion that the woman was really a man in drag.

The house front door was quickly opened and the woman seemed to rush into the house as if she didn't want to be seen, this action confirmed Ray's suspicion, the car in the meantime had moved a little further along the road and parked.

Ray watched as the two men in it got out of it and they also made their way to the house and went in.

"Sierra Bravo from India Papa, over" Ray said as he pressed his transmit button for his radio.

"India Papa send," came the reply.

"Roger, I have seen a person dressed as a woman enter the suspect building, I believe this person to be our target, this person is accompanied by two males, over."

"Roger, wait out till I get further instructions from above."

"Well don't make it too long just in case this person doesn't stay around," Ray advised.

Two minutes later the SB inspector's voice came over

the radio,

"India Papa, this is Sierra Bravo we have dispatched the local DMSU (Divisional Mobile Support Unit) to make a sweep of the area and to carry out the arrest, over."

"Roger, I'll stay in position until this has been completed, then I'll return, over."

"Roger and out," replied the Inspector breaking the radio link.

Ray sat and watched as the DMSU moved into position around the house, as he trained his binoculars on the house front window he saw one of the men look out through it.

The man must have seen one of the Police Officers approaching as he quickly moved away from the window and seemed to be saying something to someone else in the room with him.

By this time the DMSU snatch squad had kicked in the house front door and rushed inside, shortly afterwards he saw the three men and a woman who was obviously PJ's mother being taken away and put in four separate landrovers.

When they had all left the area Ray made his way back to the Police station, this time however rather than go in through the back gate he walked in the front entrance.

"Hello Ray, where the heck have you been?" asked the man behind the enquiry office counter whom Ray had been sitting with earlier.

"Just fancied doing a bit of shopping, got bored so I went around town for a walk, tell you one thing though, there ain't much to buy in this place," he replied as he went into the office part of the building.

Ray carried on walking straight through the building and out to the locker room where he got changed back into his uniform, no sooner had he done this than a message came over the station intercom.

"Constable Rutherford report to the Special Branch

Inspector," the message was repeated.

"Frig, now what do they want?" Ray thought to himself. He made his way to the office where the Inspector was elated at seeing him.

"Well done Ray, you done a great job, come here and lets have a quick dram to celebrate," he said opening the door to his own office.

Ray followed him in and sat in an easy chair in the corner of the room, while he was just getting settled the station Sub Divisional Commander came in.

"I see you're starting to earn your keep? That was a good little job you've just done, I am impressed," he said holding out his hand for Ray to shake.

"I'm glad that I have pleased you, as for future things that might be coming my way, perhaps you'll turn a blind eye to some of my methods of working?" Ray replied shaking the Superintendents hand.

"Providing you don't go OTT (over the top) I'll be quite happy if what has just taken place happens all the time."

"I can't promise that Sir, but I'll try," Ray smiled.

CHAPTER – 6 - NIGHTSHIFT

Roughly a week later Ray's section was on night shift, he loved this shift because it meant that he could sit in the entrance to a lane way and watch the movement of traffic.

His friend Jimmy liked Ray doing this because not only was there a good chance of catching someone either breaking the law or any of the local terrorists driving past, but he could also relax and shut his eyes for half an hour or so.

Ray always parked in one of the many turnoffs on the Omeath road watching for traffic coming into Newry.

On this particular night he saw a Ford transit van drive past the end of the road, he thought that it looked a bit suspicious so he decided to follow it, on pulling out onto the Omeath road he saw that the van was travelling at speed, so he put his foot down on the accelerator of the Police car and gave chase.

As the police car started to draw up behind the van, the van's rear doors suddenly opened and he could see three men in the back of it, they were all pointing Kalashnikov AK47 assault rifles at his car.

"Shit Jimmy it's time we weren't here!" Ray said stamping on the foot brake pedal, and then hand braking the car around to face the direction in which they had just come from.

"Drive like hell, get the hell out of here," Jimmy screamed as he picked up the cars radio microphone to pass the information on to the station communications room.

"Hotel Delta, Hotel Delta, this is Hotel Delta 71 over," Jimmy said into the microphone.

"Delta 71 from Hotel Delta send over." Was the reply?

"Roger Hotel Delta, we have just attempted to follow a Ford Transit van along the Omeath road headed towards the town centre, on pulling up behind it the rear doors opened and we saw three men inside the back armed with AK47's," Jimmy says.

"Where is this vehicle headed now? Over," came from the communications officer.

"Roger it is headed into the town, over."

"Could you give us the colour and VRM (vehicle registration mark) over."

"Only the colour which is dark Blue, the VRM I am not sure of because of what took place, over."

"What you really mean to say is you shit yourself with fright, didn't you?" was heard to come over the radio, this call had been made by another patrol car.

"So would you if it was you who had come across it," Jimmy replied sounding angry with the person who had said it.

"Sorry to interrupt you little chat, but 71, what is your position now? Do you still have the van in your sight, over," came from the communications Officer.

"Delta from 71 no we are now headed in a different direction, my partner wanted to follow but I am afraid that I have a wife and three kids to think of, he doesn't have that sort of problem," Jimmy said giving a chuckle.

"Roger the Duty Inspector has told me to pass on that he wants you to head towards the town centre to see if you can find the van again, over."

"Roger will do, I'll let you know if we find it," Jimmy said unhappily.

Ray stopped the car, then turned it and started driving towards the town centre.

"I hope we can find the bloody thing again, I knew we should have kept an eye on it, God knows where it might be now," he moaned at Jimmy.

"It can be where the hell it likes for all I care, I have a family to think of," Jimmy replied.

"I know you have, but you don't think I would let anything happen to you, do you, after all you are my best mate."

"There is only one thing that worries me though?"

"What's that Jim?"

"You're a mad bastard, and getting into a gunfight wouldn't bother you but I'm afraid the idea scares the crap out of me," Jimmy smiled.

"It scares me as well, you're not the only one, the thought of taking on maybe five gunmen armed with AK47's isn't exactly pleasing," Ray told him.

"Well we'll not fall out about it, where shall we start looking?" Jimmy said as they neared the outskirts of the town.

"Let's get a quick look in the Drumalane Park patch, you never know we might have scared them just as much as they scared us, they might have gone to ground there, so keep your eyes open," Ray warned.

They drove into the Drumalane estate and headed down towards the garages at the bottom, this was part of the estate that Ray did not like to be in too often as in the garages area there was very little room for manoeuvre; the chances of being ambushed were quite high.

Once they had a quick look around they drove out of the estate and headed towards another, which was called Barcroft Park, to get to it they drove towards the Monaghan Road, one of the main roads in the town.

As the drove towards the Monaghan Road Ray took a quick glance down a small side street, which is called Pound Street, this street is the smallest street in the town, as he looked he spied the van.

"There it is Jimmy, it's parked in Pound Street," he said as they drove across the top of the entrance into it.

"Keep going and park a little further along, I'll just radio in," Jimmy advised.

"Well I wasn't exactly going to go and have a look at it," Ray replied sarcastically.

"Hold on a minute, pull in just here," Jimmy said when

they were roughly two hundred yards from the street. Ray turned the Police car around so that they would have a better view of the entrance to the street, he then stopped the car.

Jimmy was just about to speak into the main radio microphone when Ray said to him.

"Don't use that radio use the chat net one, if those guys from the van happen to have a radio tuned into the main set they'll know what is happening."

"Shit you're right, hold on," Jimmy said picking up the chat net microphone.

"107 alpha, from 107 bravo," Jimmy called into it.

"107 bravo, 107alpha send," was the reply heard coming from the radio.

"Roger, can you RV (rendezvous) with us near the junction of Pound Street, we have found the van," Jimmy says.

He then called the communications officer and made him aware that they had found the van.

"Roger, duty Inspector and Sergeant on their way, all cars this is 107, proceed to Pound Street RV with the duty Inspector," the communications officer directed the other patrol cars.

Within five minutes Ray observed in his car's rear view mirror the duty Inspector and Sergeant's vehicle pull up behind his, Ray got out of his car and met the Inspector.

"The van's parked down Pound Street, at the bottom of it in the cul-de-sac, it's up against the fence to Haldane and Shields builders merchants," Ray told him.

"Have you been near enough to get a good look at it?" the Inspector wanted to know.

"No Sir, I saw it as we passed the top of the Street and we decided to stop here, I didn't want to give the game away by going to look at it."

"Could the men still be in it?"

"I wouldn't know Sir, maybe they have a safe house

somewhere here in the street and thought that if they parked here we wouldn't find them."

"They could have, I wonder, tell you what I'll get the duty SB man to run a check for us before we do anything else, meanwhile just you stay here in case they come out to go somewhere else," the Inspector told Ray.

"Okay Sir, but what about these other cars?" Ray said pointing to the other patrol cars that had arrived.

The Inspector signalled with his hand for the other patrol car drivers to come to him, when had done so he told them to leave the area and to park in the main Monaghan Road just around the corner and wait for further instructions.

When they had gone he told Ray to get back into his patrol car and wait until he, the Inspector had more information from the duty SB man, the Inspector then left to go back to the Station.

Roughly fifteen minutes later the Sergeant returned he was looking a little bit confused.

"Ray, we've had a chat with the SB man and he tells us that there are no known sympathisers in Pound Street, I was just wondering whose house they could be in or if they haven't just dumped the van because you saw them."

"All we can do then Skipper is to wait until they either return for the vehicle or see if they come out of one of the houses," Ray suggested.

"If we do that it would mean leaving a car here nearly all night, I don't think the Inspector would be too pleased about that."

"You don't have to leave a car here, I'll skirt my way around the back yards of the houses on foot and get behind the fence to the builders yard and keep an eye on the street, then Jimmy can take one of the spare men in one of the other cars with him."

"That would be a bit risky for you, what if they catch on

that you are there?"

"I have taken bigger risks in my life Skipper, providing I have my radio if anything develops I can always give you a shout," Ray assured him.

"That's all well and good saying that but what if you don't get the chance to use your radio?" the Sergeant says worriedly.

"Then you'll hear the shooting because I won't go without a fight, or better still if you get a strong smell of shit around the town it means I'm in trouble," Ray laughed.

"Okay I'll let the Inspector know, but you don't move until I give you the word, the Inspector might say no," the Sergeant says leaving Ray's car and going back to his own.

"I think your bloody bonkers, I'm damned if I would take the sort of risk that you're going to take," Jimmy said in disbelief.

"If you're not in, you can't win, anyway it will be better than sitting in a car all night listening to you snoring," Ray told him laughing.

"I don't sleep in the car I am only inspecting the insides of my eyelids, you cheeky sod, I should slap you for that remark," Jimmy joked.

"Hotel Delta 71, Hotel Sierra," the Sergeants voice was then heard to come from the radio.

"Sierra, send, over," Jimmy answered.

"Roger, inform your partner that what we were previously talking about, is a go, over."

"Roger and out," Jimmy replied.

"Right I'm off then, see you later, make sure and listen out to the radio just in case I need you in a hurry," Ray said as he got out of the car to make his way around the back of the houses to take up his position.

"You keep your bloody eyes open, I don't want to be coming back here with a body bag for you," Jimmy replied.

"I don't think you'll have to do that, oh and tell the others to stay away from the area, I don't want them giving the game away," Ray said as he started to walk away.

Ray walked away from the car towards a darkened part of the street, he tried to keep as low as he could and make use of what cover there was to mask his movements and the direction in which he was headed.

It was not long before he was in the alley that went the full length of the rear of the houses, he moved down it very cautiously and quietly.

At the end of the alley was the perimeter fence of the builders supply yard, the fence was quite high and there seemed to be no way of getting either over or through it, at least without making a lot of noise.

"Shit, now I'm snookered," Ray thought to himself.

He stayed in the alley for a short time while he tried to work out how to get over his present problem, it wasn't long before he decided to leave the alley and try to gain access to the yard by other means.

On reaching the end of the walkway where it joined onto the street pavement Ray crouched down behind one of the garden walls and spoke into his microphone.

"Delta 71, from 71 bravo," he said into it.

"71 bravo send, over," came Jimmy's voice.

"Roger, could you pick me up at the alleyway at the back of the houses, over."

"Be with you in two minutes, out."

In what must have been under a minute Ray saw the Police cars lights coming towards him.

"What took you so long?" he joked as he got into the backseat of the car.

"We had to finish our burgers first," the driver of the car a man called Davey told Ray.

"That wouldn't surprise me, Jimmy does nothing but eat

and sleep when he's on night shift anyway."

"You are really cruising for a bruising Ray," Jimmy said sounding hurt.

"And you are always getting ambition and ability mixed up Jimmy," Ray retorted.

"Well up the pair of you, I can see that I won't get any backup from Davey, so I may as well get back to sleep," Jimmy says settling back in his seat and closing his eyes as if going to sleep.

"So what do you want to do now Ray?" Davey asked.

"Do either of you know a way to get into that yard where there is little chance of being seen or making enough noise to wake the dead?"

"I do," Jimmy said sitting forward again.

"Well I can't mind read, so do spill the beans."

"Do you know where the speakeasy bar is, it's just off Merchants Quay, well if you go into the lane where it is there's a big double gate which is the rear of the yard, you might be able to climb over them."

"Right Davey lets go," Ray told him.

Davey drove towards the main Dublin Road, he then turned left at the junction towards the Merchants Quay Road, no sooner had he got on it when he took a left turn and turned into the Street that Jimmy was talking about.

They went towards the end of it and Ray could see the two big double gates Jimmy was referring to.

"Okay, turn around and drop me off somewhere where it's a bit darker than it is here just in case anyone should see me," Ray said.

"In case you hadn't noticed Ray there are no streetlights in this place, it's dark all along it," Davey pointed out.

"I'm glad you told me that I was beginning to think I'd gone blind," Ray says to him sarcastically.

"Now don't start fighting Girls, we'll drop you off here Ray, will this do?" Jimmy wanted to know.

It was nearly 150 yards from the gates so Ray agreed. "Switch your lights off Davey and slow down, don't stop, I'll get ready and just step out of the car, you can then just carry on, I'll let you know how things are going, that's if I can get into the bloody place," Ray laughed. Once they had dropped Ray off the car left and Ray crouched into a kneeling position he took a quick look around to see if anyone was watching him or had seen him.

After two or three minutes he got up and made his way towards the gates, when he reached them he noticed that the wall on either side of them had broken glass bottle pieces which had been cemented onto the top of them, the gates were about nine feet high.

This would mean that he would have to go either through or over the gates, however on the top of the gates there were three strands of barbed wire running across them.

He looked at the side of the gates and noticed there was a slight indentation in the brickwork of the wall where part of a brick had been broken, it would mean a bit of a stretch but he managed to lift his leg high enough to put the toe of his boot into the hole.

Lifting himself up he took hold of the top of the gate, which was metal, and then he started to untwist the end of the barbed wire. It was not easy, as he had to try to keep his foot where it was and hold on with one hand while trying to untwist the wire with the other.

It took a bit of time but at last he succeeded and he pulled himself up and over the gates, he lowered himself down the other side.

When his feet touched the ground again he turned and looked around the yard, it was pitch black and he could only make out the rough outline of things that he had to manoeuvre around.

Slowly and gingerly he started to make his way over to

where the perimeter fence edged the end of Pound Street.

He had only walked about twenty yards when he nearly tripped and fell over a small pile of road kerbing stones, he stopped in order to try and see if there was anything else he might be able to see that might cause this to happen again.

As he looked he suddenly heard something move over to his right; he knelt down at the same time he drew his magnum from its holster ready just in case there was someone waiting to ambush him.

Trying hard not to breathe too heavily, he bent his head lower down so that anything higher than his head he could see silhouetted by the skyline.

Slowly he turned his head to scan the area immediately to his right, as he turned it he saw something move against the skyline, he strained his eyes even more and then got a shock, he could make out what looked like to be the shape of a dog's head looking in his direction.

"Oh frig, now I've had it," he thought to himself.

Just then he heard Jimmy's voice in his radio earpiece.

"71 bravo from 71, over."

This was all he needed now, Ray knew from his experience of working with dogs that not only could he hear Jimmy but also the dog would be able to pick the slightest sound up, now he was between the devil and the deep blue sea.

He knew that if he didn't answer Jimmy, then Jimmy would think that something had gone wrong, on the other hand if he did answer him then the dog might take it into his head to attack.

Fifteen or twenty seconds later Jimmy called again, Ray had to answer him, so keeping an eye on the dog's head he said into his throat microphone.

"71, send, over."

"Roger, just thought I would give you a little bit of info,

they usually have two guard dogs in that yard overnight, over."

"Now you bloody tell me, I'm looking at one now, I don't know where the other is, hopefully he's off on the sick," Ray replied.

"Did you say you are looking at one now," Jimmy wanted confirmed.

"Roger, Yes to that, over."

"Oh boy, are you in the shit now," Jimmy said, sounding as though trying not to laugh.

"If I get out of this I am going to wring your neck, and that's a promise," Ray told him.

"Well, I'll let you get on with things, let us know if you have any difficulties, we'll have an ambulance on standby, over and out," Jimmy said ending the transmission.

Knowing that time was not on his side Ray decided to try and continue towards the fence, as he started to move he could hear the dog growling, realising that unless he got out of the yard, or tried to pacify the dog he wouldn't be able to do the job.

He stopped and turned in the dogs' direction and made a noise with his lips as if he were dealing with a cat.

He noticed that the dog had stopped growling and so he made the noise again, Ray squinted his eyes and was almost laid flat on the ground, anything to get the advantage of being able to see the dog.

After a short while the dog was within five feet of him, sniffing the air and obviously getting the scent of Ray, it advanced to nearly three feet of him with its nose pushed forward sniffing even harder.

Trying not to show any fear Ray softly called to the dog, "Come on, good boy, good dog, here boy."

To his surprise the dog started to come even nearer, he slowly put out his hand and the dog started to move his nose towards it.

Ray gave a few more words of encouragement and the dog moved right up to him, he gave the dog a light pat on its shoulder and continued to talk to it.

It wasn't long before Ray got back up on his feet and started to make his way to the fence, the dog seemed to be quite friendly towards him and walked ahead, a couple of minutes later they were both laying in hiding behind the fence.

Ray had managed to find a small gap through which he could see the whole length of Pound Street, looking at his watch he saw that the time was 03.10am, he spoke into his throat microphone.

"Hello 71, this is 71 bravo, over."

"71 bravo, send, over."

"Roger I am in position, and can see all of the street, over."

"Those guard dogs can't be up to much, over" came the reply.

"They just know a good man when they see one, over."

"I'll get the buggers sacked in the morning, over."

"You have me to contend with first, now whose laughing? Over."

"Not Jimmy that's for sure," was heard on the radio from the Sergeant.

"Too true Skipper, I'll get off the air now and give you a shout if there's any movement, over," Ray told him.

"Roger, keep alert, out."

While Ray lay in hiding the dog was laying down beside him and seemed quite content, every so often Ray would stroke it and give it a pat, it didn't bother him that the other one might come about, as he knew that the one he was with would probably help to protect him.

He had been in position for around forty minutes when he saw one of the downstairs lights in one of the houses go on, fifteen minutes later he watched as a man came out of the house with a cup of tea in his hand and walk over to the van.

The man looked through the driver's side window into the van, then put his hand into his trouser pocket and pull out a bunch of keys, after sorting through them he put one of the keys into the door lock of the van and opened it.

"Delta Sierra, from 71 bravo, we have movement at the van, over," Ray said as quietly as possible hoping that his throat microphones picked up his message.

"Bravo from Sierra, roger I will have the others take up their positions, you stay where you are, we will be moving now, out," was the reply.

Ray just settled into his hiding place more and waited, as he watched the man he saw the house door open again and another man came out.

"Hey Seamus, what are you doing?" this man called to the one at the van.

"I'm just checking Paul, to make sure everything is alright."

"Good idea, we don't want anything to go wrong, it was a good job we lost those bloody cops last night."

"I bet the thick fuckers have combed the town looking for us, I don't think they would ever find us here."

"Well it's a good thing we opened the back doors, it scared the shit out of them, did you see the way they turned their car, and the speed they drove off at? Yellow bastards." Paul says.

"Let's be honest though, I think it would have the same effect on me as well, I don't think I would be too brave staring down the end of an AK." Seamus admitted.

Just then the dog started to growl and gave a slight bark.

"What's that?" Seamus asked Paul.

"Och! They have dogs running around inside that yard every night to stop people breaking in," Paul answered him.

"I thought that someone was behind the fence."

"Not a fucking chance, if anyone went over there in the night those dogs would bloody eat them."

Just then two other men came out of the house.

"Hiya Paul, Seamus," one of them said.

"Hi, Pat, Tony," came from Paul.

"What are you two at?" Tony enquired.

"We were just checking the van and talking about the dogs over the fence, Paul says that they would eat anyone climbing in there at night," Seamus told him.

"You're bloody right, I don't think they feed the bloody things, they're a right pair of vicious brutes, I've seen them," Pat informed him.

"Well I ain't scared of them, watch this," Tony says walking over towards the fence, as he did so he fumbled with the front of his trousers, on reaching it he took out his penis and began to urinate against the fence.

"Oh but you're brave, if that dog didn't have the fence between you and it, your balls would be in its mouth," Paul laughed.

At this point Ray heard the sound of cars coming along the main road heading in his direction.

"We are just about to turn into the top of the street Ray," he heard the Sergeant say in his earpiece.

No sooner had this been said than the headlights of a Police car illuminated the whole street.

The four men were caught in the open and stared at the car with a look of disbelief on their faces.

"I'm out of here, every man for himself," the man Tony said as he ran towards the fence.

"Those dogs will have you if you climb over that fence, you're better off staying here and giving up, we aren't armed so they can't shoot us," Paul advised him.

"No fucking way, I'll see ya," Tony replied as he started to scale the fence.

At this point Ray stood up ready to put a stop to his

escape, as Tony put his face over the fence he met Ray's rifle butt coming towards him, it hit him square in the face causing him to fall back on the other side in a heap on the ground with blood pouring from his nose and mouth.

Ray started to climb the fence to get into Pound Street.

"Are you alright Ray," the Sergeant asked as he saw Rays head and shoulders appear above the fence.

"No problem Skipper, a good nights work eh!"

"Well Tony boy, is your face sore, why did you try to kiss my rifle butt? You little tinker," Ray said as he dropped down off the fence to join the other policemen.

The men were handcuffed and a Police search team went into the house to search it for the weapons and any other terrorist equipment.

"Right let's get this little lot off to the holding centre in Gough Barracks, make sure they all get a separate vehicle, then they can't concoct a story," the Sergeant says to them.

The Duty Inspector arrived at the scene just as the men were being driven away.

"Well done Ray, another good job, the Superintendent is in his office."

"Why what's wrong has he shit his bed or something," Ray joked.

"No he's waiting to see you and Jimmy so don't keep him hanging around, you can go now, I'll see you back at the Station Okay?"

"Yes Sir, we'll see you before we knock off, come on Jimmy lets go," Ray said as he went to the Police car.

Once they had put all their kit in the car they set off back to the station, as they drove through the station rear gates they could see the Superintendent just coming out of the canteen carrying a cup of either tea or coffee.

He saw them pull up and decided to wait until they got

out of the car, as they did he says, "Well done you two, come with me," as he headed in the direction of his office.

"Christ he's as happy as a pig in shit, we'd better follow him quickly just in case he changes his mood," Jimmy says quickly following.

"No take your time, savour the moment, he thinks we are the best thing since sliced bread, we couldn't ever do anything wrong in his eyes now, I bet if we were to ask for a couple of weeks off duty he would probably give us a month," Ray laughed.

"I don't believe in pushing my luck like you do, come on get a move on," Jimmy moaned.

When they had reached the office Ray knocked on the door that was slightly ajar, "Come in, don't hang around outside, I want to hear all the details, take a seat make yourselves comfortable," the Superintendent says pointing at some easy chairs.

When they had settled Jimmy started to tell what had taken place, the Superintendent sat looking at him as if mesmerised, taking in every detail.

When Jimmy had finished the Superintendent looked at Ray, "Thank you for your report Jimmy you can go now, Ray you just hold on a want a wee word with you please."

Jimmy got up and left, as he went out of the door the Superintendent waited a few minutes as he listened to the sound of Jimmy's footsteps fading then he focused his attention on Ray.

"The reason that I have held you back Ray is that I have to tell you that I have had orders from Headquarters that you are to be moved to the town of Lurgan, this is because they have been informed from a reliable source that you are on an IRA hit list, and they are going to try to murder you."

"Why me, how come my name is on the list is there any

other cops names from here who are on it?"

"I am afraid not, just yours."

"That's strange, I haven't been here as long as half the others in this place."

"Apparently from what I have been told, one of your informants has done the dirty on you and has told the local top IRA men that you are the main threat here, obviously after what happened here tonight they'll go out of their way to kill you especially when they get to know that you were involved."

"What if I don't want to go?"

"You have no choice, you're going whether you like it or not, I tried my best to keep you but I'm afraid that I can't argue with a Chief Constable, even I have to obey some orders," the Superintendent smiled.

"Oh well," Ray sighed, "When do I have to go?"

"When you have finished this week's nightshift you can take a week's leave that should give you enough time to move your kit and take it over to Lurgan."

"Okay Sir, thank you it was nice working here I was just getting into my stride, someone from HQ probably knew that I was enjoying myself and didn't like it so they thought of this to piss me off, so I'll be seeing you Sir thanks for your help and co-operation," Ray said to him offering his hand for shaking.

"It annoys me Ray, like I said there was nothing I could do, but it was good to have someone like you here, take care and goodbye," the Superintendent says shaking his hand.

CHAPTER – 7 - MOVED

At the end of Ray's week of nightshift rather than have to come back and move his kit during the weeks leave that he had been given, he decided that on the last morning when his shift finished he would pack his car and take his equipment straight over to Lurgan.

It took him a bit of time and then he was on his way to his new station, he wasn't pleased in leaving and had even tried himself to get his movement order rescinded, but it was to no avail, someone was determined to have him moved.

On reaching Lurgan Police station he reported to the Station Sergeant who in turn showed him where the locker rooms were telling him to take his pick of any empty one that he might find.

Having found one Ray proceeded to move his kit from his car to the locker, whilst he was doing this another policeman came into the locker room.

"Hello mate, are you new here? Or just passing through?" he asked Ray.

"For my sins I have just been transferred in, I wish I was only just passing through, I can assure you I hope not to be staying here too long," Ray answered.

"What section are you with?" the man asked.

"I haven't a clue I don't officially start here till next week."

"Heck, you're keen, if it was me I wouldn't be here, I'd still be on leave I would've brought my kit on the first day of duty, then it would give me an excuse to skive a little."

"I'd rather get it all moved now at the start of my leave then I wouldn't have to worry about it or still have the job of unpacking it all."

"Oh! Sorry excuse my ignorance, my name's Billy," the man said offering his hand for shaking.

"And I'm Ray."

"You must be Ray Rutherford, you've just been sent here from Newry, am I right? I've heard all about you from my mate Jimmy, he used to work with you," Billy told him.

"Jesus Christ, news travels fast in this job doesn't it?" Ray replied shocked.

"From what I have heard of you, we need your sort here, apparently you've been quite busy in Newry, let's hope you have the same success here," Billy says.

"I hope bloody not, I could do with a rest."

"You'll have little chance of a rest, this place is a hornet's nest, the IRA are always very active about here," Billy assured him.

"If that's the case then I had better make sure to enjoy my leave then," Ray told him as he finished putting his kit in his locker closing the door and putting a padlock on it.

"Well no doubt I'll be seeing you next Monday, have a nice time, I'll see you then," Billy says leaving the locker room.

"Yeah, see you," Ray replied, while thinking to himself, "From the frying pan into the fire."

He left the room himself and decided to go for a stroll round the station to try and get to know the place, as he came up the stairs from the locker room he bumped into a plain clothes man.

"Hello, how are you? You must be new here I haven't seen your chops about here before," the man said to him.

"Yes I'm the new cannon fodder, I've just moved my kit over from Newry I'm starting here next Monday," Ray told him.

"You must be the famous Ray Rutherford we've been told about, my names Pete I'm in the SB here, if you've got a few minutes you can come with me and I'll introduce you to the rest of them."

"Only if you're making the coffee, I need something to try to keep me awake, I only finished nightshift in Newry this morning, and I'm knackered."

"No problem, come on follow me we'll use the lift," Pete said walking to what were obviously the lift doors.

Inside the lift Ray noted that Pete pressed the button for the second floor, about twenty seconds later they were getting out of it and Ray followed him along the corridor to the SB office.

"You have to knock to get into this place," Pete informed Ray as he knocked on the door, on entering the Office Ray saw that all the walls that would have pictures and details of all the local terrorists on had screens covering them.

"Look what I found wandering around downstairs," Pete says pointing at Ray.

"Ray this is Terry, Graham, Paul, Sean, and this gentle man here is the Boss, he runs the place," Pete said indicating to a man who was in another room, which was just off the main office.

"Ah! Ray come in and lets have a little chat," the man who was called the Boss invited Ray into his room.

"How do you do Sir?" Ray said walking in.

"Close that door Ray," the Boss indicated to the room's door.

When Ray had done this the man introduced himself, "My names Steve, it's good to have you here, I hope you can do for us the same as you did in Newry, I've been made aware of your real purpose for being a cop by the Chief Constable."

"I was thinking that I might get a bit of peace, it's just that too many people are getting to know about what I have been up to when I was in Newry, all it takes is one load mouthed cop in this place to, shall we say, let things slip and I'll have to be moved again."

"I know how you must feel, yes you're right, however we

need someone in this station who can play these terrorists at their own game,"

"I can't promise that, but I'll give it a good try, just one thing though I think you had better let the Superintendent know the reason for my being sent here, it caused a bit of shit to hit the fan in Newry when the Super. there tried to have me disciplined for upsetting the natives," Ray informed him.

"That's a good idea, are you free to go and have a chat with him now, or do you want to wait till you come back off leave?" Steve wanted to know.

"Well providing it won't take long we can go and see him now if you want?"

"Right, follow me, we'll see if he's in yet," Steve said getting up from his chair and leaving the office.

They walked along the corridor and followed it around a right hand corner passed through a set of double doors and stopped outside of a door with a nameplate on it saying Sub-Divisional Commander, (S.D.C.).

Steve knocked on the door and opened it, putting just his head inside with the door half open, Ray heard him say, "Good morning Sir, I have brought a Constable Rutherford along with me to see you, we have something to tell you."

"Yes Steve come in, you'll have to bear with me I've only just got in, had a bit of a late night you know," the SDC says.

When Ray entered the room Steve introduced him, "Sir this is Ray Rutherford, he has been transferred here from Newry, at present he is on leave and starts with us in a week's time."

"Hello Ray nice to have you here," the SDC says shaking Ray's hand, "you had both better take a seat," he said indicating to some chairs.

"Thank you Sir," they both said sitting down.

"Now what have you got to tell me?" enquired the SDC.

"Well Sir I don't know if you know anything about Ray so I'll let you into a few things, to start with, Ray is not just an ordinary cop, he is also a member of the SAS, his job is to collect and collate information on known terrorists moving and working in this area and also South Armagh," Steve told him.

"Wait a minute Steve, I already know this I was briefed by the Assistant Chief Constable of the Special Branch, he told me yesterday when I had a meeting with him, I know all about Ray and his, um little traits."

"Thank God for that I nearly got in to a bit of bother in Newry because the SDC there knew nothing about me," Ray told him smiling.

"Have no fear, I am well aware of what your real purpose is in this force, and I might add I am very pleased that you are here, no doubt that whatever you get up to I'll be kept informed, oh! and try not to break the law while carrying out your little tasks won't you," the SDC winked at Ray.

"But of course Sir, what is that saying, 'Do unto others?" Ray smiled.

"Well thank you for coming to see me Steve, Ray, but I have some very important things that I have to be getting on with, no doubt I'll be seeing you when you start here, have a nice bit of leave Ray, make the most of it, until then goodbye," the Superintendent says getting up from his seat and seeing them both to the door.

Once they had left the office Steve turned to Ray saying, "That's it then I'll see you after your break, like the Super. says make the most of it, you'll find it rather busy around here."

"I'll leave my phone number in the control room, if you need me before my leave ends don't be shy to give me a call, I promise I won't bite," Ray smiled walking away towards the stairs that lead down to the control room.

When he had reached the control room he went into the telephonist's area and put his name and telephone number in the contact register then left the station to make his way home.

On entering his house he found that Pauline was not in so he made himself a cup of tea, which he took up the stairs to drink in bed while he watched the television before falling asleep.

He only slept for a few hours before he was awakened by the sound of the front door of the house being opened, he listened to see whom it might be coming in, just in case it was someone who shouldn't be in the house he picked up his Magnum revolver which was on the bedside cabinet beside him.

Not being able to determine whom it was he shouted out, "Who's that down there?"

"It's only me," he heard Pauline say in reply.

"I thought you were at work, what are you home for?" he asked her getting out of the bed and walking to the bedroom door.

"I had an appointment at the doctors, I haven't been too well, I've got a bit of morning sickness."

"Is it bad? I hope everything is ok,' Ray said sounding concerned.

"Oh it's nothing too serious, it's just normal sickness that you get, I have been told by some of the other women, that the Doctor can prescribe some kind of medicine for it." Pauline answered.

"Would you like me to come with you?" Ray asked.

"Not really but you can if you want."

"Well give me five minutes to get dressed and have a quick wash and I'll be with you."

"Okay Darling I'll wait for you downstairs," Pauline said as she went into the living room.

After Ray had finished getting ready he went downstairs to meet her where he gave her a quick peck on the cheek saying "I'm ready shall we go?"

They both walked out of the front door towards Ray's car, after getting settled into it they drove to the doctors.

On their journey Ray told her about how he had moved his kit to Lurgan.

He had never told Pauline the real reason why he had been moved and was a little bit wary of letting her know, but he decided to tell her.

"I know I should have told you earlier but there is a reason why they have moved me, it's because Intelligence have good information that the IRA are out to get me and they were going to try and ambush me on my way to Newry."

"Why didn't you tell me earlier?" Pauline wanted to know.

"Because at first they were not sure, and they had to get it confirmed from other informants," Ray answered.

"How serious is it? Will they be coming to our house?"

"As far as I know they do not know where I live however I would suggest that from now on you stay more alert as to what is going on around you." Ray told her.

"Well at least I now know why you've been moved, I only hope that we don't end up having to leave Richhill cause we have only just got settled in," Pauline said sounding peeved.

"Well if I hear any more and things are starting to sound too risky I'll tell you as soon as I find out," Ray assured her.

Now that he had enlightened Pauline as to the reason why he had been moved Ray felt a little bit better, however he had only lightly touched on the subject and knew for a fact that things were a little bit more serious as quite a few of his informants had let him know that not only his life but also the life of his wife were in danger.

It was beginning to worry him and he had many sleepless nights worrying about Pauline and his future child's lives.

It was okay for him because he knew what the possible outcome could be for him, but the last thing that he would want would be to have his family involved.

After the visit to the doctor they called in at Pauline's parent's house to let them know how things were going. On entering Pauline called out to her mother "Mum it's only us, we've just come from the doctors as I am having a lot of sickness."

"I'm glad you've come, because I was going to ask you have you thought of any names for the baby," Bet asked.

"Not yet as we don't even know what it is going to be whether it'll be a boy or a girl I have to go to the hospital in two week's time to get a scan so I will know then." Pauline told her.

After a cup of tea and a bit of general chat Ray and Pauline left, while they were driving back to their own house Ray began to think about his new post in Lurgan. He knew from working in Newry that there was a lot of contact between the Lurgan IRA unit and that of the ones in Newry, the good thing was he knew exactly who was seeing who, so it wouldn't be hard to keep an eye on them.

Just to refresh himself on their faces he went into a room in the house that he used as a study and after turning on a computer in it he selected a file that he had with all the sightings and photographs that he had accumulated on the Lurgan suspects.

Most of these not even the Lurgan SB had ever seen, Ray had always used a computer to record any information on things that he might hear or see on these people.

This was not only to refresh his own memory but also it

came in handy when he had information to pass on to 14 Intelligence section.

While checking through the information that he had on them he would change the details that he had found different, things like if they changed their cars, houses, friends or associates.

The one thing he always enjoyed was changing the dead or in jail part, as he saw it, there would be one less to take up space on the computer's hard drive.

His weeks leave seemed to pass very quickly and it wasn't long before he was parading for his first days duty in Lurgan, as he sat in the station briefing room he turned his head each time the room's door opened and one of his new work colleagues walked in.

Not one of them said good morning or even let on that they saw him, this made him begin to wonder if he was wearing the right after shave or not.

It didn't take him long to catch on to the fact for some reason or other the Regular Professional Police Officers who were career men sat nowhere near the Full time Reserve Police Officers.

As a matter of fact they didn't even look in each other's directions; Ray found this very strange because in Newry the comradeship was second to none and everyone mixed and chatted with each other.

The duty Sergeant was the last person through the door and he took up a position at a lectern in front of them all, he detailed Ray to be the observer in an armoured Tangi Landrover.

He would be with two other men who were called Bobby, and John, Bobby was detailed to be the driver and John was to be what was known as the rear gunner.

The rear gunner's job was to give cover to the observer whenever the observer was out of the vehicle dealing with something he was basically the observers eyes and ears.

After the briefing as they all left the room the Sergeant stopped the three of them telling Bobby and John to carry on, as he wanted a chat with Ray.

Ray went with him to the Sergeants office where the Sergeant told him to sit down on a nearby seat.

"Right Ray, first off welcome to the section, my name is Joe, it is good to have you with us I have heard a little about you and your exploits in Newry."

"Oh! And what might they be?" Ray asked guardedly.

"Well rumour control has it that you seem to be having your own little war, that you have a nasty habit of appearing or being anywhere that there might be a little trouble taking place, is that right?"

"I don't know what you mean Sergeant, I only do my job," Ray replied a bit confused, wondering what the Sergeant was getting at.

"The section Inspector tells me that he knows you and what your methods of policing are like, he told me to let it be known to you that if you so much as breath wrong while you're here he will have you dismissed from the Police."

This angered Ray and he felt his temper rising, he didn't need this kind of hassle, after all he had only just arrived.

"What do you mean by that Sergeant? Is it you that has said this? or was it really the Inspector?"

"I am just passing on what I have been told to tell you," the Sergeant said looking sheepish.

"Is the Inspector in at this moment?" Ray wanted to know.

"Yes he's probably having his morning coffee now, he doesn't like to be disturbed while he is having it."

"Well with all due respect to your rank Sergeant, sod him, please excuse me I'm gonna see him now and what's more I don't give a toss whether he's having is bloody coffee or not," Ray said getting up from his seat and walking out of the office.

As he walked along the corridor to the Inspectors office he switched on a Dictaphone tape recorder that he had in his top inside pocket of his Dartex jacket.

He had a small microphone that had been specially made for it pinned under the lapel, he often switched it on when he was going to be talking to any of the terrorists whom he might happen to stop in the street this was to record their conversations.

It didn't take long before he was knocking on the Inspectors door, there was no answer to his first knock so he knocked a bit harder, he heard someone moving behind the door and it was quickly pulled open.

"What do you want? Don't you know I see no one till I've had my coffee," the Inspector snarled angrily.

"So sorry to have troubled you Sir but if you wouldn't mind sparing me a few minutes of your precious time Sir, I would like to have a little Pow-wow with you after what the Sergeant has just informed me of," Ray told him sarcastically.

"Right come in, stand there," The Inspector ordered pointing to a spot in front of his desk, Ray done as he was told and the Inspector started the conversation. "What has he told you?"

"He made me aware that you know of me and didn't like my methods of policing and you told him if I so much as breathe wrong you will have me dismissed from the job, is that correct Sir?"

"As a matter of fact it is, you seem to forget Rutherford I was in Newry before I was transferred here so I know all about you, if you start your tricks here you'll rue the day, I don't want anyone in my section rousing the locals."

"I'm sorry Sir but I don't quite see what you mean," Ray says acting dumb.

"I mean I want to do my time in this station with the

least amount of trouble, if you start doing the sort of things here as you done in Newry the local IRA just might decide to start shooting or bombing the town."

"But I thought that one of the policing jobs in all of the towns was to try and apprehend the terrorists and stop that sort of thing happening?"

"Well let's just say I don't want to be bloody killed just because you want to be a Cowboy, if you start any trouble with the natives you'll be out of here and maybe the job before you can blink, do I make myself clear."

"So what you are telling me Sir is that I am to have nothing to do with the local terrorists, is that correct Sir?" Ray wanted to get confirmed on the tape recording.

"Are you bloody stupid, yes that is exactly what I mean, watch my lips, LEAVE THE TERRORISTS ALONE," the Inspector said louder as he mouthed each word.

"Okay Sir I have it now, I'll do just that," Ray told him smiling.

"Right that's good, now carry on with your duties, goodbye and remember what I have just told you," the Inspector warned him pointing to the office door.

Leaving the office Ray made his way down to the locker room where after taking a quick look around and seeing no other cops there he rewound the tape and played it back.

He could hear the whole conversation very clearly and was pleased that there were no blank or muffled bits on the recording.

"Gotcha, you yellow bastard," Ray thought to himself as he listened.

Happy with the result he took the small tape out of the machine and left it in his locker and replaced it with another one.

Once he had put the recorder back in his pocket he proceeded to make his way to the Operations and Control room to have a call sent out to get the vehicle that he was assigned too, to return and pick him up.

As he stood in the Control room looking out through the bullet proof window at the stations big armoured gates waiting for the vehicle to return he started to think about what had taken place.

He was trying to decide whether to give the tape recording to the station Superintendent now or to the Special Branch Assistant Chief Constable (ACC) at the next Tactical and Co-ordination (TAC) meeting.

One of the problems was that if he gave it to the SDC and the SDC was a good friend of the Inspectors then it would not go any further and the Inspector would get away with what he had said, Ray was not in favour of that happening especially because the Inspector told him he would have him thrown out of a job.

He made up his mind that he would pass it on to the ACC then that way the shit would be coming down from an even greater height and no doubt the ACC would tell the Chief Constable who would make life very hard for the Inspector.

Roughly ten minutes after the call was sent to the police car Ray saw it being driven through the station gates, it came down the hill towards the station then followed the road round to the side of it to the station backyard.

Ray picked up his equipment and left the Control room to go to the backyard, as he walked along the corridor he passed the Sergeants office.

"Ray have you got a minute?" the Sergeant asked him when he saw him.

"Yep, no problem Skipper," Ray stopped at the office door.

"Come in a minute, sit yourself down." Ray entered the office and sat back down on the seat he had not long parted from.

"What can I do for you Skipper?"

"Look Ray, what was said to you this morning is only

what the Inspector wants, it's not what I want, all I want is to get the job done properly I'm not like him, all he is interested in is to go up the ranks without any bloody problems, as far as I'm concerned you just carry on the way you did in Newry, balls to him," the Sergeant says pointing in the direction of the Inspectors office.

"I wasn't very impressed with him; as a matter of fact I think that he and I will have a few arguments with the way he thinks."

"All I can say is don't worry about him, I'll try to keep him off your back," the Sergeant promised.

"Right okay skipper I had better get down the backyard they'll be waiting for me, I'll see you later," Ray said getting up and leaving the office.

He continued along the corridor and as he rounded the corner at the bottom he bumped into Bobby.

"It's all right I am just coming," Ray said to him.

"There's no rush Ray, we're in to get our breakfast, I'll see you in the canteen. I'm just going for a pee," Bobby replied carrying on.

Ray went into the canteen where he saw John sitting at a table with two other men.

"Hi there," he said sitting down at the table with them.

"Hello Ray this is Geoff and this is Will," John introduced him to them.

"Hi guys nice to meet you," Ray shook both their hands.

Looking around the canteen he saw some of the other members of the section sitting at another table.

"What's up with that lot? Have you all got a disease that I don't know about or something?" Ray enquired.

"No in case you haven't noticed, we all have the dreaded big letter 'R' on our shoulders, as you know it means that we are full time Reserve Constables so we're not good enough to be sitting with them," Will informed him.

"What a load of shit, you lot are just as good as them, there's no difference in my eyes." Ray told him.

"That's because you've come from the border where you have to stick together, here it's different, if you carry on sitting with the 'R' Cons they won't take it too kindly."

"One thing my man, nobody tells me who I can sit with or talk to, as far as I can see we are all the bloody same 'R's or no bloody 'R's on our shoulders," Ray replied angrily.

"We could do with more Regulars like you here," John put in.

Just then Bobby came into the room. "Hey Bobby, I have a seat for you here," Ray says to him pointing at a chair.

"No you're all right Ray, I have a cuppa here," Bobby replied indicating to the table that the other men were on.

"Well bring it over, or can't you lift it?" Ray laughed.

"No like I said, I'll sit here," Bobby answered sitting down at the other table.

Bobby's attitude and that of the others on that table annoyed Ray, as he was not used to this sort of behaviour, he had always been accustomed to everybody mucking in together and not really caring whether a man was a Reserve Constable or a Regular Constable.

Although there were other people in the canteen besides the section members he thought it was best that he let the other guys know of how he felt and in a raised voice he said to the men on the other table.

"What the hell is wrong with you lot? Do you think that you are something special just because you're not Reserve Constables? You all seem to forget that we are all fighting the same bloody war here, I have only been in this station for a couple of hours, and I think the section I'm in is full of shit. It would do you a lot of good to be sent down to South Armagh then you might realise that the guy next to you in a shooting might just be the guy that saves your life, whether he's a Reserve Con or not."

Ray's outburst caused a deadly silence in the canteen; everybody sat stunned looking in his direction, and even the duty Inspector who was just coming through the door with the Sergeant stopped with his mouth open. After a minute of silence Ray saw the Inspector muttering something to the Sergeant, who in turn called over to Ray.

"Ray, can I see you in my office?"

Back in the Sergeants office he says, "Ray you've only been here a short while, it's your first day and already you're starting to make waves."

"I suppose the Inspector has told you to have a word with me because he doesn't like what I said."

"You've got it in one, you're not really doing anything to help yourself you know, the thing between the Cons and the 'R' Cons has been going on even before I ever came to the section, there is no love lost between them you might have noticed."

"But that shouldn't be the case, the thing is we are all cops, it shouldn't matter, so what's the problem?"

"I think it's because the Regulars have to do three months training and the Reserves only do six weeks."

"I think the whole thing is bloody stupid," Ray told him.

"Well just do me a favour Ray please try and keep the peace."

"I will Sergeant, I'm sorry for the outburst but I have had my say now so I won't be doing it again."

"Good now let's go and get the breakfast, I'll see you in the canteen," the Sergeant says.

Ray made his way back to the canteen and went to the table that he was sat at, John and the others were still drinking their teas and coffees.

"No doubt you got a rollicking?" John said to Ray as he sat down.

"Only a little one he told me to behave myself."

"So you'll be sitting with the others from now on then?" Will asked.

"Does it look like it?"

"No but then again the others haven't managed to twist you to their little ways yet, you wait they'll have a try."

"They can try all they want, nobody picks who I want to sit with, I'm afraid that I will sit with whom I like," Ray told him.

"Well it's good to know that there is at least one Regular Constable who doesn't mind our company," John said.

"Right who wants another tea or coffee?" Ray asked getting up and making his way to the counter.

"If you're buying I'll have one?" John answered.

"And me," came from Will.

"None for me I've got to go back out to do gate guard," Geoff told him.

Ray ordered the drinks and once they arrived he returned to the table, to get to his he had to pass the one the Regulars sat at.

As he passed he heard one of them say loud enough for him to hear, "He only sits with them because he isn't good enough to be with us, besides he's a fucking Englishman anyway."

Ray ignored what had been said and carried on to his own table, on reaching it he took the drinks off the tray that he was carrying them on, turned and made his way back to the Regular's table where he pulled up a seat and sat down with them, quietly he said.

"I don't know which one of you Yellow Bastards said that as I was passing, but if he has a grievance because I'm English then we can always talk about it in the backyard, that's if he's man enough?"

"If you must know I said it," one of them replied.

"And what's your name?" Ray asked.

"If you must know that as well, it's Damian," came the reply.

"Well Damian I can't help being English just as you can't help being a Catholic so really we are both outsiders being as all this lot are probably Prods, so if I was you I would keep my fucking mouth shut before someone like me slaps you into being good looking."

"Are you threatening me?"

"No I don't make threats, I'm bloody promising you, one thing though just watch who you're messing with because one day I might be in a position that you'll need my help and believe me by the time I've thought about giving it to you, you might be dead." Ray assured him. With these words he got up and went back to his own table, he felt the look of hatred boring into his back from the men as he left.

"What did you say to him? Because the looks he gave you when you left should have turned you to stone," Will asked Ray as he reached his table.

"I just advised him that he was being a very silly saying naughty things about me and that because I am English I'm no different from him," Ray smiled.

"Don't look now Ray but he's gone to speak to the Inspector," John warned.

"I don't give a toss if he speaks to the Chief Constable, neither of them can make me pregnant and if they do I don't have to keep it."

"I think we should go back out on patrol before the shit hits the fan, shall we go or wait a few minutes more?" John suggested.

"No I think you're right John lets go before it starts," Ray replied.

Finishing off their drinks they both got up gathered their equipment and made their way towards the canteen door, Bobby noticed this and done the same, on leaving the building they walked to the Tangi where John opened the back doors on it and climbed in.

Ray went to the front passenger seat put his clipboard

hat and Ruger rifle into the front foot well before getting in; once settled he picked up the radio microphone and carried out a radio check.

They left the station compound and made their way up through the town centre, Ray half turned in his seat to look over into the back of the vehicle to speak to John. "Right John start giving me a run down on the town, if you see any scrotums that I might need to know about let me know will you?"

"Yep no problem, now if you look to your right you will see a public toilet block in the centre of the street, this is the town meeting place for both factions. Every summer all the shitheads from both sides meet here and have a great little battle, it's fun to sit back further up the street and watch."

They travelled up one side of the town and as they came down the other and were passing the Master McGrath public house John leaned over Ray's shoulder and pointed to a youth stood not far from the pub doors. "Do you see that wee twat there? He is one bad wee fucker his name is Declan he always stands in a position so that he can see who is coming out of the station, he's probably taking notes of policemen's car numbers, I think we'll have a word with him, pull over Bobby let's see what he has got to say for himself," John says as Bobby pulls into the side of the road.

Ray and John got out of the vehicle and John walked over to the youth. "Well good morning Declan, and how are you this fine day?" he asked him.

"I was alright till you pair of bastards turned up," he replied with venom.

Ray stood to one side taking note of them both and looking Declan straight in the eye.

"Let's have a wee look at what you have in your pockets shall we?" John says to him.

"I've got fuck all, why don't you just piss off and leave

me alone."

"Now, now, that's not a very nice way to talk, empty your pockets," John ordered.

Declan realising that he wasn't going to get anywhere decided to turn attention to Ray as he had noticed that he had been staring at him.

"What are you bloody staring at?"

"I was just trying to work out when I last saw somebody who has a face as ugly as yours, you were certainly at the back of the queue when looks were given out, you are just so ugly, how do you manage it with just one head?"

"Fuck off you big bastard," Declan spat back.

"This is getting away from the subject, nice try though Declan now empty your pockets," John requested.

Declan with a bit of hesitation started to do as he was asked, Ray kept an eye on him and noticed that he didn't even try to empty what appeared to be a pocket in the lining of his jacket.

"Hold on just a minute Declan there's one of your pockets that you didn't look in, it's this one here," Ray said grabbing hold of him and opening the jacket and pulling the zip back from the pocket.

On closer inspection of the paper John saw that there were some car numbers on it, most of them were those of cars belonging to some of the policemen in the station, he showed the paper to Ray who noticed that his own car registration number was on it.

"Right you little fucker get in the back of the Rover, you are under arrest for gathering information likely to be of use to terrorists," Ray said pushing Declan to the back doors of the vehicle.

"I'm going nowhere, and you can't make me," Declan told him pulling away and standing still.

"OOOOOH! You shouldn't have said that I think you might be very sorry the way you're carrying on, the big lad here," John said pointing at Ray, "has just moved up here from South Armagh and he would shoot you rather than look at you, so if I was you I wouldn't make him angry 'cause you wouldn't like it, now do yourself a favour and get in the Rover," he advised.

Declan took the advice and got in the back.

"What'll you do if I jumped out and ran away?" Declan said to Ray.

"I'll blow your fucking head off," he replied aggressively.

"You're not a very friendly guy are you?"

"Not for arseholes like you I'm not, now do yourself a favour and shut your trap or I'll shut it for you." Ray told him.

The trip back to the station was not long and on their arrival Ray booked Declan into the Station occurrence book while John telephoned the SB office to have one of them know of the arrest, this was so that one of them could come and interview Declan.

CHAPTER – 8 – TIP OFF

Now that Ray had actually had dealings with Declan whenever he was on duty he would keep an eye out for him, this was not only to see what he was up to but also he felt that he could befriend him.

It took about five weeks of Ray continually stopping and chatting with him before Declan started to talk to Ray without any bitterness or hatred towards him.

As Ray was on the beat one day he saw Declan walking towards Lurgan Park and he told the other policeman who was with him to wait where he was, while he went to catch up and stop him.

"Hey Declan, come here a minute," Ray called to him. Stopping and hearing his name called Declan turned to face him, "Hello Ray what do you want me for this time?"

"Nothing much just wanted to have a little chat to see how you are."

"I'm not too bad just cruising along."

"So what have you been up to?"

"Not a lot, I'm a bit pissed off though,"

"Yeah you don't look too happy what's up?"

"I can't tell you."

"Why? Is it as bad as that, you know if I can help you I would," Ray assured him.

"Look Ray we can't talk here, I don't need anyone seeing me talking to you, if the wrong person saw me I would get a beating or maybe even worse a knee capping."

"Surely not you, after all your brother is one of the top IRA gunmen in the town?"

"I know that but it wouldn't make any difference."

"Okay then we'll have a natter some other time, when you feel you want to let me know and we can arrange to meet somewhere that you feel safe," Ray told him turning to walk away.

"Ray before you go, if you want I can chat with you later

tonight, where shall I see you?"

After a bit of thought Ray told him, "I'll be in the Warringstown area tonight sometime after eight o'clock exactly what time I couldn't be sure, if I see you let's say near the war memorial I'll stop then we can go somewhere for a talk, how about that?

"Sounds good to me, I'll see you later then alright?" Declan says moving off in the direction he was already going.

Ray went back to join his partner who this day was a man called Colin.

"Right we'll have to go back to the station there's something I need to do," he told him.

"That's all right by me, I could do with going back I need a good crap and a cuppa tea with a sticky bun," Colin said.

Roughly twenty minutes later they entered the station where they parted company, Colin headed for the canteen while Ray went up in the lift to the second floor to the Special Branch Office.

Steve answered his knock on the door.

"Hi there, are you busy? I've a little something to tell you," Ray informed him.

"Got all the time you want Ray come in," Steve replied. Sitting down and getting comfortable Ray started to tell him about his meeting with Declan.

"He wants to meet me at the war memorial in Warringstown, tonight, I told him if he was there sometime after eight I would be there."

"You didn't give him a definite time then?"

"No I only told him after eight."

"Do you think he's genuine?"

"Well let's just say he seemed positive to me."

"How do you know he isn't setting you up to get you shot?" Steve asked worriedly.

"That's a risk I'll have to take, mind you I don't think

he'd be that stupid."

"You never know with someone like him, he could be setting you up for the brother."

"Well what do you suggest?"

"What we could do is put some of my men in and around the area to keep an eye open to see who happens to be moving about there."

"I don't want them being seen and maybe scaring him off," Ray told him.

"Nobody will even know that they are there."

"Yeah but if Declan sees any of them, his trust in me will be blown."

"Look we will only be seen if we want to be, so what if he sees any one of them he might think that the man is only out for a walk."

"How about getting the SB from Portadown in the area, Declan wouldn't know any of them?"

"Right that seems a good idea, I'll give them a ring, they'll probably be glad of the overtime they don't get a lot there," Steve laughed.

"I would rather you done that then get this all screwed up, this could lead to other things, you never know how helpful Declan might turn out to be."

"I see your point, the only thing is that I don't want to have to report to the Authorities that we've let you get killed."

"Once I have picked him up I will take him for a drive in the Banbridge area, that should put him at his ease, oh and just one thing I wouldn't like any of your men to be seen following just in case he notices."

"How will we know where you are, and if you are alright?" Steve wanted to know.

"We'll just have to trust that things won't go wrong, wont we?" Ray smiled.

"There is one way to keep in touch with you?" the SB man Pete said.

"And what might that be?" Steve answered him.

"Well if Ray was to go over to Mahon Road camp and see the Tactical Support Unit (TSU) they could put a bug and radio tracking device in his car then we could listen to what is going on and also be able to follow at a long distance." Pete told him.

"That's a bloody good idea, what do you think Ray?"

"Fine by me, but will they be able to do it with such short notice?"

"We'll soon find out," Steve says picking up his phone and dialling a number.

At the end of a conversation with the person who had answered the phone in Mahon Road Steve turned to Ray.

"Right that's it then they have agreed to put it is as soon as you get your car over there, they haven't much on, so away you go," he told Ray and pointed at the office door.

"Just one thing Sir, what do I tell my Inspector?"

"Leave that with me I'll get the SDC to tell him that you're to go home re some problem," Steve assured him.

Ray left the office went to the locker room and got changed then went to his car to drive to Portadown Mahon Road camp.

On reaching it he made contact with the TSU Inspector who told him to drive his car into a big green coloured Nissan type building which they were using as a workshop.

The work only took a few hours before Ray was on his way back to Lurgan, when he reached the station he reported straight to Steve.

"Right Sir that's me all set up."

"Dead on, I suggest that you go home now and if you can report here at, let's say 1845hs tonight," he said looking at his watch, "then we can finalise what is going to take place, is that alright?"

"It's fine by me, I'll see you later then," Ray says as he

goes out through the office door.

Ray returned back at the station at around 1815 where he went to the canteen to get a cup of tea as he entered it he saw a number of uniformed men who were not from the station but were from the Headquarters Mobile Support Unit. (HMSU)

This unit was a specialist team that had been formed to mainly deal with terrorists; their sole purpose in life was to either arrest or eliminate any persons involved in the commission of terrorist acts.

They were the uniformed branch of another special unit called E4a who worked in civilian clothes, Ray had actually made application to join E4a but had been refused, the senior officers of the unit thought that he wouldn't be good enough for them.

He often inwardly laughed at them as these guys really thought they were god's gift to undercover work, little did they know that the terrorists more or less knew exactly who was in the team.

As he sat drinking his tea on a different table one of the HMSU men spoke to him,

"Hello Ray long time no see, what brings you in at this time of the night are you working overtime?"

"I suppose you could say that, what are you lot here for?"

"We can't tell you that, it's a need to know basis and you don't need to know," another of the HMSU men told him.

"Oh is it? And who do you think I'm going tell? In case you didn't notice I wasn't asking you anyway," Ray replied a bit annoyed at the man butting into the conversation.

"I'll have you know that I happen to be a Sergeant, so I would watch what you say to me."

"Is that because you think you're something special?"

"Let's just say we all happen to be a cut above the ordinary cops like you," the Sergeant says haughtily.

"I'm sorry I didn't know you were a Sergeant, I don't see any rank displayed on you, I think you're pulling my leg," Ray smiled.

"We don't show our rank, we don't have to because we all know who is who, that's what you get when you work in a tight knit unit like ours, we tend to work on the same sort of thing as the SAS."

"I see I didn't know that," Ray told him as though unknowing.

"Here is another bit of info. for you, the training we have to do for this unit is based on the same as the SAS."

"Boy! I see what you mean by maybe being a cut above the ordinary cop, you must have really trained hard?" Ray said to him while laughing inwardly.

"You'd better believe it, so the best thing you could do is take yourself off, when you're up to our standard of training then you might be good enough to sit with us," the Sergeant says.

The Sergeant's attitude annoyed Ray but he didn't say anything he just got up and left the canteen to make his way down to the main briefing room, as he entered it he saw Steve already there waiting.

"Hello Ray, do you have everything ready?" Steve asked.

"Yeah, I see that the cowboys are up in the canteen."

"We only called them so that they could do cover, the Divisional Commander told us to task them."

"I thought that it would only be SB who would be doing the cover work?" Ray said a bit put out.

"So did I but the powers to be decided otherwise," Steve replied sounding apologetic.

"I think the next time I have to meet someone I'll keep it to myself."

"That could be a bit dangerous Ray, I wouldn't advise you to be doing that sort of thing, you'll stand a good chance of getting killed that way."

"Warringstown will wonder what the fuck is going on

tonight if anyone sees all the bloody roughty toughty Police running around," Ray told him.

"Like I said Ray there's nothing I can do about it, well look I'm just going up to my office to get my briefing notes, I'll be back in a minute," Steve says leaving the room.

Ray stayed where he was sitting and waited, he was not alone long when the first of the HMSU men came into the room closely followed by the Sergeant that Ray had dealings with before.

"We meet again," the Sergeant says to him.

"We'll have to stop meeting like this, people will be starting to talk about us," Ray said smiling.

"I'm afraid you'll have to leave as we are getting a briefing here in about ten minutes by the SB, you'll be able to come back after, is that alright?" the Sergeant said pointing to the door.

"Oh! I see, sorry," Ray says getting up to leave.

As he was going through the door Steve was coming in with two other SB men and the Divisional SB Superintendent.

"Where are you going Ray?" he asked.

"I've been told that I am not supposed to be here as this is far too important for me, I'm not good enough," he replied looking around at the HMSU Sergeant.

"Who told you that, this whole thing revolves around you," Steve says.

"Well if the HMSU Sergeant doesn't mind I'll stay then," Ray smiled knowing that he had dropped the Sergeant in the shit.

"Right Ray give your bit of briefing, you can tell the HMSU what their duties are," Steve told him.

"Okay thanks Sir."

Ray told the HMSU what he wanted and explained to them that their presence in the area was not to be known he wanted them to stay in their positions until they were either stood down or if they were called for, at the end of the briefing he asked.

"Are there any questions?"

"Yes I have one," the HMSU Sergeant says.

"What would you like to know, I thought that someone who had been SAS trained would have found my briefing quite straight forward."

"It was but what I would like to know is, what is the actual job?"

"I'm sorry but that is a need to know basis, and I am afraid you do not need to know, all you have to do is make sure you carry out your part of it," Ray told him smiling, as were some of the other HMSU men.

"I think we had all better go to my office," Steve said noting that there was a bit of friction between them.

Roughly five minutes later they were in Steve's office, "Right I don't know what's going on between you two, but I think I can guess, how do you feel about me letting the Sergeant in on our little secret Ray?"

"It's up to you, boss, mind you I hope he knows how to keep his mouth shut?" Ray says.

Steve went on to tell the Sergeant what Ray's true role was in the Province.

"Now that you know what it is, I will just tell you that if word ever gets out about what you now know you'll be in deep shit, so mums the word, is that understood?" Steve informed him.

"I seem to owe you an apology Ray," the Sergeant offered.

"We'll not fall out about it, however I think in future you should always be a little more careful how you treat the ordinary cops," he smiled.

"Now that you two have kissed and made up let's get on with the task in hand, shall we return to the briefing room?" Steve said as he opened the office door.

Five minutes after reaching the briefing room the

Sergeant led his men out to their vehicles to drive out to Warringstown and take up their positions.

At twenty minutes to eight after Ray had made sure that his radios were working by doing a radio check, made sure that his Revolver was properly loaded he made his way to his car.

When he got to it he opened the car boot and took out a false set of number plates and proceeded to put them on his car.

Ray had three sets of false plates that he could put on the car and he changed them around every week or ten days, this was to cause confusion to any of the terrorists who might have his cars details in order to carry out a hit on him.

It wasn't long before he was driving out through the station gates and headed in the direction of Warringstown.

As he drove along he kept an eye out to see if Declan might be on his way to the village.

He was hoping he might see him, as it would mean that he wouldn't have to meet him at the rendezvous point, this would cut down the risk of possibly being murdered.

It wasn't long before he saw the village boundary sign and he slowed down to the thirty miles per hour speed limit for the village.

Whilst driving through the village towards the meeting place he kept his wits about him and gave nearly everything a second look, on turning a corner the war memorial came into his view and he could see Declan there waiting for him.

Just to be on the safe side rather than stop there and then Ray continued to drive past and follow the road up the hill from the war memorial towards the town of Banbridge.

He caught sight of Declan in his rear view mirror looking at his car and watching him, Ray continued on his way and drove up and over the hill, when he knew he was out of Declan's sight he turned his car around and stopped.

After waiting for a few minutes he pressed a button which had been fitted on the underside of his steering wheel, the button was a radio transmission switch, the microphones were hidden in the lining of the car doorposts.

"Bronze 1, from Alpha 1 over," he said.

"Alpha 1, from Bronze 1 send," he heard the reply.

"Roger, I am about to meet with our subject, how are things your end? Over."

"All is well here, nothing moving, over"

"Right I'm on my way, out," Ray said ending the transmissions.

Before continuing to the meeting he leaned over and flicked another switch under the dashboard, this switch turned on a vehicle tracking device so that the vehicles direction of travel could be seen by the SB men who would be following him as backup in case anything went wrong.

It also started a tape recorder so that anything said in the vehicle could be recorded for future reference.

Ray drove back over the hill towards where Declan was waiting, as he done so he kept an eye on the side of the road or any places where he might be ambushed.

On nearing Declan he pressed the button in his car that wound down the electrically operated windows.

"Right come on get in," he said to Declan as he drew up beside him.

"I didn't think you were coming," he says getting into the car.

"We'll take a wee drive, I don't want to be sitting here just in case someone sees you with me and you get your knee caps shot."

"Where are we going?" Declan asked.

"I think we should take a drive out towards Tandragee, It's in the arsehole of nowhere so nobody should see us there."

"Yeah that's a good idea, I haven't been in Tandragee for quite a while."

"So what do you have to tell me?" Ray asked as he started to drive.

"It's about my brother Colin, as you probably already know he's the top IRA man in Lurgan."

"Tell me something new, we've known that for a very very long time."

"Yeah but did you know that him and yer man Clooney are planning to do a shooting at Craigavon cop shop?"

"No I didn't, now that is new, how do you know all this?" Ray asked.

"I was in the house the other night and overheard them talking when I was in another room, so I put my ear to the door to hear more and caught all they were talking about."

"When are they going to do the job?"

"Clooney is sussing the movements of the cops when they turn up for duty, as you know the station doesn't have a car park inside the station grounds and they all have to park outside the perimeter wall, well that's when it's going to happen," Declan says.

"I know all that but when is it going down? Is what I asked."

"Sometime in the next two weeks, Clooney says that he'll need that much time to work out the change of shift patterns."

"How is Clooney keeping an eye on the station?"

"He's watching from a flat overlooking it."

"I don't suppose you know which one by any chance?"

"I haven't a clue, all I know is that it belongs to someone who is part of the IRA unit, I think it's a woman, who she is I don't know, however I do know that her name is

Bronagh."

"I suppose it will be a sniping job, will it?"

"No apparently Colin is going to do it on a motorbike, he is going to do a ride past."

"Is he going to shoot anyone in particular," Ray wanted to know this as then the cop concerned could be moved out of the area to another station.

"No just whoever gets in his sights at the time, you never know Ray it could be you or any cop calling there."

"Are you sure it's definitely going to happen?" Ray asked, as he was not sure if Declan was telling the truth.

"I am dead positive, apparently the top brass of the IRA in Belfast want the Lurgan ones to do something as they haven't done anything for a while."

"So the Lurgan boys have got to prove that they aren't sitting back on their arses doing nothing eh!"

"That's right so my brother is going to give them something to talk about."

"There is just one thing puzzling me Declan, why are you telling me all this?" Ray wanted to know.

"Because believe it or not I am getting fed up with all the bother he is causing to my mom and dad, the police are never off the doorstep."

"Well why do you do the lookout jobs for him? All you're doing is getting yourself a bad name that is why all the cops in this town give you a hard time."

"If I don't do want he wants I'm worried that he'll maybe shoot me or get my knee caps blown off."

"Ah! So by telling me what he is up to you are hoping he either gets killed or he ends up being arrested, so then you won't get as much hassle, am I right?"

"I mean to say Ray, the cops are nearly always on our doorstep and searching our house every two or three weeks just because of him it's really annoying."

"Okay I'll see what can be done, well let's drive back to Warringstown then I can drop you off, or do you want me to drop you nearer Lurgan?"

"No drop me near where you picked me up, by the way you'll not tell anyone what I told you will you?"

"What you tell me stays with me, if you hear of anything else coming down you can always tell me, Oh! I forgot, how are you off for cash? Do you need any?" Ray offered.

"I'm not doing this for money I'm only doing it too get that bastard brother of mine out the way, money is the last thing on my mind."

"I realise that but a few extra quid always helps doesn't it?"

"I suppose it does."

"Here's twenty pounds, that should keep you in cigarettes for a while, if you have any really good info. then I can see you getting a lot more than that." Ray assured him.

"Now that sounds good to me, thanks Ray."

By this time they had reached Warringstown and Ray dropped Declan off near the memorial, then he made his way back to the station to attend a debriefing by Steve.

CHAPTER – 9 – DEBRIEFING

When Ray had parked his car and turned off all the devices he made his way up to the SB office where Steve was sitting with two other men whom Ray knew as members of the Tactical Co-ordination Group (TCG).

"That was a good job, well done Ray," Steve said as Ray settled down into a chair.

"I only hope he wasn't pulling our pissers, if he was he'll rue the day," Ray replied.

"Do you know these gentlemen? They are Brad and Pete, from the TCG they're very interested in what is happening," Steve says introducing the other men.

"Nice to meet you gentlemen, and to what do we owe this pleasure?"

"We have been after cracking the IRA unit in this town for quite some time," the man called Brad says.

"And no doubt you find this an opportunity to do so?" Ray smiled.

"Let's just say that this would be the best chance we get to possibly put away their leader, it would be good to have him permanently out of the way or maybe in prison for a long time, either way doesn't matter."

"I'm all in favour of that," Steve told him.

"Aren't we all?" Ray muttered.

"So how are we going to deal with this problem?" Pete asked.

"The thing is Declan's brother is going to do a ride by on a motorcycle, this could be a big problem especially as we don't know when," Steve says.

"We do know it will be within the next two weeks and at a shift change over time, but which changeover?"

"Well he's got three every day, the thing is can we justify the cost of extra manpower to keep close observation on the station?" Brad said.

"What about using the HMSU, as far as I know they have very little work to do, the Sergeant was telling me that tonight's job was the first real tasking that they had done for quite a while, most of the time they are training," Ray told them all.

"That's a good idea all this training they have done can be put into practice, then we can see if they are as good as they profess to be," Steve says in agreement.

"I don't know, it would have to be cleared by the divisional operations officer, he might not want them to be doing this sort of work," Brad informed him.

"Why not? after all they are supposed to be an anti-terrorist unit and we are dealing with terrorists here." Steve answered.

"Yes but they have been formed to act as uniform support for the E4a branch," Pete added.

For the unknowing E4a are another branch within the force that has the sole responsibility to gather intelligence, carry out surveillance on terrorists, and try to find weapons stored by the IRA or other terrorist organisations.

They work like the Codie and Boyles of the television program the professionals, however most of the police officers in the force felt that with their sort of professionalism they would be better off being called the Codeine and Boils.

"I think that surely trying to save a cops life is more important than whether the HMSU can work for us rather than being the sole property of E4a," Steve says sounding annoyed.

"You don't understand Steve it's not as simple as that, the HMSU are mainly for taking out groups of terrorists not just one," Brad tells him.

"What are you saying here? Just now you told us that it would be good to have Colin out of the way and that this was a good opportunity to do it?" Ray says coming to Steve's support.

 "Yes I know I said that but I thought that there would

be more than just one of the IRA unit doing the job," Brad admitted.

"Well I'm so bloody sorry that there aren't more for you, so where do we stand in regards to trying to stop one of the policemen in Craigavon being murdered?" Steve said angrily.

"Well you could ask operations if the local DMSU (Divisional Mobile Support Unit) could be spared," Brad suggested.

"I don't believe I'm hearing this, are you telling us that a cop's life means nothing to you?" Ray asked.

"All I can say is that knowing the local IRA unit here they'll probably cock it up any way," Pete says.

"And what if they don't? It means some poor cop dies just because you can't be bothered to stop it happening," Ray seethed.

"It would just be a glitch in the overall plan that we have for this area," Brad says.

"It's nice to know that you lot have an overall plan, but what about the poor wife and family of the cop that gets it?" Ray wanted to know.

"That is not of our concern, you know what it's like, his family would be well looked after and his wife and kids will probably better off than if he was still alive."

"I'm not listening to any more of this crap, I'm off," Ray said getting up and heading for the office door.

"No don't go yet Ray I want a chat with you after these so called gentlemen have left, we can discuss how best to deal with things," Steve said.

The men from the TCG took the hint and gathered their jackets and notes then made their way out of the office while Ray sat back in the chair that he was in.

"We have a heck of a problem," Steve said as he closed the office door.

"Only because of those bastards," Ray replied.

"Let's forget about them, we'll try and sort something

out." Steve says.

"I only hope we can or some poor cop ends up dead."

"Do you have any ideas or anything that might help get us out of this tangle Ray?"

"First of all we need to know which flat Clooney is using, then hopefully if we manage to catch him in the act of watching the station we can pull him in for a few days to Gough Barracks interrogation centre."

"Yes, I have already told my men to get a good look at the electoral register for a woman in the surrounding flats whose first name is Bronagh."

"Hopefully if we find her we can get Clooney, failing that we could get the Divisional Mobile Support Unit (DMSU) to do civilian clothed surveillance in the area." Ray suggested.

"They would probably quite enjoy doing it, it's different from what they would normally be up to," Steve agreed.

"The biggest problem we have though is how the hell do we cover the men at the shift change over times, as you know, they all have to park their cars outside of the station the chances of one of them being shot are quite high." Ray pointed out.

"What about having them all come here to Lurgan, and then transporting them to Craigavon in an armoured Landover?"

"The only thing with that is, the IRA would know that we had got wind of something going on, however I think that the idea is a good one, at least we won't be attending any funerals."

"Right that's what I'll do then I will see the SDC and have him pass on the order that all members of Craigavon police station will report to Lurgan for transportation to and from their station for security reasons," Steve decided.

The transportation went on for the next ten days and no attack or attempt to attack the police coming and going from the station materialised.

On the eleventh day while Ray was performing mobile patrols of Lurgan an emergency call came over the car radio informing all vehicles that a member of the Craigavon Criminal Investigation Department (CID) had been shot at while getting out of his car to enter the station.

Ray immediately drove towards the Kilwilkee estate in Lurgan which was a very strong Republican estate and where Colin and Clooney lived.

He was hoping that he could catch Colin on the motorbike to either arrest him or if needs be shoot him. As he entered the estate he drove down past Colin's house but there was no sign of him, he also went past where Clooney lived he also did not appear to be around, so Ray decided to keep up surveillance in the area.

He had only been in the area for roughly half an hour when he heard that Colin had been stopped and arrested by members of the DMSU, a little put out about this he left the estate and carried on with patrolling the town.

When he got home later that night Pauline met him at the door, after giving him a peck on the lips she said "I have an appointment for the hospital on Thursday for a scan so then we will know if we are going to have a boy or a girl," she informed him.

"That's fantastic I'm really pleased about that, so we'll finally know, all I hope is that it has all of its fingers and toes and is okay," Ray answered.

"To be quite honest with you darling I just can't wait, I'm so excited."

Thursday soon came around and they went to Craigavon hospital for the scan.

As the doctor moved scanner across Pauline's stomach we started to tell them what he saw.

"Well Mrs Gray from what I can see here you are going to have a girl."

"How do you feel about that Ray?" Pauline asked as she looked him in the face.

"To be really honest with you darling I don't mind at all, mind you I would love to have had a boy, however providing like I said before she has all of her fingers and toes I'm more than happy and no doubt I'll be quite proud to be walking with her hand in hand when we go shopping," Ray told her.

Once the examination was over Ray and Pauline returned home and it wasn't long before Pauline was on the phone to her mother.

When she had finished her conversation and replaced the receiver she turned to Ray, "So now we have to think of names for a girl, what would you like to call her?"

"Well providing it is not after anyone in the family I don't really mind, because that is one thing that will cause an argument in any family when someone names their child after a relation because then the other ones feel a bit put out," Ray said.

"I will have to get a little book with children's names in it then maybe we can pick one, or better still I can ask my friends at work if they have any suggestions."

Ray at this time, with other things on his mind did not really want to get into choosing the baby's name.

"Well we have plenty of time to choose one so let's not rush into it shall we?" He remarked.

"Okay we'll wait until later," Pauline agreed

CHAPTER – 10 - HMSU

Roughly ten weeks after the hospital appointment Ray was told he was to attend an Interview with a senior officer of the E4a department in Mahon Road military and police camp in a town called Portadown.

After parking his car outside of the E4a offices he went to the buildings front door where there was a uniformed police officer waiting for him.

"Hello, you must be Ray?" the man enquired.

"Yep that's right, I have an interview with your boss where do I go?"

"Hold on a minute and I'll let you in," the man said going over to the building door and pressing some buttons on a combination door lock, when the door opened he said, "Go straight down this corridor and turn left, the boss has his office the second door on the right."

Ray followed the directions and was soon knocking on the office door.

"Come in," could be heard in answer to his knock.

He entered the office and saw three men sitting around a big square desk, "Constable Rutherford Sir, I believe you sent for me?"

"Yes I did Ray, this is Chief Inspector Allen, and Inspector Greaves, I am Superintendent Murphy, please sit down," the man in the middle of them told him indicating to a chair opposite them all.

"I suppose you are wondering why we have sent for you?" the Chief Inspector says.

"Let's just say I am a little curious," Ray told him.

"The thing is Ray we know all about you and we feel that keeping you on ordinary police duties is a bit of a waste of your sort of talents, so we think that you would be better employed putting them to good use with this unit, how do you feel about that?"

"To be honest Sir I wouldn't like it at all, I'm quite happy working in Lurgan."

"The job would mean that you wouldn't be up to your eyes in paperwork," the Inspector said trying to entice him.

"I don't get that bogged down with paperwork anyway Sir," Ray replied.

"You are being offered a very good job here, you would be a fool not to take it, just think you'd be able to really get to grips with the terrorists," the Superintendent put in.

"If that was all I ever thought of I could get to grips with them in Lurgan, as you know I have some very good touts there Sir."

"We know that but we feel that you should be with this unit, we are asking you, rather than ordering you move here," Said the Chief.

"If you had me moved here just so that I would be with you then you would have one unhappy cop, mind you I could mention this to authorities a little bit higher than the ranks present here, and I am sure that they would listen to what I have to say," Ray threatened.

"Alright Ray, you can't blame us for trying," the Superintendent conceded.

"The thing is Sir that if I am taken away from Lurgan how will I be able to keep in touch with my touts?"

"We see your point it would be hard," he admitted.

"Also Sir can you recall the last incident that took place at Craigavon cop shop?"

"Yes the one where they tried to kill a CID man?" the Inspector says.

"That's right Sir, well I can remember being in the SB office in Lurgan when the E4a men were there and we told them what was going to happen and they didn't want to know, hopefully the next time they might be a little bit more interested, it shows my informants are giving me the right stuff."

"Yes we know that now, if you get any more good info.

like that Ray then I'm sure it will be acted upon," the Superintendent said looking at the other two men as if he had been kept in the dark about it.

"Oh! I see that I have mentioned something I shouldn't have, have you finished with me Sir?" Ray asked.

"Yes I think that will be all, however if something else does come up you'll be notified," the Chief said dismissing him.

Ray got up from his seat and left the office, as he walked back to his car he started to smile, as he knew that the Superintendent would be rollicking the Chief and the Inspector.

Around two weeks after this Ray was out on foot patrol in Lurgan when he saw another of his informants, this man was known to the police as being the second in command of the IRA unit.

Ray had managed to recruit him as an informant because he stopped him one day while he was on mobile patrols and found the man to be drunken driving, a deal was made between them that he would let Ray into a few secrets if he would let him off.

"And what about ya?" Ray said approaching him.

"Not too bad Ray and you?"

"I'm fine thanks, have you anything to tell me?" Ray enquired.

"There is something coming down soon, three men from the Taghnevan estate are going to carry out a hit on a UDR member, who lives just outside of Portadown," he said looking around him to see if anyone was watching him talking to Ray.

"You're looking a bit restless, would you like to chat somewhere else?" Ray asked.

"Anywhere but here in the street, you never know who might see us."

"Tell you what you take a walk into Lurgan Park and I'll meet you there in about twenty minutes by the cricket clubhouse, is that alright?"

"It's a lot better than here, I'll see you soon," the man said carrying on in the same direction he was going in before he was stopped.

When the man was a safe distance away Ray retraced his steps back to the Police station where he went up to the SB office and spoke to Steve.

"Hi there, guess what? I am about to meet with Biff, he has something to tell me apparently there is a job coming down in Portadown," he told him.

"Bloody hell, don't tell me you've got him telling you stuff as well?" Steve said shocked.

"It's amazing what you can do when you have something on someone," Ray smiled.

"I'm surprised you haven't managed to get Colin to work for you?"

"Not yet but I'll work on it." Ray laughed.

"Tell me what's going on then?" Steve asked.

"Some UDR boy is going to be murdered at his home, he lives just outside of Portadown," Ray replied.

"When are you going to meet Biff?"

"I have to meet him in about fifteen minutes outside the Lurgan cricket club in the Park."

"Right I will have men in the park to cover you, you had better leave now," Steve advised.

Ray quickly made his way out of the station and walked briskly towards the Park.

As he passed through the park gates near the Grand Orange Lodge hall his eyes scanned the area looking for anything that might be out of place or anybody whom he might know to be suspect.

Even though Steve had said that he would have men in the area to cover him Ray knew that it didn't take long to shoot someone especially if the sniper was holed up in one of the Rhododendron bushes that littered the park. He walked along the tarmac pathway towards the club watching everything around him to make sure that no one was watching him, as he neared the club building he turned off onto a rough gravel pathway to bring him behind it.

Before walking around the corner of the club house he loosened his magnum revolver in its holster and took hold of the pistol grip, he turned on his pocket tape recorder then went over to the side of the building and peered around it to see if there was anyone there, when he saw there wasn't he continued around the back.

About halfway around the back Biff suddenly appeared out of a recessed doorway, Ray speedily drew his pistol from its holster.

"It's only me," Biff shouted nervously.

"I nearly blew your bloody head off then," Ray told him.

"I was shitting myself as well, I didn't know who was coming, I thought that someone had seen me hiding here." Biff says.

"As far as I can see we are the only ones here, so let's make it quick, what's coming down?"

"Like I said there is going to be a hit on a UDR man who lives just outside of Portadown."

"Where? Just outside of Portadown?"

"Do you know the roundabout just past Shamrock Park heading towards Armagh?"

"Yep I sure do."

"Well if you go up the hill just over it there is a road on the right if you go along it there are a number of bungalows, he lives in one of them," Biff says.

"And who is going to do the job?"

"Three boys from the Taghnevan."

"When?" Ray wanted to know.

"They have it planned for Friday."

"What time? Do you know?"

"Yep they will be leaving the estate at about nine o'clock Friday night they hope to have the job done by ten thirty."

"What sort of guns are they going to use?"

"They will have with them an Armalite, an AK47, and an Uzi."

"What sort of car will they be in? And what's the registration"

"It will be a Red Toyota, it has an English Registration, I'm not sure what it is but it is the only one on the estate."

Ray knew the vehicle that Biff was describing as he had seen it on several occasions being driven through the town and around the estate.

"You had better not be pulling my leg you know what will happen if you are," Ray warned him.

"I'm not, I know what you'll do if I'm pissing you around," Biff smiled knowingly.

"I don't suppose you know what route they will be taking do you?" Ray needed to know this so that the authorities could set up a vehicle checkpoint to get the car stopped.

"Ah come on Ray, you should know that I wouldn't know that, only the men who are going to do the job and Colin would have that sort of information" Biff laughed.

"I would have thought that with you being second in command of the IRA unit here you would know?"

"It works that only those involved in the job know all the details, that way the least amount of people who know the less chance of anything leaking," Biff says.

"Right that will do for now, how are you off money do you need any?" Ray asked him.

"I could do with a few quid how much do you want to give me?"

"Would twenty quid do for now and if this comes off and we bag them I'll see to it that you get a lot more how's that?"

"It'll do for now, but I hope it will be a fair bit more afterwards," Biff told him.

"It will, here you are," Ray said taking a twenty pound note out of his wallet and handing it over.

"Thanks Ray, it's nice doing business with you," Biff says taking hold of the money and putting it in his pocket.

"Right I'm off, I'll go this way," Ray says pointing ahead of him, "And you go about ten minutes after I have left, alright?"

"Yep, if I get any more info. I'll see you in the town," Biff assured him.

Ray walked briskly away back towards the station, as he walked he took the pocket recorder out and re-wound it, then played the recording of the conversation that he had just had with Biff.

On reaching the station as he made his way to the SB office he bumped into his section Inspector who was in the corridor that the office was off.

"What are you doing back in the station? Shouldn't you be out on the beat?" he scowled at Ray.

"Yes Sir, I have just to drop off something for the SB Inspector," Ray answered.

"You could have waited till your break time to do that, I suggest that you about turn and get back out on patrol."

"It would only take a minute Sir," Ray assured him.

"Just do as I have ordered you," the Inspector said in a raised voice.

"Okay Sir I'm going," Ray told him as he turned around to leave.

Just then the SB office door opened and Steve put his head out, "What's going on here? What's all the noise?" he asked Rays Inspector.

"I was just sending Ray back out on the beat where he should be," he replied."

"Did you get that thing I asked you for Ray?" Steve asked him.

"Yes I did Sir but I have been told to wait until my break time to see you," Ray told him knowing that it would drop his Inspector in the muck with Steve.

"Well I'm here now so you had better give it to me," Steve said.

Ray went over to him and handed over the tape recorder.

"Thanks Ray, now I think you had better come into the office and tell me what went on in the park."

Ray's Inspector went ballistic when he heard Steve say this.

"I have just told him to go back out on patrol, how dare you countermand my orders, he is one of my men not yours," he raged.

"Who the hell do you think you are talking to? Unless you have forgotten I happen to be the Senior Inspector here," Steve informed him.

"Right I'm going to see the SDC about this," Rays Inspector said, storming off before Steve could say anything more.

"Come on in here Ray," Steve said walking into the office.

Ray followed him and sat down in a chair then placed the tape recorder on Steve's desk.

"There's some good stuff on that, it cost me twenty quid with the promise that there would be more if things work out," Ray said pointing at the recorder.

"Don't worry, I'll see you get your money back and that you will get the extra if it all works out," Steve assured him.

Just then there came a knock on the office door, Steve got up and opened it to find the SDC there.

"Good morning Sir, I was expecting a call from you," Steve said to him.

"I have just had Rays Inspector crying to me that you countermanded his orders is this right?"

"It is Sir, Ray was doing a little job for us, I think you'll be quite pleased with the outcome."

"Well what is it?" the SDC asked.

Steve re-played the tape recording of the conversation while the SDC stood listening intently to it, when it had finished he said.

"That's good information you've done well yet again Ray, I can see now why you needed Ray to come and see you pronto."

"Okay I will overlook what has gone on, keep me informed of any further developments or anything I can do," the SDC says leaving.

"I wish there was something I could do to get your bloody Inspector moved from this station, I hate the bastard," Steve enlightened Ray.

"What does the SDC think of him?" Ray enquired.

"As far as I can tell he is only looking for the excuse to get rid of him."

"Well if there is no love lost I might just be able to help out there," Ray said.

"Oh! What do you have up your sleeve?"

"You see that tape recorder, I have it on me at all times now when I first came here I was threatened by the Inspector that if I stepped out of line he would have me thrown out of the job, and also that I was to leave the terrorists alone, luckily for me I taped the whole conversation," Ray sat smiling.

"Where is the recording you made?" Steve said sounding eager to listen to it.

"It's in my locker downstairs."

"Brilliant now I've got the git, go and get it will you?"

Ray got up and went to his locker, it wasn't long before he returned with the recording and they both sat and listening to it.

"Boy but you are one crafty sod, wait here I'll be back soon," Steve said going out of the room headed in the direction of the SDC's office.

It was roughly fifteen minutes later that Steve returned

with a big smile on his face.

"You look a lot happier now than you did earlier," Ray said to him.

"Let's just say your Inspector won't be here for much longer, he's really shit the nest the SDC was raging when I left him."

"Good perhaps now I will get a bit of peace, he has made my life hell since I came here he has seen to it that I get all the shit jobs," Ray informed him.

"You won't have that problem anymore, now then I will have to pass on this information about the hit on the UDR man on to the TCG then we can work out what is going to happen," Steve said smiling.

"If you don't need me anymore then I'll go now being as it's my lunch break," Ray told him looking at his watch.

"Okay Ray I'll let you know what they decide to do about it, see you later," Steve said as Ray went out through the door.

Ray went down to the canteen where he had a cup of tea and a light salad for his lunch, he was pleased about what was going to happen about his Inspector, but was really overjoyed that the men who were going to carry out the murder of the UDR man were going to be caught, he would only have to wait for three days to see what the outcome would be.

The following morning when he reported for duty Ray was told by the Sergeant that he was to do paperwork that day as people were coming to see him.

While sitting in the canteen at approximately 9.30am a message came over the station intercom system that he was to go to the SB office, he finished his breakfast first and nearly ten minutes later went up to it.

After knocking on the door he was let in by the SB man Pete.

"Hi Ray, you've got some visitors, they're with Steve in his little hidey hole," Paul said to him walking over to

Steve's door and opening it.

As Ray entered the room he saw the three men who had tried to get him to join the HMSU sitting drinking coffee with Steve.

"Hello Ray we meet again," the Superintendent says.

"Good morning gentlemen how are you all?" he replied.

"We are all fine and really pleased with the information you've got for us," the Chief told him.

"Well Chief it's all part of the game, I like to do my little bit," Ray says smiling.

"That's funny you should talk about doing your little bit because we want you to do a little bit extra, we would like you to be in on this task, after all you know the area well and who we should be watching for and all the details about the car and so forth, so how do you fell about that?" the Superintendent asked.

"It seems alright to me, what role will I play in the job?"

"We are going to put men in around the area where the car is to keep an eye on it, when it's taken anywhere we can determine who the driver is and who is with him, this way we can get a positive ID on them so we know whom we are dealing with, I would like you to be in that car," the Superintendent suggested.

"Who will be with me in the car?"

"It will be two E4a men that you'll be with."

"There is only one problem that I can see, and that is where the car is situated now it is in a cul-de-sac, the only way to keep an eye on it is to have your observation car parked near enough to keep an eye on the entrance to it and believe me a strange car hanging around that area will soon be noticed," Ray informed him.

"We have already thought of that and so we will have cars in hiding at all the junctions to be able to note any cars coming in and out of the estate."

"You seem to have everything sewn up, so when do I

join the E4a men?" Ray asked.

"You can go and get your civilian clothes on and join them now, they'll be out in the backyard waiting for you," the Superintendent told him.

"I take it my Sergeant knows all about this?"

"Yes he's been told that we want you for special duties, mind you he's not been told anything more, we have also informed your boss in HQNI and they have agreed that we can use you on this job."

"Okay then Sir I'm on my way," Ray said getting up from his seat and leaving the office.

It didn't take Ray long to get changed and he was soon out into the backyard of the station where he saw the Superintendent talking to two men in a battered looking Mazda car.

"Ah! There you are Ray, this is Alan and John you'll be with them," the Superintendent introduced them.

CHAPTER – 11 – THE JOB

"How are you doing gentlemen, nice to meet you," Ray said as he opened the back door of the car and got into it.

"It's nice to meet you as well, I didn't know that we had members of your Regiment working over here covertly," Alan says.

"I had a rough idea that they did, but now this confirms it," John told Alan.

"Haven't I seen you before Ray?" Alan asked.

"Yes you have, I came across you when you were on your training course at Hereford, I was the guy that was instructing you on the camouflage and concealment techniques."

"This sort of work should be old rope to you then?" John said.

"The only problem is how do you camouflage a car? It's a lot different from hiding in a field or jungle" Ray laughed.

"I think you could be right," Alan said as he started the car and began to drive out of the station.

They left the station compound and followed the one way system into the town centre, then made a right turn along Union Street driving towards Craigavon along the Tandragee road to the Drumbeg Roundabout.

At the roundabout they took the third exit onto the Tullygally East Road then passed the fronts of the houses of the Tullygally Estate.

Nearly 400 yards from the roundabout they turned right onto the Old Portadown Road to drive past the Horseshoe Bar then into the Taghnevan estate.

As they travelled across the top of the cul-de-sac John and Ray looked down towards the bottom of it.

"Well the car is still there," John said.

"I tried to get a look at the registration number on it but I couldn't see it," Ray told them both.

"I think we'll try and take a drive past nearly every twenty minutes or so, that is of course providing no one starts to pay any interest in us," Alan says.

"I would leave it longer than that, it doesn't really matter if we don't see it go anywhere as the other cars in hiding will be bound to pick it up, the car can't move without at least one of us clocking it," came from John.

"I just hope they don't miss it, it will be interesting to see who is in the bloody thing, at least then we know what we're up against," Alan said.

"We have from today Wednesday, till the supposed day of the attack on Friday in which to find out, we are bound to know by then who all is involved," Ray put in.

"I do know one thing that the Tactical Support Unit (TSU) is going out tonight to try and put a tracking device on the car," John informed him.

"That would be a great help just in case it does manage to slip past any of us, could you imagine if it did? we would all be running around like chickens with our heads cut off and I don't think the boss would be too happy either," Ray replied.

"It would be alright for you, it would be us that gets it in the neck," Alan said.

"By the way how long are we going to be doing this for?" Ray wanted to know.

"We will be on till about three in the morning then another lot relieve us, after they relieve us we all go back to Lurgan station for a shower and something to eat and a bit of sleep, Why? Alan asked.

"I was just wondering, my wife will be thinking that something has happened to me when I don't get home after my duty," Ray told him.

"I think we had better take a quick trip back into the station so you can ring your missus to let her know that you won't be home for a while," John suggested.

"That is a very good idea, come on let's get back," Alan

agreed.

It wasn't long before Ray was on the phone talking to Pauline telling her that he wouldn't be home for maybe three days at least as he had been detailed to take part in a VCP operation.

"Why will it take that long?" she asked.

"They have been planning it for ages now, it's mainly over in this area and Craigavon, I don't know for sure but I think they have had word that the local IRA are moving a lot of explosives and weapons into the patch," he lied to her.

"How many of you are going to be doing it?"

"I can't say over the phone, but a lot is all I can tell you."

"What are you going to do for clean shirts and your washing and shaving kit?"

"I'm sure I will be able to arrange something, look I've got to go now I only rang to tell you so that you weren't worried," Ray told her.

"I think you've got another woman somewhere haven't you?" Pauline said sounding suspicious.

"No I haven't if you want to check up on what I am up to you can ring here any time you like and ask to speak to the Superintendent, he'll let you know that what I am telling you is for real, anyway I've got to go now my love bye," Ray said replacing the phone.

"Right that's that done, shall we go?" Ray said turning to Alan and John who were standing nearby.

"I think before we go back out you had better go and see the Superintendent to let him know that your wife might be ringing here," Alan told him.

"I suppose I better had, won't be long," Ray told them as he walked away headed towards the SDC's office.

Almost ten minutes later he returned to where he had left them to find that they had gone, wondering where they could be he began to look around the nearby offices.

After looking in them all and not finding them he went to the SB office to see if they had gone there, as he entered it he saw Pete sitting drinking a cup of coffee at his desk.

"Have you seen Alan and John anywhere Pete?" Ray asked him.

"They were here a few minutes ago, then when they heard that our typist was going to the canteen for a cuppa they went with her," Pete informed him.

"Right thanks Pete, see you soon," Ray said turning around and leaving him.

He walked along the corridor down two flights of stairs and was soon walking through the canteen doors, as he looked around it he saw Alan and John sitting around a table with a few of the typists.

"I was wondering where the heck you two had gone to, I looked all over the station for you," Ray said as he approached the table.

"It's nice to know you missed us, sit yourself down Ray have a cuppa and settle down, you'll have a heart attack if you're not careful" John told him pulling a chair away from another table for Ray to sit on.

As Ray sat down one of the typists who was called Sonia asked him, "Would you like a cup of tea or coffee Ray?"

"I could murder for a cup of tea with two sugars please if you don't mind," he answered putting his hand in his pocket to get out some money to pay for it.

"Don't bother about the money I'll get it for you," she told him.

" That's one I owe you." Ray told her.

"I'd rather have a proper drink," she replied smiling at him as she walked to the counter to get the tea.

She soon returned with the tea and placed the cup with two sachets of sugar and a spoon down in front of him.

"Thank you sweetheart, I'll really enjoy this," Ray told

her ripping open the sugar sachets and emptying them into his cup.

"I myself would rather have a good whiskey and water," Alan said.

"I like a very big Bacardi and cola, no ice just a piece of lemon," Ray retorted.

"Me I like anything that gets me pissed," John put in.

When they had all finished drinking their drinks and the typists had left they all went back to the car and it wasn't long before they were driving out of the station heading down Billy Street towards the Taghnevan estate. As they reached the set of traffic lights that were just prior to the entrance into the estate John spotted the Red Toyota coming out of the estate and heading towards Craigavon with three men in it.

"Looks like they are going for a wee jaunt, we'll follow them, I'll just let the others know, Blue three from one, over," Alan said pressing his radio transmission button which was disguised as a car cigarette lighter.

"Blue one send," came over the radio.

"Blue three target vehicle is on the move and heading in your direction, over."

"Roger we see him, we'll pick him up."

"It shouldn't be too long before we are with you, we're just waiting for the lights to change, out" Alan said ending the connection.

"For christs sake hurry up and change," John muttered looking at the lights that were still showing Red.

"Patience, patience dear boy," Alan told him.

"They'll be well away out of our sight before the lights change," John groaned.

"Blue 3 at Roundabout 1 will pick them up, you'll see," Alan informed him.

At this moment the lights chanced in their favour and Alan drove on.

"I wonder if they are going to do the job now' Ray asked

in general.

"No I would think that they're either working out the route or maybe doing a dummy run." John answered.

"Just to be on the safe side I think we had better let the rest of the cars know so that we'll have back up in case it gets shitty," Alan suggested.

"All cars this is Blue 1, target on the move headed in the direction of the job, move to and take up your positions," he said pressing the cigarette lighter again.

"Blue 1, this is Blue 3, target has just driven around Roundabout Four past the Craigavon shopping centre still headed in the right direction, over," was heard on the radio.

"It's definitely looking like a dummy run," Alan said.

"At least we might be able to get a good idea of the route they'll be taking on Friday night," Ray replied.

"I can't see them coming this way, I would have thought that they would have gone via the back roads, it could be a little too risky for them they run the chance of being stopped at a VCP being carried out by the local cops," John put in.

"That's if the local cops are doing their job properly," Alan laughed.

"Blue 1, this is Blue 3 we are now travelling the Northway and the Army are setting up a VCP on the Shillington Bridge, just for your info, out." Was heard coming over the radio.

"Shit that's all we need now," John said sounding exasperated.

It was not long before they reached the VCP and were stopped by one of the soldiers.

"Good afternoon gentlemen, would you have any means of Identification on you please?" the soldier asked Alan.

"I have my driving licence is that any good?" he replied.

"Could I see it Sir?"

"Here you are, don't laugh at the picture on it," Alan said

handing over his licence.

The soldier looked at the licence picture then back at Alan.

"I see by this picture here that you have grown a bit of a beard and long hair since this photo was taken, why would that be Sir?" the soldier says, obviously suspicious that Alan should want to change his appearance.

"I got fed up with shaving and having my hair cut."

"Could you wait here please Sir?" the soldier said before walking over and showing the licence to another one of the army men who must have been a superior.

They both looked over towards the car and the superior soldier could be seen talking into a radio microphone.

"It looks like they're checking the cars number plate, once they have found out that they've stopped a cop car they'll soon let us go," John said.

No sooner had he said this than the soldier returned to their car and handed the licence back to Alan.

"Here you are Sir sorry for the delay," he said waving them on.

As they pulled away from the VCP Blue 3 came back on the radio.

"Blue 1, from 3 target vehicle now on return journey, we will meet you back at the Station, over."

"Roger, where are they now? Over" Alan replied.

"Heading back in your direction."

Roger we'll pick them up and carry on surveillance till they get back home, see you in the nick," Alan told them ending the transmission.

He continued to drive along the Northway too the roundabout at Rectory Park where he drove around it to double back the way he had come.Just as they entered onto the roundabout they all saw the Toyota enter on to it as well coming from the direction of Armagh.

"We're just in time," John said smiling.

Alan continued to follow the Toyota staying roughly 150

yards back from it,.

"This should be fun when they come across the VCP," Ray brought up.

"It might be moved by the time they get there," John replied.

No sooner had John said this they came onto part of the road where they would be able to see the VCP.

"Would you bloody believe it, they're packing the VCP in, that's you putting the jinx on it" Alan says to John.

"What did I tell you, it's called sods law," John replied.

They continued to follow the Toyota back towards Lurgan however this time on the journey the driver of the car instead of driving straight on at Roundabout number 2 to Roundabout 1, took the second exit at number 2 to take them onto the Tullygally Road.

"I wonder what they are up to now?" Ray queried.

"Hmm, this is interesting," Alan remarked.

"They might be trying to see if anyone is following them," John suggested.

"They could well be, I'll tell the other cars to watch out for them and we can turn off into Legahory towards the Craigavon cop shop," Alan told them.

"Blue 2 and 4, this is Blue 1, target vehicle is travelling along the Tullygally Road keep your eyes skinned and try to pick it up, we'll meet you back at Lurgan when you've finished, over" Alan transmitted.

"Blue 2, roger."

"Blue 4, roger," came the replies.

After this Alan turned off towards the Craigavon Police station drove past it and onto the Drumgor road where he arrived back at roundabout 3 and headed back towards Lurgan.

They were not long back at Lurgan when the other two cars arrived the driver was a man called Howie.

"Well Howie how did it go?" Alan asked him.

"No sooner had you passed your message than we

picked them up at the Drumgask Roundabout where they got onto the Brownlow Road drove straight through the next Roundabout and back into Taghnevan Estate."

 "I wonder what route they will be taking on Friday night?"

"I wouldn't have a clue but mind you we should have a good idea after the TSU boys have bugged the car tonight," Howie answered.

"What time are they doing it?" Ray asked.

"I haven't got a clue, but I would imagine the early hours of the morning," Howie replied.

"Well I suppose we had better get out again just in case they decide to go for another wee jaunt," Howie says turning and walking away.

"Yeah okay we'll see you later, we won't be out for a while I've something to sort out about what is going to happen," Alan tells him.

The car was not moved again for the next two days, meanwhile the TSU had managed to successfully bug the car and put a tracking device on it.

When the Friday came all the men who would be involved were briefed on what roles they would play by a Superintendent at Mahon Road camp, when they were all assembled he began.

"Good evening gentlemen, as you know we have an operation on tonight because of information that we have received that a member of the UDR is going to be murdered at his home not far from here.

For the members of the HMSU as you are by now aware we in the E4a have been doing a surveillance job of a house in the Taghnevan estate in Lurgan. These three men are believed to be the parties who will be carrying out the job study these faces," he says switching on a projector which showed pictures of the men that also had below them their Dates of birth and home addresses.

"These men are very dangerous, we have no reason to doubt that they will be armed, it is from a good source that they will have an Armalite rifle, an AK47, and an Uzi so be bloody careful.

We have decided that rather than let them get anywhere near to their victim we will stop them at Roundabout number 2 in Craigavon, just in case they try to make a run for it the members of the HMSU will be in hiding near the Roundabout, take note of these positions," the officer said clicking a button which brought up a plan of the roundabout and the proposed positions of the ambush on the screen.

"There will be men here, here, and here," he said pointing at parts of the plan with half a snooker cue that he was using as an indication rod.

"We are not exactly sure which way they will be approaching the roundabout from, however be prepared to adjust your positions accordingly, the E4a will have cars following them and should be able to give you plenty of notice, are there any questions?"

"Yes Sir, do we carry out a normal vehicle stop like we do at a VCP?" one of the HMSU Sergeants asked.

"Yes everything must look proper, I don't want them being made suspicious that we know what they are up to."

"What if they don't or won't stop?"

"Then it's up to you to make them stop."

"What if they turn around when they see us?" another HMSU man asked.

"Then the E4a vehicle will block their escape."

"What if they start shooting?" the HMSU Inspector wanted to know.

"Let me just say if they do that, remember, 'dead men tell no tales' do they?" the Superintendent told him.

"If it comes to that, what do we do afterwards?"

"You get the heck out of the place quick, and the local

boys can take over from there, they will be informed as to what is going on and have already been told to stay out of the area until it's all over."

"I take it that means we come back here?"

"Yes I will be here listening to your radio transmissions, if you do have to resort to shooting them don't worry because we have your statements already prepared, you'll look like angels."

"Aye, angels of death," one of the men muttered.

"If that is all gentlemen then I suggest we all take up our positions, and good luck, Oh by the way like they say in Hill Street Blues, "BE EXTRA CAREFUL OUT THERE," I don't want any of us getting hurt," the Superintendent says smiling.

All of the men left the room to make their way to their vehicles; it was not long before

Ray, Alan, and John were leaving the camp heading towards Lurgan, as they travelled towards Craigavon Ray asked.

"What did the Superintendent mean by already having our statements prepared?"

"Well let's put it this way, the guys in the car we are going to stop are going to die tonight, we have been after them for some time, they showed no mercy towards the people they have murdered and we are going to show them no mercy, so just to make it all look legal everyone who is involved tonight will have to make a statement." Alan answered him.

"Yeah and it helps if we all have roughly the same thing in them, once we have cleared off back to Mahon Road we just pick up a copy of our statement which has been prepared and sign it then we are given a photocopy of it for us to read and memorise just in case any enquiry should come about," John said.

"Then that way everything looks above board, we done the same after the job at Mullacreevie park in Armagh a few years ago when we got two more of them, there are still bits of paper flying around about that, only this time we will be ready," Alan informed him.

By this time they had reached the Taghnevan Estate where they drove around the different Streets just to kill a bit of time until the men who were going to be committing the murder of the UDR man were on the move.

"I wonder what time they are going to leave to do the job?" Ray asked.

"It's ten thirty now I would imagine that they'll be ready soon," John says looking at his watch.

At that moment a call came over the car radio.

"Blue One, from Tango Sierra, target vehicle on the move heading towards the Old Portadown Road, over."

"Roger we're on our way," Alan replied while having to turn the car around in the road to head back the way he had just come.

On reaching the Old Portadown road he got back on the radio.

"Tango Sierra, we can't see the vehicle yet, give me an update as to its location now, over."

"Roger Blue One, it's now travelling along the Tullygally East Road towards the Drumbeg Roundabout, over."

No sooner had the TSU man told them this than a set of rear car lights could be seen ahead of them.

Alan speeded up so that they could get near enough to see if these lights were those of the Toyota.

"There you are my little beauty," John said leaning forward in his seat and picking up his MP5.

They followed the Toyota along the Road to the Drumbeg Roundabout where it travelled along the Brownlow Road to the Ardowen Roundabout.

At this Roundabout it took the Third exit onto the Tullygally Road and headed towards Roundabout Number 2.

"I think we had better sit back a bit just in case there are any stray bullets," John said to Alan laughing.

"I think you could be right, hold on a minute," Alan said pressing the radio transmission button, " Bronze 1 vehicle approaching you now," he warned the HMSU before turning into the entrance of the Rowan Park estate and stopping.

All three of them wound down the cars windows in order to hear how things were turning out.

Ray had only just got his window down when he heard the sound of gunfire.

"Damn, I'm glad I'm not receiving that lot," he remarked.

"You're right there, listen to it they must be trying to make the bloody car into a sieve the amount of shots they are taking," John said.

"It's what you call in America, overkill," Alan laughed.

After about two minutes the shooting stopped.

"I think we had better get out of here," Alan said winding up his window and driving out of the estate onto the Tullygally Road and heading back towards the Brownlow Roundabout.

"Yep it's time to sign our statements," John said sitting back in his seat.

When they reached Mahon Road camp they reported to the Superintendent.

"Hello Sir, it sounded like another successful adventure, were any of our lot hurt at all?" Alan asked him.

"No, only the one that was knocked down by the Toyota," the Superintendent replied winking and smiling.

"That's good to hear, I love it when things go to plan," John said.

"I suppose it's time to take a look at my statement,come on you two you can get yours as well, let's go and see what the CID have for us," Alan said leaving the office.

It wasn't long before Ray had his copy of his statement

and was soon on his way home, As he opened the front door to his house he found Pauline was entertaining two of her friends.

"Oh hello Darling, how did the VCP operation go?" She asked.

"It went fantastic we manage to stop a lot of people and got quite a few prosecution cases out of it," Ray lied.

"Would you like a cup of tea and something to eat?" Pauline enquired.

"No thanks my love I am completely knackered and all I want is to get into my bed, so I'll see you in the morning if that's okay, so good night ladies," Ray said making his way to the stairs which lead up to the bedroom.

When he got into the bedroom he took out his copy of the statement and started to read and memorise it just in case an enquiry should take place into what had happened.

CHAPTER – 12 - SONIA

The following day Ray was on what was called an early turn, which meant he would be on duty from 8am to 4pm, at around 10am he went to the station canteen for his breakfast.

While he sat drinking a cup of tea, having finished his meal he heard the canteen door open, on looking up he saw Sonia come through it, Sonia saw him and smiled then walked over to where he was sitting.

"Hello and how are you today?" she asked.

"Not too bad, just ticking along, and you?" he replied.

"I'm fine, is there anybody sitting here?" she asked him pointing at a chair across the table from him.

"No you can sit there if you want, as a matter of fact it will be nice to have a pretty face to look at, rather than some big hairy arsed cop," Ray smiled.

"Thanks for the compliment, I'll just go and get a coffee no doubt you could do with another cup of tea?"

"Just like the last time we met, I wouldn't say no."

"I'll be back in a minute," she said walking up to the counter.

Ray was quite pleased that she had decided to sit with him, as it would be somebody to talk to while he was having his breakfast as most of the other cops seem to shy away from him.

It wasn't long before she was back and sitting down opposite to him.

"By the way we were not introduced the last time we met, my names Ray," Ray introduced himself.

"And I'm Sonia, how do you do?" she replied shaking his hand.

"So you're one of the typists? No doubt you see a lot of badly written reports and probably most of them are mine," Ray joked.

"As a matter of fact I don't see many of your files, I take it you don't like paperwork, as a matter of fact your

Inspector came up to the typing pool the other day and he was checking on how many files you had submitted for typing," she informed him.

"Yes for some reason he doesn't like me and I think he is trying to find enough reasons to have me fired, I thank you for your information I suppose I better watch out as it looks like he is gunning for me." Ray said.

"Anyway enough of that tell me a little bit about yourself Ray," Sonia asked.

"Well if you must know I am ex-British army I used to train sniffer dogs, guard dogs and security dogs as well as drugs detection dogs and tracker dogs," Ray told her.

"I believe you were stationed in Newry before you came here, is that right?"

"Yes I really enjoyed myself in South Armagh, I was really happy there."

"I heard that they had to move you as the IRA were after you because you were catching too many of them, is that right?"

"I suppose you could say that but I was only doing my job and now because I done it so well I'm in this godforsaken hole." Ray said in defence.

"Why? don't you like it here?"

"On my first day of duty I saw the hatred of the regular Constables towards the Reserve Constables and I didn't like it, as far as I am concerned we are all in the same job there is no difference between us."

"Yes I heard about you having a go at some of the Regular Constables, I wish I had been here to see the looks on their faces," Sonia said smiling.

"One thing I have learned about this station is that, there is more danger inside here than there is out on the streets."

"I must agree there is a lot of back stabbing goes on in this place," Sonia says.

"I would love to take half of the Regular cops and put

them in Newry or on the border then they would learn what comradeship is all about," Ray told her.

"I know how you feel, I hate this place for all the back biting, I think a few months on the border would do them all a lot of good." Sonia agreed.

"Tell you what, let's stop talking about them it only depresses me, let's talk about you, you'd be a more interesting subject," Ray laughed.

"What would you like to know?"

"Let me see, are you married, divorced, engaged or courting?" he asked.

"Take a look at these do you see any rings on them?" Sonia answered showing him her hands.

"No I don't, so that means you must be courting, am I right?"

"No wrong again I don't have a boyfriend."

"Now that surprises me because I couldn't imagine a good looking girl like you not having a man in your life," Ray told her.

"I did up until about ten days ago, but then I found out that he was two timing me so I told him to piss off."

"Oh! I'm sorry to hear that," Ray sympathised with her.

"I'm not sorry I'm just glad that I found out before things went too far."

"Like they say it's no use crying over spilt milk, you've got to just get on with life, when something like that happens to me I just say 'die dog shite the licence' and carry on," he laughed.

"That's exactly what I am doing, now that is enough about me tell me a bit about you?"

"For starters I am married, my wife is called Pauline and she's expecting our baby girl in March," Ray informed her.

"Have you thought of a name for her yet?" Sonia asked.

"No not yet we're working on that, I told my wife that one thing I do not want is for her to be named after someone in the family, and that's the only stipulation I have."

"Well if I can think of any good ones I'll let you know okay?" Sonia offered.

As she said this Ray looked down at his watch, "I had better go before the Inspector comes in and sees me sitting here, it would give him something more to moan about and get on my case for," Ray said getting up from his chair.

As he left her sitting at the table and went through the canteen door walking straight into Steve who on seeing Ray said, "Ahh! Ray I want a little word with you, can you come to my office when you are free?"

"Yep no problem as a matter of fact I'm free now I can spare you five minutes or so now if you want?" Ray told him.

"Fine, then follow me up to my office."

When they reached the office Ray took up his usual seat opposite Steve.

"So what can I do for you, boss?" Ray asked.

"We have been tipped off that there are a number of weapons in the area ready for use in a shooting in the town somewhere, as of yet we don't know what or whom the target might be, I was wondering if you knew or if any of your informers might be able to throw a little light on the subject?"

"I'll see what I can do, I'm going back out now so if I see any of my touts around I'll find out if they know anything," Ray assured him.

"It would be most appreciative believe me, so I'll see you later bye for now," Steve said showing Ray to the door.

Ray left the building and went out to the station back yard to where the patrol car was parked with a man called Bobby who had been detailed as driver of it for the day sitting in it waiting for him to arrive.

"Where the heck have you been? I've been waiting here for nearly ten minutes now, we've got a call to go too in the Kilwilkee Estate, apparently some guy is beating the crap out of his wife," Bobby told him.

"How long ago did you get the call?"

"About fifteen minutes."

"Christ by now he will either have killed her or they will be screwing like two bunnies, either way there's no rush," Ray laughed.

It wasn't long before they were at the house that they had been sent to, Ray knocked on the house front door and his knock was answered by a woman who had blood coming from the side of her mouth.

"Good morning madam I believe you sent for the Police?" he said to her.

"Yes I did but there is no need to bother now we've sorted it all out."

"Could I speak to your husband please?" Ray asked her.

"Hold on a minute I'll just get him," She replied turning away from the door and going into the house.

It was not long before the woman's husband came to the door, he appeared hot and was sporting a swollen lip, he looked as if he was drunk.

"Yes Constable what can I do for you?" he asked.

"I have received a report that there was a bit of a fight going on here between you and the wife, is that right Sir?"

"Yes but it is all over so you can fuck off now."

"That's not a very nice way to talk Sir, I was only enquiring as to how things are and making sure that nobody was hurt," Ray told him.

"The only person who is likely to be hurt is you mate, that's if you don't piss off out of here pronto," the man threatened.

Ray was not very pleased by the attitude and decided that because of the way the man had spoken to him he was going to push the man into swinging a punch at him then he would have a reason to arrest him.

"You are a terrible man, why are you being nasty to me I only came here to help and all you have done is threaten and curse at me," Ray said to him very sweetly.

"Are you some kind of fucking queer?" the man raged stepping out of the house onto the porch way.

"My, my, you are a ruffian aren't you?" Ray mocked.

"Look if you don't bugger off you'll find out how much of a ruffian I am," The man replied walking towards Ray with his fist raised.

"Now don't be silly Sir, we can be friends if you want?" Ray said backing up as far as the house garden gate.

"I'll show you how bloody friendly we can be," the man said rushing at Ray and swinging his fist which missed Ray by a whisker.

By this time Ray, on seeing the man coming towards him backed out of the gateway and onto the path outside the garden, the man followed him still swinging his fists.

"Now you're mine pal," Ray said to the man returning the punch and hitting him straight in the face.

When the man went down Bobby ran over to help Ray take hold of him.

"Guess what ball bag, this queer is now arresting you for assault on Police and disorderly behaviour you can either get in the back of the car yourself or I can put you in it, let me tell you this much, if you try any more of your nonsense you'll be a very sorry guy, do you understand?" Ray told him.

"Yeah ok I'll come quietly," he replied walking over to the car.

It did not take long for them to get back to the station where Ray took the man in through the back door to the custody suite, once the prisoner was placed into a cell to sober up before being interviewed Ray and Bobby went to the canteen.

As they entered it they saw the Sergeant and Inspector sitting together having a break, Ray walked over to them.

"What are you two in at this time for Ray?" the Sergeant asked him.

"We've just brought a prisoner in for assault on police and disorderly behaviour."

"Oh! I see, well you had better both get a coffee, what sort of a mess is he in?" the Inspector wanted to know.

"He has a few facial marks that he received while resisting arrest and also given to him by his wife."

"His wife!" the Sergeant exclaimed.

"Yes we had to go to as family dispute, by the time we got there they had just finished punching the living daylights out of each other," Ray smiled.

"Okay get yourselves a drink and then go back to the cell block area and interview him then we can throw him back out," the Sergeant told them.

"We can't do that just yet he has been drinking and is slightly drunk, also we are waiting for the Force Medical officer to arrive to examine him."

"If that's the case then wait up here until the custody Sergeant sends for you, Bobby you go and tell him where you'll be," the Inspector says.

"Will do Sir, Ray will you get me a coffee I'll be back in a minute," Bobby said walking away through the doors they had just come in.

Ray went over to the counter and ordered the drinks then went to sit at a table towards the back of the room, it wasn't long before Bobby returned.

"Tell me this Ray, why did you arrest that bastard in the cell? It's not like you to take on any paperwork unless you really had to," Bobby asked him as he sat down.

"I thought it would be a good idea because then we could spend the rest of the day sitting on our arses drinking tea and coffee, rather than being out driving around the bloody town."

After their coffee they both went to what was known as the Constables work room, this was a room with two desks in where the police officers could write up any reports or prosecution files and update their note books. No sooner had they settled down to their paperwork than the room door opened and Sonia walked in.

"Hello you two, I see you're slaving away," she said in general.

"Me and Ray are the hardest workers in this place, if we didn't come here half the crime in this town wouldn't be detected," Bobby told her.

"You've got to be joking, the only people that work in this place are the civil servants, you lot only sit on your bums driving around in a car all day," Sonia retorted.

"You've got that wrong, what do you say Ray?" Bobby said.

"I'm keeping out of this just in case she starts to swing the fists, I would hate to see you getting a good hiding from her," Ray told him.

"Oh! Thanks mate it's nice to know who your friends are," he replied.

"Well let's put it in this way Sonia is better looking than you," Ray chuckled.

"Why thank you Ray," Sonia said sounding pleased.

"By the way I don't suppose you have had a chance to think of any names yet have you?" Ray asked her.

"Not really I've been too busy, we have a lot of work on," She replied.

"Names for what?" Bobby butted in.

"Names for my daughter, do you have any suggestions?"

"None that spring to mind but I will give it a bit of thought," Bobby told him.

"Good, now where were we Sonia before we were so rudely interrupted?" Ray asked.

"I was just telling you that we are rather busy up in the

typing pool and I haven't had chance to think yet," she answered.

"Well if you do think of any good ones I'm open to suggestions and I can tell the wife."

"I will, I promise you, I had better go now I have a lot of work on I will catch you later Ray see you soon, and you Bobby," Sonia said as she left the office.

After she had left Ray and Bobby set about their paperwork, a couple of hours later they went down to the cell block to interview their prisoner on their way there Ray said to Bobby "I hope this guy has sobered up otherwise we might have to work a little bit longer."

"I hope he has as well my wife is expecting me home on time tonight as we are going to visit some friends," Bobby replied.

On reaching the custody suite Ray approached the Sergeant asking "do you think my prisoner has sobered up enough for me to interview yet?"

"Well the last time I looked about five minutes ago he was still fast asleep snoring like a pig," the Sergeant answered.

"I suppose I had better go and check, do you have the key to his cell?" Ray enquired.

"Yeah it's hanging up over there," the Sergeant said pointing to a key rack "it's number 4."

Ray found the key and went to the cell number four on opening the door and called out to the man "hey Sean, rise and shine, it's interview time."

At first Sean did not seem to respond so Ray took his foot and gave it a shake "come on Sean time to go," he said.

Sean is slowly began to sit up, he took one look at Ray and said "I see it's you again, you big bastard why don't you just leave me alone?"

"Because you have slept long enough and it's time to throw you out now that you have sobered up," Ray told him.

"So what do we do now?" Sean asked.

"Well first of all we have to go to interview room to fill out a bit of paperwork, then you'll be free to go how does that sound?" Ray informed him.

"Okay lead the way," Sean replied disgruntled.

Ray led the way to the interview room and Sean followed with Bobby behind him, on reaching it Ray pointed towards a seat, "There you are park your arse there."

As Sean got settled into the seat Bobby looked at Ray and quietly asked him if he really needed him to be present at the interview.

"No it is okay for you to go if you want, I can deal with this," Ray told him.

Once Bobby had gone Ray closed the interview room door and took up a seat opposite Sean and pulled open a draw in the desk taking out a number of forms that had to be filled in.

Before he had a chance to commence his interview Sean said, "Is there any way that I can get out of this?"

"How do you mean?" Ray asked him.

"Well you know, if there's any way I can help you with things would you be prepared to turn a blind eye as to what I have been doing?"

Making it seem that he did not understand what Sean was meaning Ray said, "I'm sorry but you've lost me there what sort of things are you talking about?"

"You know things that the IRA are up to," Sean said sounding exasperated.

"Why are you so worried about this little incident?" Ray asked him.

"When you see my record you will understand, I have a bit of a list and if I go to court for this I will probably get two years in jail," Sean told him sounding worried.

This was news to Ray as he had no idea as to Sean's criminal history, now that he knew he decided to try and turn him into an informant.

"Well let me see," Ray said lifting his head to look at the ceiling, "It will all depend on how good the information is, and how useful it is to me."

"It's good info. believe me, and I know for a fact that some weapons have been brought into the area and there is going to be an attack made on the police," Sean informed him.

"Well when is this going to happen?" Ray asked.

"I'm not sure of the exact date however I can try and find out for you," Sean replied.

"Okay I'll tell you what, if you can find that out for me shall we say within a couple of days I will hold this file up, however if you don't come up with the goods I'll go ahead with it and you can spend your next 2 Christmases in jail, how's that?" Ray told him.

"Before I go do you promise?" Sean asked worried.

"You have my word on it believe me, but remember you only have a couple of days before I go ahead."

"Okay it's a deal," Sean said reaching his hand across the table to shake Ray's.

"Right, before you go I will tell you this much if when you get home you argue with your wife anymore and hit her I'll have you put in jail tonight," Ray said.

"You can rest assured Sir, I won't touch her I promise," Sean assured him.

"Right then where shall I meet you for you to give me the information?"

"I'm not sure is there anywhere you would like?"

"How about meeting you by the sugar Island petrol station?"

"That's fine by me, I will meet you there in about 2 day's time at around 11 o'clock in the morning how does that sound?"

"It seems okay to me however if you try to set me up to have me shot I won't be too happy," Ray let him know.

"I am not that stupid that I would leave here and tell the IRA about our conversation, they would kill me on the spot," Sean said sounding worried.

"Okay well I will see you in two days, just make sure the information is good and believe me don't give me any bullshit or the IRA would be the least of your troubles do you understand?"

With this Ray got up from the desk and walked with Sean to the custody Sergeants office to have Sean released.

After having all the paperwork complete Ray escorted Sean up to the enquiry office door and let him carry on his way home.

He then went to the Special Branch office to speak with Steve and inform him of what had taken place.

On entering the office he immediately went to Steve's door, he found Steve sitting at his desk looking at some paperwork.

"Hi boss I have some good news for you," Ray told him.

"I bloody hope so I am so pissed off with all this crap that I am getting about those weapons being moved into the area," Steve replied.

"Well I have just been speaking with a guy that I arrested this afternoon and he has told me that if I drop the charges against him he will find out where those weapons are and who or what is the target."

"That's brilliant how soon will we know?" Steve said excitedly.

"I gave him a couple of days and told him that if he didn't know by then that I would go ahead and prosecute him."

"Do you really think he'll come up with the information?"

"Well let's put it this way if he doesn't he could spend the next two years of his life in jail, now with that hanging over his head I think he'll play ball," Ray answered.

"That has really pleased me I'll sleep better tonight, mind you I'll sleep even better when he supplies the information," Steve smiled.

"So what did you arrest him for?"

"We got a call to his house where there was a family dispute, being as I wasn't really in the mood for any work I decided that if I pushed him into taking a swing at me then I can arrest him and spend the rest of the day here in the station," Ray laughed.

"So basically you got him for disorderly behaviour and assault on police is that right?"

"You bet your arse I did," Ray informed him.

"Like I've already said, I hope he comes up with the information then that will be a load of our minds."

"I hope so as well because then we can lay out an ambush and catch the bastards that are going to carry out the hit." Ray suggested.

"Yeah the HMSU will have something to do, mind you we have kept them pretty busy this past couple of weeks."

Two days later Ray met with Sean, "So what do you have to tell me Sean?"

"All I managed to find out was that some weapons had been moved into the area as they are going to shoot some cop who works here in Lurgan, apparently this guy is not really a cop they think he is a soldier in disguise,"

"I wonder who that could be? As far as I know there is nobody in this station like that, mind you the way things are over here you never know who it could be," Ray replied putting a puzzled look on his face.

"Well I don't know any names, but I do know one thing they have said that if they can't get him they might get his family instead," Sean replied.

"Why his family?" Ray wanted to know.

"I think it is because his wife is also Army, she's supposed to be in the UDR."

"I'll tell you what, do the best you can to find out the

name and I'll give you some money if you can is that alright?" Ray told him.

"Okay, I had better go now before I get seen talking to you I will try and let you know tomorrow, see you then," Sean said as he walked away back towards Lurgan.

With the information that he had just received Ray became a very worried man, he knew exactly who the IRA were talking about, it was him.

He got back into the police car and returned to the police station where he immediately went up to the Special Branch office.

On entering it he signalled to Steve that he wanted to speak to him alone, they both went into Steve's part of it

"I have just found out from Sean who the target is," Ray informed him.

"Oh yeah, and who is it?"

"Believe it or not it is me, apparently the IRA know that I'm not a cop and that I'm a soldier undercover," Ray answered.

"Shit, how the hell did they find that out?" Steve exclaimed.

"I don't know but they have also said that if they can't get me they'll get my family and to be very honest with you that has really pissed me off," Ray said sounding exasperated.

"Shit I see now why you are looking so worried, I didn't think they would resort to also attacking a man's family, however I certainly would'nt put it past the bastards," Steve said.

"I would love to find out who it was that told them about there being a soldier undercover."

"I wonder if they are just guessing?" Steve suggested.

"I'm not sure but I can certainly tell you this much I am bloody worried, my wife has just found out she is pregnant and believe it or not it would tear me apart if anything was to happen to her and our baby." Ray told him starting to get a bit frustrated.

"Maybe you should think of taking some leave till things cool down."

"I suppose I could, I haven't had any days off for quite a while, as a matter of fact it is a good idea I think I will." Ray agreed.

"Rather than have you ask your Inspector we'll go straight to the SDC and let him know what is happening, then that way your Inspector can't say anything," Steve informed him.

They both left the office and went to speak with the SDC, once he was made aware of the situation he granted Ray immediate leave for two weeks.

On leaving the SDC's office Ray went down to the locker room where he started to get changed into his civilian clothing, as he did so Bobby came into the room.

"What are you up to?" Bobby asked.

"I'm getting changed and going home, the SDC has granted me two weeks leave starting as of now," Ray replied.

"You lucky sod I wish I could get leave whenever I want it like you," Bobby said sounding downhearted.

"It's like I have always told you Bobby, it is not what you know, but who you know."

Just then a call came over the intercom directing Ray to his Inspectors office.

"I wonder what the hell he wants now?" Ray said in general.

"I don't know probably he is going to chew your arse out because the SDC gave you leave and it didn't go through him," Bobby answered.

Ray finished getting dressed and then made his way to the Inspectors office where he found the Inspector and the Sergeant talking, he knocked gently on the door before going in.

"You wanted to see me Inspector."

"Yes I do, who the bloody hell do you think you are? Going over my head and asking for leave from the SDC, have you forgotten that there is a chain of command?"

"Yes I do Inspector however getting this leave was very important to me and I am sorry if you're feeling bad about it, however my leave has been granted and I am going now, I will be back in about two weeks," Ray informed him.

"Well I have a good mind to put a stop to it, I'm getting just a little bit fed up with your attitude and work."

Just as Inspector said this Steve came to the office and heard what was said.

"Are you still here Ray?" He asked.

"Yes I am Sir my inspector wanted to see me and he just told me that he is getting my leave cancelled."

"I see, well I would like you and the Sergeant to just wait outside of the office while I have a word with your Inspector if you don't mind," Steve said indicating for them both to leave the office.

Ray and the Sergeant left the office and waited outside, no sooner had they closed the door when they heard Steve raising his voice at Ray's Inspector.

"Let me tell you something, if it wasn't through cops like Ray there would be a lot more murders going on and the last thing a man like him needs is a bloody dickhead like you on his back," Steve said.

"I don't care what you say he is in my section and he will do what I want, when you are his boss then you can say what he does, so I would just mind my own business if I were you," Rays Inspector was heard to reply.

"I don't give a toss if you are his Inspector and if you want to take this up with the SDC, he's in his office now so come on let's go," Steve said opening the office door.

"No I'm going nowhere so just get out of my office," the Inspector said waving his hand towards the doorway.

"I'm going up to see him now and tell him what an

arsehole you are and that you are trying to get Ray's leave cancelled which I can assure you will never happen," Steve said as he turned to walk away.

At this point Ray did not know what to do so he turned to look at his Sergeant asking him "What the heck should I do?"

"I think you had best go along to the canteen until something is worked out," he advised.

Ray made his way to the canteen where he brought himself a cup of tea and sat waiting to see what was going to happen, roughly half an hour later the Sergeant came in with a smile on his face and walked over to him.

"Right Ray you had better go home to start your leave and I'll see you again in about two weeks okay," he said.

"So tell me what happened?" Ray wanted to know.

"I'll let Steve tell you that, he knows better than I do apparently the SDC was not very impressed with our Inspector."

"Okay then Sergeant I'll see you after my leave, take care," Ray said getting up from the table and walking towards the door.

It wasn't long before he was in his car and driving home, as he drove he began to think of how he was going to explain to Pauline what was taking place.

He knew she would be worried and really the last thing he wanted to do was to get her all upset, another problem was that she might start to ask questions as to why he in particular would be the target.

However he decided that he would just play things by ear.

CHAPTER – 13 – SILLY WEE MAN

After his two weeks leave had ended Ray reported back to the station for duty he was detailed to accompany one of the other cops whose nickname was Stoner in one of the mobile patrols, after gathering all their equipment together they went out to the police car that they would be using for the day.

Just as they were about to drive out of the Station a call came over the car radio telling Ray that he had to go and see the Special Branch Inspector.

"Bloody hell I wonder what they're wanting me for now?" Ray moaned.

"When you need me I will be in the canteen, I might as well have my breakfast while I am waiting for you," Stoner told him.

"Hopefully I won't be too long but you never know, do me a favour Stoner and get in touch with the communications room to let them know we are not on patrol," Ray said.

"Yep no problem I'll do that before I get something to eat," Stoner say's walking off in a different direction.

Ray made his way up the flights of stairs to the special Branch office where his knock on the door was answered by Paul.

"Boy, they are panicking here something is coming down and Steve is running around like a chicken with his head cut off," Paul whispered to Ray.

As Ray walked through the door Steve caught sight of him.

"Ray, come into my office we have got to do some serious talking, there is something going on and it is supposed to be happening soon, have you heard anything from any of your informers?"

"I haven't had the chance I only started back to work today," Ray told him.

"Well it is vital that we get some up-to-date information

quickly the word on the street is that there is something going to happen soon, and to be quite honest we haven't got a clue to go on."

"Like I said boss I haven't seen any of my informants, all I can do is just take a chance that I see one on my patrols," Ray told him.

"Don't you know where they live because you could call on one of them and try to find out what's happening."

"I'm not going to just knock on their doors because that would put them at risk, and I'm sure they wouldn't thank me for it."

"We have to do something?" Steve said sounding worried.

"I realise that but there is nothing I can do at this moment in time, anyway what rumours have you heard?" Ray asked.

"We have heard that there are more weapons in the area that are being hidden somewhere either in the town or somewhere on the outskirts, the info is a bit sketchy but it comes from a reliable source."

"I hope you are not paying your informant because if you are you're being conned out of your money anybody could say that sort of thing and be right nearly 90 percent of the time," Ray laughed.

"I know that but at the end of the day beggars can't be choosers," Steve replied.

"What I'll do then is take a drive around the estates to see if I can find any of my touts walking about."

"I only hope you do see one, then at least we will be in a position to try and stop anything happening."

"Right well I had better get back out on patrol I'll see you later Sir," Ray assured him as he left the office.

Ray made his way back down to the canteen where he found Stoner tucking into a rather large breakfast, seeing that it would take Stoner probably quite a while to finish eating it he went to the counter and ordered himself a breakfast.

Once he had got it he walked over and joined Stoner and sat opposite him.

"So what's all the panic about?" Stoner asked as Ray sat down.

"They've heard a rumour that somewhere there are some weapons hidden by the IRA and that they're going to be used in a shooting and they wanted to know if any of my touts might be able to let us know who or what is the target."

"I take it then that we are not going to be doing much other than try and track down one of your informants today."

"You've got it," Ray said.

"Well I suppose it's better than having to deal with things like traffic accidents and family disputes," Stoner smiled.

"Anything is better than that, mind you I have a few assault cases to deal with but there is no rush for the paperwork so chasing up my touts will be a nice break."

Just shortly after that they had finished their breakfast and after gathering their equipment together they went out to the police car, it wasn't long before they were driving out of the Station gates.

"Let's take a little look around the Kilwilkee estate just to see who is about," Ray suggested.

"Do you know what time it is?"

"Yes it is 9.30 in the morning, why?" Ray wanted to know.

"Just for your information you won't find any of those lazy bastards out of their beds at this time of the morning," Stoner say's.

"I suppose you're right there," Ray agreed with him.

"What we could do is go and get some papers and then find a little place where we can park up and have a read after all we have nothing much to do." Stoner suggested.

"Now that's a great idea let's go to the newsagents," Ray told him.

As they were on their way to the newsagents a call came over the radio asking them to attend a road traffic accident on the Dollingstown road.

"Shit that's all we need," Stoner moaned.

"Just radio back and tell them that we are tied up with something else, then the other mobile patrol can deal with it," Ray said.

Stoner done as Ray had said and it wasn't long before they were parked up in a nice quiet spot reading their papers.

After about half an hour when they had finished reading their papers they decided to go for a drive around the Kilwilkee estate, no sooner had they driven into the estate than Ray spied one of his informants.

"Do you see that man on your right Stoner? Just pull up beside him I want a little chat he might be able to help me with something."

"I take it he is one of your touts?"

"Let's just say that he helps me with a few things now and again."

No sooner had Ray said this than the car pulled up beside the man Ray opened his door and called the man over to him.

"Hey Fats, long time no see where have you been hiding?"

"Oh! It's you Ray, I haven't been hiding anywhere."

"Well come and stand with me over here I think we need to have a little chat," Ray said getting out of the car and walking to the back of it.

"What do you want to know Ray?"

"I have heard a whisper in the town that there is something coming down, is this whisper right?"

"I don't know I haven't heard anything," Fats replied looking nervous.

"Now you're not telling me porkies are you?" Ray asked him.

"No, no honest to God I'm not," Fats answered seeming more nervous.

"Well you know what would happen if you were, or if I found out you were telling me lies? I would have to remember the time that I caught you in the car that you had stolen and then you might just end up in jail," Ray reminded him.

"I was hoping that you had forgotten all about that after all I have always given you any information about anything that's going on," Fats replied.

"I suggest then that you start to try and listen into a few conversations whenever you are in the company of any of the local IRA men, because like I have already told you I've heard a whisper that something is going on and I want to know what it is."

"If I do manage to find anything out what's in it for me?" Fat's wanted to know.

"Depending on how good the information is I'll definitely forget about the stolen car episode, and you never know I might even slip you a few pennies."

"I would appreciate that very much especially a few pennies in my pocket, I haven't got a job at this moment in time and they would come a very handy," Fat's said feeling pleased that he would have the chance to get some money.

"So, it's all up to you, don't go letting me down will you?"

"I'll try and find out as soon as I can, I promise."

"Right I'll see you later then," Ray said getting back into the Police car.

As the car pulled away Ray watched Fat's walk along the street and head towards in the house of a well-known IRA member.

"Was he any use to you?" Stoner wanted to know.

"He wouldn't tell me anything so either he is too scared to say, or he doesn't genuinely know a thing," Ray answered.

"So where do you want to go now?"

"Take a left turn here and we'll drive past Declan's house on the off chance that he'll be out of his bed."

As they cruised past the house both of them looked at the building, in one of the downstairs windows Ray got a glimpse of someone looking out, when this person saw the police car they quickly stepped back away from it.

"Well someone's up and out of bed I'm not too sure who it was," he told Stoner.

"If you want we can park up by the garages just around the corner, we should be able to keep an eye on the house front door to see who's coming and going," Stoner suggested.

"That's a good idea, go too it."

Stoner drove into the garage area and parked up near the entrance and left the engine running, this was a precaution just in case they should come under attack then at least they would stand a good chance of getting away.

Luckily for them things were not very busy so it gave them a chance to stay in the area, after approximately 35 minutes Stoner nudged Ray's arm.

"Here we go someone's coming out of the house."

"Let's hope it's Declan," Ray replied looking at the house.

As they sat watching the place they were both shocked to see Clooney come out through the door.

"Well what do you know? I wonder what he's doing in there at this time of the morning?" Ray remarked.

"Perhaps he's shit his own bed and decided to spend the night with Colin," Stoner laughed.

"Now this is very interesting, I'm glad we saw this I wonder who else is in the house?"

"It is a pity that we didn't have a reason to knock on the door then we could find out," Stoner says.

"I wonder if any of the others need to see Declan or his brother about anything then that would give us a reason to pay them a little visit."

"I could always give the other cars a call if you want?" Stoner offered.

"Hmm that's a very good idea, go to it Jerry," Ray said smiling with a devious look on his face.

Stoner leaned forward in the car and took hold of the radio microphone and holding it to his mouth he began to call the other cars.

It wasn't long before John's voice came over the radio telling Stoner that he had to call at Declan's house on an inquiry about a shoplifting matter, a rendezvous was arranged for the two cars to meet on the road which led into the estate.

"Now we will get to see who else is in the house," Ray said as Stoner started the car.

"It should be quite interesting, I only hope it doesn't turn into a shooting match I have to go to a party tonight and I would hate to miss it just because I'm full of holes," Stoner said laughing.

They drove away from the garage area to the main road where as they arrived they saw the other car that John was in coming slowly down towards them.

It pulled up and stopped opposite them on the other side of the road Ray got out of the car and walked over towards John's, as he approached the car John opened his car door, Ray knelt down beside him.

"Well what can I do for you Ray?" John asked.

"There's something fishy going on at Colin and Declan's place, I saw Clooney coming out of it early this morning he must have been there overnight," Ray informed him.

"I see what you mean it is a bit odd they've probably
Been doing a bit of planning as to who they are going to

murder next."

"I'm very curious to see who else is in the house so that is why I need someone who has the reason to be knocking on the door to make a few enquiries about something."

"Well I have to speak to Declan about a shoplifting case so if you want you can come with me while I talk to him," John said.

"I would appreciate that very much that's if you don't mind?"

"Right come on let's go round there now it's getting near my break time, I'll see you round there shortly," John said closing his car door.

It wasn't long before both cars were pulling up outside of Declan's house Stoner and Billy who was John's driver for the day stayed with the police cars while John and Ray went to the house front door.

They both took up positions either side of the door then Ray put his arm out and knocked on it, the reason they knocked on the door in this manner was for their own security as on previous occasions it had been known for terrorists inside of the house to shoot through the door. Colin appeared to be a bit nervous when he answered the door.

"Yeah and what do you want?" he asked them in an aggressive manner.

"Is your brother Declan at home?" John enquired.

"I think so," was the reply.

"Would you tell him that I would like to speak with him please."

"Okay hold on I'll get him," Colin said attempting to shut the door, however this was in vain as Ray quickly put his foot in the way to stop it closing.

Colin called out Declan's name and soon Declan joined them.

"Yeah what can I do for you?" He asked looking

nervously at Ray.

"I would like to ask you a few more questions about the shoplifting case that I'm dealing with, can I come in?" John said as he moved to walk into the house causing Colin and Declan to both step back.

"Well you're already in aren't you?" Colin said.

"Oh! So we are, I hope you don't mind, mind you it's very nice of you to invite us into your house it's a lot better than just talking on the doorstep don't you think?" John smiled.

"We didn't bloody invite you into the house so you can both just get back out before I throw you out," Colin said taking up an aggressive stance.

"Now don't be like that Colin, Declan invited us into the house didn't you Declan?" Ray said looking him straight in the eye threateningly.

"Err. yes I did," Declan replied a bit worriedly as he felt intimidated by Ray and would also be scared by what his brother might do to him after Ray and John had left.

Realising that the two policemen were not going to go away Colin left them with Declan in the hallway and went into the kitchen at the back of the house.

Ray watched him as he left and noted that Colin seemed to give a slight nod of his head as if there was someone in the kitchen who Ray couldn't see.

While John stood talking to Declan, Ray slowly moved into the hallway of the house still keeping an eye on the kitchen.

In order to get a better view of the kitchen doorway he positioned himself to stand beside Declan's shoulder.

As he looked towards the kitchen he could see Colin looking in his direction as Ray looked at him he noted that there was a bit of the shadow of the wall which would indicate that there definitely was someone else in the room.

To make it look that he had'nt noticed this Ray started to

talk to Colin.

"So how are things with you these days Colin?"

"They're not too bad, at least they were alright until you bastards turned up."

"Now that's not the right sort of attitude to have we are only doing our job," Ray told him.

"Well I think you lot must drive around in your cars all day trying to work out who you're going to hassle next."

As Ray talked with him he noticed that the other person in the room was moving around as he saw the shadow keep moving.

"No we have a lot of better things to do than mess around with you lot, you and your cronies are just a pain in the arse."

"That works both ways mate," Colin said.

"And what does the person who is in the kitchen with you think?" Ray asked as he left his position and quickly made his way to the kitchen doorway and looking into the room.

The other man who was in the room was caught by surprise and looked at Ray.

"Well, well, well, look who we have here? if it isn't my old friend Phely from Newry, and how the devil are you?" Ray asked him.

"So this is where they sent you, it's nice to see you again Constable Rutherford the boys in Newry will be glad to know where you are," Phelim replied sounding threatening.

"That sounds like a little threat," Ray remarked.

"No Constable I don't need to threaten you because when I tell the boys where you are they would only be too willing to come up here and do things for themselves."

"Let me tell you this Phelim if I happen to see any of them here in Lurgan there will be a few more funerals in Newry," Ray warned.

By this time John had finished speaking to Declan and had taken up a position next to Ray.

"Do you know this man? Have you ever seen him before" Ray asked John.

"No I've never met him before who is he?"

"His name is Phelim, he and I know each other very well he is one of the Newry IRA."

"No I'm not I haven't been convicted or charged with anything to do with the IRA so you can't accuse me of that," Phelim said in his defence.

"Don't bloody lie you're involved in nearly all the terrorist attacks in Newry if you're not actually pulling the trigger you are pressing the tit that sets off a bomb," Ray retorted.

"Maybe I am, but you have to prove it and until you can I'm a free man," Phelim sneered at him.

"One day you'll come unstuck and then we'll see whose laughing and I know it won't be you unless you're smiling while you are laying on the slab at the mortuary full of holes."

"You might be there before I am so you'll never know will you," Phelim said.

"You had better hope I am, anyway enough of this what are you doing up in this neck of the woods?" Ray asked him.

"That is for me to know and for you to find out."

"If I was you I wouldn't be so smart we can always take you in under the emergency provisions act and have a little talk for a couple of days, that's if you want?" Ray threatened him.

"Do whatever the fuck you like it won't bother me I have been held for seven days before and they never got anything out of me you see the law helps me more than it does you, you're the poor fuckers to have to live by the law whereas I don't," Phelim smiled again.

At this point of the conversation Ray turned to John and

told him to write down Phelim's particulars so that the information can be passed on to the station criminal intelligence officer.

As John took out his notebook and flicked through the pages to where he could write down Phelim's details Ray walked away and over towards Declan, he stood in front of Declan with his back to Colin and Phelim.

When Declan looked at Ray's face, Ray winked at him and silently mouthed the words that he wanted to meet him at their normal rendezvous, Declan gave a slight nod of his head to indicate that he had understood what Ray had mouthed.

It wasn't long before John had finished recording the details and both of them returned to their police cars prior to getting into them Ray arranged to meet John back at the Station canteen.

"What took you so long it's getting bad whenever I let you out of the car you don't know when to come back," Stoner moaned at Ray.

"I met an old friend in there from Newry he was one of the IRA men that were out to murder me that is why I was transferred here," Ray informed him.

"I bet he got a right shock when he saw you."

"Not half as much as I did and he recognised me straight away I would love to know why he is in this area, especially why he is staying at Colins house?"

"I would imagine that the Special Branch will be very pleased to have this little piece of information," Stoner said.

"That's why I would like you to take me straight back to the Station if you don't mind, that is unless you have something you'd like to do?"

"I've nothing to do and it will be good to get back as I am dying for a cuppa."

It didn't take them long to arrive back the Station as they pulled into the backyard and parked up Ray told

Stoner to get the tea's in while he went up to the Special Branch office to let them know about Phelim being in the area.

Ray quickly went up the stairs to the SB office and was soon sitting at a desk telling the SB Sergeant about what had taken place at Colin's house.

"Now that is nice to know, is he still there?" he asked Ray.

"Well he was when we left why?"

"Because there was a terrorist attack on a part time member of the UDR in Newry last night and the poor guy was killed so maybe Phelim done the job and then came up here to lie low until the heat was off."

"You could be right there, would you like us to go back around and bring him in for questioning?" Ray offered.

"No not yet I think we should get the DMSU to call at the house and lift him, if you want you can be parked somewhere near to keep an eye open just in case they get the wrong man," the Sergeant told him.

"Okay Skipper give me a call on the radio when you want me to follow the arresting party, we'll either be in the canteen getting a cuppa and something to eat or back out on patrol I'll see you later," Ray says as he leaves the office.

He went down to the canteen where he joined Stoner taking up a seat opposite him.

"So what's the score?" Stoner asked him as Ray sat down.

"The SB are going to get Phelim lifted for the suspicion of the killing of a UDR part timer last night in Newry," Ray informed him.

"Who is doing the arresting?"

"They are going to get the DMSU to get him, we have to be nearby just to make sure they get the right man."

"Well if the Dimsu (police slang for DMSU) are doing the job we may as well have a meal while we are waiting for them to come over from Portadown, you know what they're like they always turn up when the horse has bolted," Stoner smirked.

"I can't see why we have to wait for them there are enough men here on duty to be able to go and get him here and now, that's if he's still there since we left?" Ray moaned.

"Yeah I think we should be the ones to arrest him, after all it would mean a nice trip over to Armagh Gough Barracks Interrogation centre," Stoner agreed.

"I know at least it would be a break from driving around this dump," Ray said.

They had a meal and just as they were about to get up and leave to go back out on patrol the SB sergeant came into the canteen looking for them.

"I'm glad I caught you before you went back out I have a bit of news for you there has been a change in plan," he told them.

"Don't tell me, the Dimsu can't come and we have to go and get Phelim ourselves am I right?" Ray guessed.

 "You've got it, when can you go?"

"We can go now, hold on a minute while I check to see what the other car's doing they can come as back up."

"Right I'll leave it in your hands, let's just hope he hasn't scarpered," the Sergeant said as he left them.

Ray called John's car on his portable radio that he had attached to his gun belt, he arranged to meet up with them on the road leading into Kilwilkee.

Nearly ten minutes later they were all discussing what tactics to use and the best way to effect the arrest, John was a little wary as he felt that because they were at the house earlier Colin and Phelim might be expecting them back.

"I think this could turn into something like the showdown at the OK corral, I hope to Christ they don't have any weapons in the house," he said.

"If they do and they start shooting then it's open season on terrorists, anyway you and your driver can go round the back of the house and me and Stoner will knock on the front door," Ray told him.

"What if he comes out the back do I arrest him or do I just keep him there till you arrive?"

"If he tries to run away then stop him in any way you can, if he doesn't run then hold him until I get there."

"If he is armed then just shoot the fucker we'll all say that you told him to put his weapon down, and carried out the proper procedure before shooting him," Stoner laughed.

"Let's hope it doesn't come to that," Ray said as he started to get back into the police car.

"Right Ray we'll follow you in, see you in a bit," John says getting into his car as well.

Both cars drove into the Estate and as Ray's car pulled into the street that would take him to the front of the house, John's carried on to the street that would bring him to the back of it.

Stoner drove very slowly along the road until John's voice came over the car radio telling them that he was ready and in position.

"Right let's go for it," he said to Ray as he speeded up and stopped outside the front of a house a few doors away from Colin's house.

Ray and Stoner quickly got out of the car and almost running went and took up positions on either side of the house's front door, Ray knocked on the door and it was opened by Declan.

"Hello again Declan, where's Phely?" Ray asked him.

"He ain't here, he's gone."

"Then you won't mind us coming in and checking will you?"

"You're not coming in again you've no reason to," Declan says trying to close the door.

"Well we are so get out of the bloody way or I'll shoot you," Ray said pushing him aside and up against the hallway wall.

As he did so he heard someone open the house back door, he quickly made his way past Declan and on reaching the doorway into the kitchen he tentatively ducked down before looking into the room.

He saw that the back door was open and made his way over to it, on looking in the back garden he saw John standing over Phelim who was laying on the ground with blood coming from his mouth.

"Silly wee man, fancy trying to bite the butt of my rifle, you'll hurt yourself that way," John said smiling from ear to ear.

"Hi Phely," Ray said standing over him and twiddling his fingers in a wave, "now why are you trying to run away? Have you something to hide?"

"I'm saying nothing," Phelim replied spitting some blood from his mouth.

"Well get on your feet we're going for a little drive to Gough Barracks in Armagh and I thought we would take you with us," Ray told him.

"And what if I don't want to go with you?"

"Then we'll just have to make you, and I'm sure you wouldn't like that."

As Phelim got to his feet Ray carried out a search on him, when he put his hand into an inside pocket of Phelim's anorak jacket he felt a pencil and a piece of paper removing them he looked at the paper and saw on it was list of car registration numbers.

"Now what do we have here, collect car numbers do you?"

"You know what it is, it's a list of numbers of private cars that the local cops drive."

"Why would you want them," Ray asked sarcastically knowing that Phelim would be collecting them to carry out shootings or bombings on them at some time or other.

"If you don't know the answer to that then I ain't gonna tell you," he smirked.

"This is getting us nowhere so I think then best thing to do is to get you settled into Armagh, come on let's go," Ray told him taking him by the arm.

After signalling his driver to drive around to the front of the house John followed behind and warned "If you try to make a run for it again Phely next time I won't hit you with the butt I'll just plug you full of holes."

"You'd probably miss me," Phelim laughed.

"If you want to take that chance you could always try?" Ray said.

They walked back into the house and through the kitchen as they came into the hallway Stoner was standing blocking the front doorway to stop Colin from leaving.

"What shall I do with him?" he asked on seeing them and pointing at Colin.

"Keep him there while John's driver comes round to the front," was Ray's reply.

When the car did pull up both men were taken out to them and put in separate cars.

"I think we should also take wee Declan with us as well," Ray suggested to John.

"Then I had better call up another vehicle, hold on a minute," John says.

Another vehicle was requested to assist and it was not long before it arrived, it was the station perimeter security patrol Tangi Landrover, the commander of it was a man called Al Beye.

"Boy it's great to be away from just driving round and round the outside perimeter of the bloody station, what can we do for you?" he asked as he got out of the Tangi.

"I thought you would like the break, the thing is we need

to get these three men over to Gough Barracks, and we don't want them all in the same vehicle," Ray told him.

"I will have to check with the duty Sergeant for permission to go there, I can't see him allowing it as we are now the only vehicle left to cover the town, just hang on a sec I'll give him a call."

"No don't bother what you can do is take him back to the station and after we have dropped our man off we can come back and get him."

"Okay we'll do that for you, who do you want us to take?"

"You can take Declan we shouldn't be that long, just tell the Sergeant what's going on so that he doesn't throw a wobbler, also could you let the SB know that we have the package they wanted."

"Right we'll see you in a while, come on Declan get in the back," Beye said leading him to the rear of the Tangi.

Shortly after Ray and John's car were on their way to Armagh as they travelled Ray turned to look at Phelim in the back seat.

"It's nice of you to come with us, I like these little trips don 't you?"

"I'm saying fuck all," Phelim replied.

"I would have thought that you would be pleased of the break, after all you get free meals, a good night's sleep and a lot of peace and quiet," Ray goaded him.

Phelim just ignored him and wouldn't take the bait.

"I didn't know that you and Colin were good mates or is it Declan whose your friend? after all they are both nice people to know," Ray mused.

"It certainly wouldn't be Declan, he's only a Pratt, a fucking wannabe he's a tadpole short of a swamp," Phelim retorted.

Roughly twenty minutes later they were driving through the camp gates of Gough Barracks towards the interrogation centre.

"I hope you brought your tooth brush and shaving kit, you could be here for at least a week," Ray said to Phelim.

"I will be glad to get in a cell just to get away from you, you sarcastic bastard, I hope you get fucking shot while I'm in here, if you don't I will be looking for you when I get back out."

"Now you shouldn't make those sort of threats it's not nice," Ray laughed.

"I'll promise you this much you are gonna die very soon because when I get out of here I'm coming hunting for you and I mean it."

"I'm glad you warned me, just to make sure that I got what you just threatened could you say it a bit louder just in case it didn't come out very clear," Ray smiled as he pulled the Dictaphone from his pocket.

"You think you're so fucking smart don't you?"

"I only get smart when I'm dealing with scum like you, anyway here we are hold on and I'll let you out of the back of the car," Ray said as they pulled up outside of the interrogation building.

It did not take long to book Phelim into the custody suite then Ray and Stoner were soon on their way back to Lurgan happy that their day had been quite eventful.

CHAPTER – 14 – IN THE KNOW

When they got back to the station Ray went straight up to the SB office to speak to the Sergeant to let him know that they had delivered Phelim to Gough barracks.

"Well skipper he's safely behind bars for a week and guess what the bastard said to me? He told me that when he gets out he's coming looking for me," Ray said.

"I bet that scared you I can see your knees knocking from here," the Sergeant laughed.

"Well I am going back out on patrol so unless there's anything else I'll see you later."

"The only thing I need to know now is where are they stockpiling those weapons if I knew that I would sleep better at night."

"Well I have Declan being held downstairs, I told him that I wanted to see him later on so hopefully I might have a little bit of info for you then."

"As soon as you do let me know, okay?"

"I will no problem, bye for now," Ray said as he left the office.

He made his way back down the stairs to the custody suite to see the Sergeant and have Declan released, he didn't want to speak to him in the Station to get any information from him, so he told Declan that he would be released and that he would meet him out of town by the Silverwood Hotel rather than their usual meeting place.

Once Declan had left the Station Ray went to look for Stoner, the first place he looked was in the constables workroom however he didn't find him there so he went to the canteen where he did find him playing a pinball machine.

"Funny that! I actually went to the Constables workroom looking for you, but I should have known to come straight here to your second home," Ray said as he walked up behind him.

"Well I had a good teacher in you didn't I?"

"You've got to be joking, I have more important things to do than sit in a canteen playing pinball machines."

"Now it's funny you should say that because I've noticed that since you have been here you seem to spend a lot of time in the SB office, why is that?"

"Because I like to know what's going on and keep my finger on the pulse."

"I don't think it is that reason, as a matter of fact after a bit of thinking I have come to the conclusion that you are not just an ordinary cop, I can't put my finger on it yet but I'll soon work it out."

"Well when you do let me know, come on we've things to do," Ray told him walking towards the canteen door to leave.

When they reached the car Stoner opened his door and stopped, as he was about to get into the vehicle he said, "I know it has just come to me, what was it you used to do in the Army?" he asked Ray.

"I was a dog trainer."

"Hmmm is that all you were?"

"Of course Why?"

"You're not one of these 14 Intelligence guys are you?"

"Do I look that clever?"

"You never know from what I have heard about them they'll take anybody into that lot."

"Thanks it's nice to know when your partner distrusts you," Ray remarked as he got into the car.

Soon they were driving back out of the station Stoner for once was very quiet and seemed to be pondering on something.

"You're quiet what's up have you run out of conversation?" Ray enquired of him.

"I'm just doing a bit of thinking and piecing things together."

"I thought that, by the sound of cogs going round in

your head," Ray laughed.

"Don't you worry Ray it'll come to me, and I am sure you are not what you appear to be there is something fishy about you."

"All this thinking is doing you no good you'll end up in the nuthouse if you are not careful then Lurgan would be missing one of its finest," Ray continued laughing.

"Well I don't care what you say I'll get you sussed out yet."

"Like I said Stoner when you do, let me know, meanwhile can you drive around the Craigavon Lake area, by the Silverwood Hotel?"

"No problem what are we going out that way for?"

"Just to see if anything is happening out there after all it's very rare that we go out that way."

"Yeah you can say that again I can't remember the last time we were out there."

"It will make a change from driving around that boring town."

"I know exactly how you feel I am beginning to really hate this damn place, I wish they would transfer me out of it to somewhere that is nice and peaceful, somewhere like Portrush where I can sit and look at the women all day."

"I would imagine that if they sent you there, they wouldn't be getting much work out of you, would they?"

"You hit the nail on the head there," Stoner remarked.

At this point they reached what was known as the Silverwood roundabout on driving three-quarters of the way around it they started to head out towards the M1 motorway.

As they got roughly within 300 metres of the slip road onto the motorway Ray spied someone walking towards them on their side.

As they neared this person they noticed that it was Declan so Ray told Stoner to pull over to the side of the road and stop beside him.

"Hello Declan what brings you out this way?" Ray asked him.

"You should know? You said you want to see me."

"That's right I do get into the backseat of the car we'll go for a little drive and a chat."

Declan done as Ray had asked him and they were soon driving towards an area known as Oxford Island, which was a swampland a few miles away from the town limits. Once they had reached a spot where Ray thought they would not be seen talking by any passers-by he told Stoner to stop the car telling Declan to get out of it and follow him a short distance so that Stoner couldn't hear what they conversation would be about.

"Well Declan do you have any news for me?"

"No nothing at all."

"Are you sure?"

"Of course I am don't you believe me?"

"To be quite honest with you I think you are telling me porkies."

"No I'm not honest to God I'm not."

"Now I know your bloody lying, if there's one thing I have learned in this job it is that whenever any of you Fenian's say honest to God, I know you're lying."

"Well you can believe me or not but I'm telling the truth.

"Did you know that you are starting to look like Pinocchio your nose will soon be touching the ground, so before it does I think you had better start telling the truth."

"I know nothing believe me," Declan said shaking worriedly.

This didn't go unnoticed by Ray; "You are nearly shitting yourself what's wrong? are you scared in case the brother finds out that you are talking to me?"

"Fuck sake if he knew that he would kill me whether I am his brother or not, or he would get someone like Phely to do it for him."

"You needn't worry about Phely he is in Gough barracks for a wee holiday for about seven days," Ray informed him.

"Phely is one man that I definitely hate he treats me like an imbecile."

This made Ray have to turn away to hide a snigger as he knew where Phely was coming from, because he knew that Declan was about as bright as a five watt bulb, however that was to Ray's advantage.

"I'll tell you this much Declan, Phely was telling us on the way to Gough barracks that you will have no chance of ever getting into the IRA he says you are a tadpole short of a swamp," Ray told him knowing that this would anger him.

"That bastard had better watch out what he is saying about me as I know enough to put him in jail for a very, very long time."

"You think you know a lot about him, but I don't think you do." Ray goaded him.

"That's just where you are wrong Ray."

"How am I wrong?"

"Well for instance I know for a fact that he was the one who shot that UDR man last night in Newry."

"How do you know that for sure?"

"I heard him telling my brother when he arrived last night."

"He could have been talking about something else, or just claiming to have done it to make himself look big," Ray said to get Declan to give him a little more information.

"He told us last night that he shot the man four times in the back and then went over to his body and shot him right between the eyes," Declan seemed to knowingly boast.

"Well if you think you are that clever and know everything that is happening in the town tell me what else is going on."

"Like what?"

"I heard a little rumour that there have been a few weapons brought into the area is that true?"

Declan seemed to get a little bit worried again, "I don't know anything about that."

"I think you do Declan and I'm afraid if you don't tell me what you know I'll have to tell Phely what you just told me, and I don't think you will be living for long after I've told him."

"Please don't do that Ray, if you promise not to say anything I'll tell you, is it a deal?"

"It all depends on how good the information is that you give me."

"The only thing I know is that my brother was talking to three boys from the junior IRA who live in the Taghnevan estate, he told them that there were some weapons being hidden near here."

"I don't suppose you know where?"

"As far as I know they are being hidden in a hayshed not far from here."

"In case you haven't noticed there are hundreds of bloody hayshed's around here, what I need to know is which one?"

"I'm not sure exactly but if you want I'll try and find out."

"Make sure you do I need to know where they are as of yesterday do you understand?"

"Sure no problem Ray I'll find out as quick as I can, I'll try and find out tonight as I know one of the boys, if I do I'll meet you in the Park tomorrow afternoon is that okay?"

"Right that's fine just make sure your brother doesn't catch you trying to find out."

"I will don't worry he's the last one I don't want to know what I am doing."

"Before you go he is a little something for you," Ray said handing him a £20 note.

"Gee thanks Ray, this'll come in handy," Declan said taking the money and putting it in his pocket.

"Right let's get back into the car, where can we drop you off?"

"Don't bother I don't want to run the risk of being seen with you."

"Why's that?" Ray wanted to know, " If anyone sees you with us they will think we have arrested you."

On getting back into the car Ray told Stoner to start driving back towards the Silverwood Hotel as they passed the slip road to the M1 motorway Ray took a quick look around to make sure that nobody was in the vicinity, then he told Stoner to stop the car and let Declan out.

"I'll see you again tomorrow then Ray," Declan said as he closed the car door before quickly walking away from it.

Stoner pulled away from the side of the road and started driving towards the police station, they hadn't gone far when he turned to Ray and said,

"I think I know what you are really here for and it would take a lot to convince me that you are just an ordinary cop."

Ray pretended that he didn't hear what he said and continued to look through the car window.

"Did you hear what I said?" Stoner wanted to know.

Very reluctantly Ray looked at Stoner saying, "I heard exactly what you said so I think it is about time you knew the truth and my real reason for being in the province, then not only will you sleep better at night you won't have to keep asking me questions."

"Right now we're getting somewhere, so come on spill the beans."

"I'll tell you this much if anything that I tell you gets out you'll be in deep shit."

"Your secrets safe with me, I won't tell a soul," Stoner assured him.

Ray went on to tell him all about what he was really in the province for and why it was important that nobody knew anything about him, he also told him that if anyone found out that he knew not only would Stoner be in trouble but Ray would be moved out of the province.

"So that is why you are more interested in the terrorists than doing ordinary police work."

"That's right Stoner so you just make sure you keep what you know to yourself because I'll tell you this much if I have to leave here you could end up laying face down in a ditch with a hole in the back of your head."

"Like I said nobody will hear anything from me I promise you that." Stoner assured him.

"Now that we have got that out of the way let's go back to the station and while I go and see the SB, you can have another game on the pinball machine."

"That seems like a good idea to me," Stoner says heading in the direction of the station.

It wasn't long before they were both getting out of the car in the back of the station and

Ray took his normal traipse to the Special Branch office. After entering into them he knocked on Steve's door and walked straight in.

"Boy, have I got news for you Governor, for a start as you know I know very little about the shooting of that UDR man last night but I now know that he was shot four times in the back and once between the eyes, am I right?"

"You are spot on who told you that information?"

"I just got it from one of my touts who knows for a fact that it was Phely who done it."

"Who is this informant?"

"Sorry boss but I can't tell you."

"Wouldn't you even give me a little hint?"

"Nope not a chance, also I might have information for you about the weapons you are looking for."

"Now that is good news it's the best news I've heard all day, where are they?"

"I am not exactly sure at this moment but my tout will try and find out tonight."

"So when is he going to let you know?"

"I'll be meeting him again tomorrow hopefully he'll have some good news for us."

"What else has he told you?"

"Well he did let me know that our friend Colin from the Kilwilkee had been seeing and chatting with three of the junior IRA boys in Taghnevan."

"I don't suppose you know what he wanted to see them for?"

"No but with a bit of luck my tout will be able to find that out for me."

"Okay Ray we'll just have to wait, thanks for keeping me up to date I'll see you later,"

"If you need me within the next fifteen minutes," Ray said looking at his watch "I'll be downstairs in the canteen getting a cuppa, so I'll catch you later," he said as he left the office.

Ray made his way to the canteen to find Stoner, as he entered it he couldn't see Stoner anywhere so he about turned and headed for the Constables workroom.

When he opened the door to it and put his head inside he found Stoner was not they're either, as he closed the door and turned to walk away he spied one of the other Policemen.

"Have you seen Stoner anywhere?" Ray asked him.

"The last I saw of him was when the Inspector called him into his office," he replied.

"Thanks mate," Ray said as he made his way towards the Sergeants office to speak to him, mainly to find out what the Inspector wanted Stoner for.

On reaching the office Ray knocked on the door and heard the Sergeant call him in.

"Have you seen Stoner anywhere skipper?"

"Yes I believe he's in with the Inspector."

"You don't know how long he is going to be in there do you?"

"He shouldn't be too long now he's been in there nearly twenty minutes."

"Right thanks skipper I'll wait for him in the canteen," Ray said turning to leave the office.

"Hold on a minute Ray I'd like a little chat with you."

"Yes skipper what can I do for you?"

"Take a seat, I've been asked to have a little chat with you by the Inspector."

"Oh! What does he want now?"

"He asked me to have a little chat with you about your workload apparently he isn't very happy because he has not seen any paperwork from you for quite a while."

"Well as you know Sergeant anybody can get themselves bogged down with paperwork, but a lot of the things I feel can be dealt with by way of caution, then that way I would be spending more time on the streets rather than sitting in an office writing."

"All I can say about that Ray is, you must try and put more paperwork in, it doesn't bother me how much you put in to be honest it's just that I want to keep him off your back."

"Thanks skipper I'll go and get a few cases to keep him happy."

"Right well that's it for now Ray I'll see you later."

Ray got up from his chair and headed back to the canteen where he ordered himself a cup of coffee, just as he turned to walk away from the counter Stoner came through the canteen door.

"Hi Ray I'll have a coffee as well, being as you're

buying."

Ray got a coffee and joined Stoner at the table he had sat down at.

"I hear you had a little chat with the Inspector?"

"Yeah he collared me in the corridor as I was on my way to the toilets."

"What did he want to see you about?"

"He asked me about what we got up to when we were on patrol."

"What did you tell him?"

"Not a lot, I told him that we spent most of our time driving around the estates and sometimes out towards the divisional boundary."

"I hope that's all you told him because if you told him anymore you're a dead man."

"Don't I bloody know it, I might act stupid but I can assure you I'm not."

"That's okay then, well here, we had better get back out on patrol, drink up," Ray said as he put his cup on the table and got up from his seat.

They both made their way out to the car and it wasn't long before they were back out of the station.

"Okay where do you want to go this time Ray, Taghnevan, Kilwilkee, Mourneveiw?"

"As a matter of fact I want to go somewhere where I can get a file I've just had the Sergeant warning me that the Inspector is watching to see how many prosecution files I put in."

"Oh! He's up to the dirty tricks is he, he'll be watching in the hope that he can get you moved by saying you're not doing your job properly."

"It's looking that way, but I'll tell you this much Stoner he's messing with the wrong guy here, he'll be moved long before I am."

"You couldn't make it tomorrow could you?" Stoner laughed.

"I thought that you and him were good buddies, after all you always seem to be chatting with him, as a matter of fact I think you two are having an affair," Ray smiled. "Give me some credit, if I was a woman I wouldn't look at him twice, how the hell his wife can wake up every morning looking at his ugly mug I'll never know, she must have nerves of steel or be blind."

"Perhaps she uses the same guide dog as your wife uses," Ray said laughing.

"Right that's it I ain't saying another word, you big shit," Stoner replied sounding hurt.

"Yes it will be great, perfect peace, I should get at you more often," Ray still laughed.

As they drove along the Park Road a car suddenly came screeching out of the park entrance and onto the road in front of them where it accelerated away.

"Go get him Stoner, there's my first victim," Ray said reaching for the two-tone horns switch.

Stoner speeded up and turned on the police car headlights full and gave chase it didn't take long before he was up behind the speeding car.

"I wonder what his hurry is?" Stoner remarked.

"I don't know but he is in for a shock when he pulls over," Ray answered.

"Well no harm to you Ray he doesn't look like he is going to do that."

"You're right there as a matter of fact he seems to have speeded up a bit more, put the foot down Stoner don't lose him." Ray said with the adrenalin building.

Stoner pushed the accelerator down further and matched the speeding car; "This guy isn't going to stop you had better call one of the cars in Moira to see if they can help."

Ray got on the car radio and called for the Moira patrol car to help intercept the speeding motorist.

"Juliet Mike from Juliet Lima 71 we have a Red ford

escort XR3I trying to evade us, would you be in any position in the village to intercept him? over"

"Lima 71 this is Mike 80 we are not in the village at this present moment we are out in the cuds but we will make our way back towards you coming from the Crumlin direction keep us informed and we will do our best to assist, over," came the reply.

"Roger Mike 80 will do, we are at present just entering the village heading towards the M1 Moira roundabout."

As they speeded up to catch the Escort Stoner said, "The way this guy is driving he'll end up killing some poor sod, if not himself."

"Well just pull back a bit with a bit of luck he might just slow down."

Stoner done as Ray said and slowed the police car just enough that they could keep an eye on the Escort, the Escort driver did appear to slow his speed as well.

Once they were through the village Stoner speeded back up, as so did the Escort as both cars approached the roundabout that could take them onto the M1 motorway the driver of the Escort instead of turning left onto the roundabout decided to turn right against the flow of traffic.

"This guy has a bloody death wish, all you can do is try and follow him Stoner but be careful I'm too young and good looking to die," Ray joked.

"Well I'm going to take it easy I have two kids and a very nice looking wife at home, so I ain't gonna get myself killed for this madman."

They continued to follow the Escort around the roundabout and when it came to the Airport Road exit off the roundabout the driver of the car turned off onto it and picked up speed.

"Gotcha now, now you've had it," Stoner said gritting his teeth and pushing hard on his accelerator, the Airport Road was a good road for a car chase as it was wide and fairly straight so any oncoming traffic would have a clear view of them.

The police car was travelling at some speed and was right up behind the Escort when Stoner tried to overtake and pulled alongside of it the driver steered into the path of Stoner's car.

"The bastard, now he is getting me angry I'm gonna run this fucker off the road," he remarked.

"He is a little tinker isn't he," Ray said smiling.

"He'll be a dead one by the time I've finished."

"Let me just see where the Moira car is," Ray said picking up the radio microphone and saying into it, "Mike 80 from Lima 71 we are now chasing this car along the Airport Road headed towards Crumlin, over."

"Roger Lima 71 we are on the same road heading in your direction," came the reply.

No sooner had this been said when Ray saw the Moira car coming towards them with its full lights on.

"Now we've got the git, he'll be a very unhappy chappie in a few minutes," Ray said.

"I am just ready to side swipe him into the hedge, and you see when I get hold of him he's gonna get one hell of a talking to," Stoner promised.

Ray knew what Stoner meant as he had seen him in this sort of mood before and had also seen the result of the other man's face, it wasn't a pretty sight.

The driver of the Escort had also seen the other Police car and he drove even faster to try and make it to a turn off which was on his right, Stoner noted this and was practically standing up on the accelerator to get more speed out of the Police car.

As both cars neared the turn off junction that was on their right, the Escort started to pull across the road to turn into it.

Just as it started to enter the mouth of the junction and turn, Stoner floored his accelerator and drove the Police car crashing into the side of the escort.

The Escort was lifted momentarily up in the air and bounced sideways into the hedge that bordered the road.

Although a bit shaken by the bump Ray and Stoner were quickly out of their car and ran over to the Escort where they found the driver sitting looking like a goldfish out of water with his mouth opening and closing.

"Are you ok? Are you hurt at all?" Ray asked the man.

"Yep I'm ok nothing broken,"

"There fucking soon will be," Stoner ranted as he pulled the car door open and grabbed hold of the man dragging him out of the car and onto the ground.

"Ahhh! You're hurting me," the driver yelped.

"You're lucky I ain't killing you." Stoner raged.

As the man lay on the ground Ray recognised him as a terrorist he once had dealings with in Crossmaglen.

"Well look who it is? It's my old mate Joseph from the Castleblaney Road Crossmaglen, how the devil are you Joe? Now what would you be doing here in Lurgan you don't have family in the town."

"Oh! It's you is it, so this is where they sent you," Joe said sounding peeved.

"Yes much to your heartbreak I am now here and I don't like it when shitbag's like you come onto my patch, so like I've already asked, what brings you up here?"

"I just fancied a day out and thought I would take a look at the countryside outside of Crossmaglen."

"Okay, well why didn't you stop when we tried to pull you over?"

"Because I was frightened and wasn't sure what to do because it was the first time I ever had a cop car with its horns on coming up behind me."

"I see you still lie like a cheap watch, well now you can get into the police car and we'll go back to Lurgan station for a little chat and if I am still not happy with your story then you'll be spending a few days in Gough Barracks."

As Joe tried to get up off the ground he let out a moan and lifted his foot up obviously he had hurt it.

"Well, well, it seems as if you'll have to be going to the hospital first, can you walk on that foot?" Ray enquired of him.

"It's really painful I think I might have broken it." Joe replied wincing with the pain.

"Okay I'll call an ambulance, just sit back down on the ground till it comes."

Ray contacted the Lurgan station control room and got the radio operator to have an ambulance sent to the scene.

Whilst they were waiting for it to arrive Stoner and the driver of the Moira car took a search of Joe's car to see if there was anything in it that might have been the reason for Joe wanting to get away.

Not long after starting the search the driver of the Moira car let out a whoop of delight as he gingerly lifted up a revolver that he had found under Joe's car seat.

"Look what we have here?" he said placing the pistol on the bonnet of the escort.

"Now that is interesting, you are in very deep shit now Joe," Ray told him.

"You planted that there," Joe says sounding very worried.

"And why should he want to do that?"

"To try and stitch me up."

"I think you had better tell us what you were doing with it?" Ray said walking over and standing beside Joe's bad leg.

"I'm saying nothing till I speak to a Lawer."

Ray put his foot onto Joe's ankle and applied a little pressure on it causing him to cry out in pain.

"What were you saying just then about a Lawyer?"

"Ahhh! You bastard that hurts, I only said I ain't saying anything till I see my Lawyer."

"If I was you I would start talking to me otherwise your leg could be very sore by the time you get to see him." Ray told him applying pressure again.

"I'm saying fuck all to you, this is torture that's what you're doing to me."

"No it's not, it's called persuasion."

While Ray was talking to Joe, Stoner called the station to inform the duty Inspector and Sergeant what was the outcome of the chase and what had been found.

Ray was just about to ask Joe again why he had the pistol when the ambulance turned up and two paramedics got out of it, after Ray had explained what had happened they began examining Joe.

Their conclusion was that he had only sprained his ankle, this pleased Ray as it would mean that he could take Joe straight back to the police station rather than have to accompany him to hospital.

Not long after the paramedics had left, the Sergeant and Inspector arrived with two of the CID (Criminal Investigation Department) and a photographer, closely followed by Steve and Paul from Special Branch Ray and Stoner meanwhile after putting Joe into their car withdrew from the area and began their drive back to the station to place Joe in custody.

CHAPTER – 15 – WEAPONS INFORMATION

The following day after the arrest of Joe the Inspector gave the morning duty briefing; he detailed Ray for station duties, which meant that he would be in the enquiry office as the SDO.

This was a bit of bad news for Ray, as it would mean that he wouldn't be able to meet with Declan to get the information about the weapons that the IRA had hidden in the area.

However he did not say anything to the Inspector, as he didn't trust the man so he just went to the enquiry office and relieved the officer who was there.

Because Ray's duty day started at 07.45 it meant that there would be none of the SB men coming in till 09.00 as their job was basically 9 to 5.

There was never anything much happening at this time of the morning most of the men doing the SDO duty would get stuck into any paperwork that they had to do, Ray never took much paperwork on and so he had none. Instead he just picked up a magazine that was already in the office and settled back to read it, no sooner had he got settled than the Inspector came into the office.

"What are you doing Rutherford? Don't you have any work to be getting on with?"

"No Sir not a thing." Ray replied.

"I think that is because you just drive around all day doing nothing and turning a blind eye to anything you might see."

"I'm afraid you're wrong there Sir if you would care to take a look at the station caution book I've given plenty of cautions to a lot of people."

"Where is it? I don't believe you."

"Here you are Sir," Ray said handing him the book.

The Inspector couldn't wait to get hold of it and snatched it from Ray's hand.

"I'll take this back to my office and check it, you had

better be right," he warned.

"I think you'll find that the last four entries were made by me."

"Right while I just check this book you can make yourself busy by cleaning this place up." the Inspector told him going out of the office.

Amazed at this order Ray stood and took a look around the room, there was nothing he could see that needed cleaned so he just took up his old position and carried on reading the magazine.

At around 9 o'clock some of the administration staff of the station started to turn in for work it was like the rush hour at London's Piccadilly train station, as he watched them come in through the doors he saw Steve arrive.

"Good morning Inspector" he said to him.

Looking up and seeing Ray behind the counter Steve's face dropped, "What are you doing in here?"

"I was detailed for SDO today."

"That's no good how are you going to see your contact?"

"I don't think I will be able to today, but sure that's life eh!" Ray shrugged his shoulders smiling.

"I'll see about that stay there I'll soon be back," Steve said going on into the station.

"I a'int going anywhere, I can't," Ray told him as he sat back down to carry on reading the magazine.

It wasn't long before Steve returned with Ray's Inspector, "I would like you to put Ray out on patrol, there's something he needs to do for me," Steve told the Inspector.

"I'm sorry but I have detailed all of my men and I am not changing the duty sheet just to please you."

"Look it's vitally important that Ray is out on the streets today." Steve informed him.

"I'm sorry but no can do, having Ray in here is the only way that I know he's working."

"I take it then that all my entries in the caution book

stand for nothing then Sir?" Ray piped in.

"Oh yes it shows that you are actually bothering to get out of the car now and again."

"So yesterday's little incident was not very important?" Ray continued.

"That has nothing to do with it, what I want to see is more paperwork coming in on my desk from you."

"Right Sir, well I hardly think that I will be able to get any sat behind this counter."

"Exactly, that is the way I would see it as well," Steve said in agreement looking at the Inspector.

"Well I have made my decision so this is where you'll be doing your duty today," the Inspector said quite adamant.

"It's no problem to me," Ray told him looking over at Steve.

"Well it isn't all right with me, I'm not happy about it what I need Ray to do today is extremely important, lives could depend on it," Steve flamed.

"All I can suggest then is if you're not happy that Rutherford is working inside today you should go and see the Superintendent, but as far as I am saying Rutherford is in here today, and I detail my men, you have no say in what duties I give them," the Inspector says raising his voice.

"Right well we'll see about this," Steve said angrily as he stormed out of the office.

With Steve gone the Inspector took a quick look around the office then turned to Ray saying "You've done a good job in here, this is how this office should be kept, nice and tidy."

"Yes Sir," Ray replied laughing inwardly.

"Well Ray all I can suggest to you while you are in here with a bit of time on your hands is that you think about your future position in this job, I can assure you that if you don't start taking on a bit more paperwork and showing me that you are capable of doing it, you'll be looking for another job do I make myself clear?" the Inspector told him.

"Yes Sir you do."

"Right well just make sure you do," the Inspector says walking out of the office.

Roughly 15 minutes later another police officer came into the office, he had his paperwork tray in his hands.

"Hi Ray I've been told to come and relieve you, you've got to take my place in the car with Stoner."

"Who told you that?"

"The Sergeant did, apparently from what I hear the Inspector is not very pleased as this has come down from up high."

"I bet you're not very happy about having to be in here all day?"

"I don't mind really because it will mean I might be able to get some of this paperwork shifted out of my tray, Oh! and Stoner is waiting for you in the canteen."

"I'll let you carry on then, see you later mate," Ray said picking up his equipment and leaving.

As he made his way along the corridor towards the canteen he heard "Ray can I see you a minute please?" coming from behind him.

Turning he saw it was the Sergeant, "Yes Skipper what can I do for you?" he said walking back the way he had come.

"Come into my office a minute we've got to have a serious chat," the Sergeant says leading the way.

Once they were in the office the Sergeant pointed to an easy chair, "Sit yourself down, would you like a coffee this could take a while."

"Well rather than you make it I'll buy you one at the canteen Skipper, I was just going there to meet up with Stoner."

"No I think that what we have to talk about is best kept

between ourselves."

"Okay then I'll have a coffee NATO standard."

"What the heck is that?"

"In army slang it means white with two sugars please."

When the Sergeant had finished making the coffee he settled down sitting opposite Ray.

"I am not exactly sure where to start here, so just bear with me, the thing is it seems to me and the Inspector that you have a certain amount of power in this station and from what I have been led to believe you seem to have a lot of contacts up to the highest level in this job."

"Oh! What makes you think that Skipper?"

"Well for starters I have a friend who works up in headquarters in Belfast and I hope you don't mind this but I asked him if he knew anything about you, if your name had appeared on anyone's desk up there."

"In what way do you mean?"

"Well I was making enquiries as to the reason of you move from Newry to here, mainly to see if it was for disciplinary reasons or the like."

"And what did you manage to find out?"

"To be quite honest Ray not a thing, my friend told me that for some reason there were not even any records on you at HQ which is very strange as there should be, so just to set my mind at rest here Ray, What's going on?"

"As much as I would love to tell you I can't, all I can advise Skipper is let sleeping dogs lay, you don't really want to know," Ray said winking.

"It's just that the Inspector wanted to know and asked me to have this chat with you, me I am quite happy with what you do, so don't think it is just me."

"I know it's not you trying to dig the shit up on me, I know it's the Inspector and believe me he's messing with the wrong person, I'll have to have words with someone."

"Okay Ray we'll forget this conversation ever took place

you can go and find Stoner, thanks for enlightening me," the Sergeant said getting up from his seat and clearing away the empty cups.

"Right, I'll see you later," Ray replied leaving.

He went straight to the canteen to find Stoner as he approached the staircase outside of the canteen door he saw Steve coming down them.

"Ah! Ray, come here let me have a little word in your shell like," Steve motioned him over to him.

"Yes Sir what do you need me to do?"

"When do you see your tout?"

"As soon as I can but we arranged to meet definitely at around lunchtime if I see him any earlier I'll come straight back and let you know."

"Good, well make sure you do it is imperative that I get that information as quickly as possible, do you understand?"

"Yes of course, settle petal," Ray told him smiling.

"It's alright for you it's not your balls on the chopping block."

"I'm going out now as soon as I give Stoner a shout, when I see my tout I'll tackle him to find out what he knows, mind you Steve he might not have anything to tell me."

"I just hope he has because I have had really hot info that there is going to be an attack in this town somewhere and I need to know where or some poor sod is going to die."

"Right well I'll just get Stoner and we'll get out and see if he's anywhere about, I'll come and tell you as soon as I've met with him alright?" Ray said walking away into the canteen.

Stoner was playing the pinball machine when Ray walked up behind him.

"Right Stoner we've to go out straight away, come on get your kit on."

"Hold on a minute Ray I've just got two more balls to play and I'll be with you."

"We haven't got time, this is a rush job."

"Ah! Shit, rush, rush, rush, that's all we seem to do in this place," Stoner says moving away from the machine and picking up his equipment.

They both made their way out to the car; Stoner got in the driver's seat while Ray got into the front passengers.

"Where are we going that's such a hurry Ray?"

"We have to try and find Declan, the SB have a bit of a flap on."

"They always have a flap on, what's happened has one of them seen something in the paper he's been reading?" Stoner joked.

"No it's a little bit more serious than that, someone could end up dead."

"I see, well where does Declan fit into the equation?"

"I've asked him to try and find out where the weapons are being stashed to do the job."

"Do you wanna know something Ray, I don't trust Declan as far as I could throw him, I think you place too much trust in him."

"Not really he knows that if he crosses me he'll be signing his own death warrant."

"Oh! Yeah and what are you going to do take him for a drive to Oxford Island and shoot him?"

"No I wouldn't be doing it the IRA would do it because all I would do is let it be known that he's an informer."

"They wouldn't believe that, because his brother is one of the top men in the IRA in this town." Stoner says in disbelief.

"Believe it or not Declan hates what his brother is doing, he only goes along with him because he's scared of him."

"You could be right there, anyway where are we going now?"

"Take a drive along North Street and towards the Kilwilkee, we might be able to see him walking about."

It was not long before they were driving into the estate. "Well I don't see him anywhere, I think he could still be in bed scratching his arse and snoring," Stoner joked.

"I hope he gets out of it soon, I need to see him quickly I only hope he has a bit of good news for me," Ray said.

"Shall I take a drive past the house? You never know he might see us and realise that we need to see him."

"That might just do the trick but I don't want anyone suspecting what we are up to."

Stoner took a slow drive around the estate making sure not to go directly to the street that Declan's house was in, eventually when they did pass the house Ray looked over at it to see if there were any signs of anyone there. In the downstairs window he saw a face appear and was pleased to see it was Declan Ray didn't make any signs he only looked at him.

"Right he's seen us, I just hope he has the wit to go to where I have arranged to meet him, okay Stoner lets go for wee drive to the park."

"Your wish is my command master," Stoner replied as he drove towards the road that led them out of the estate.

"Take a slow drive up along the town we'll give him about twenty minutes to get there, that should be long enough."

"That is if we don't get called to do something or other on the way,"

"That's what I like about you Stoner you're so pessimistic," Ray remarked.

"Well if we get a call we'll have to answer it because we are lead car today, so all the work falls on our lap."

"I think finding Declan is more important, I don't care what else may happen he is my main priority."

"I'll leave it to you to tell the boss then shall I?"

"Yep I'll tell him, to be quite honest I don't think he'll say much after what happened this morning, he's on a very sticky wicket."

"Why? what has he done?"

"Let's just say that the Superintendent is not very happy with him."

"I can see why, he's an arsehole anyway," Stoner smiled.

As they drove up through the town Ray spied Declan walking towards the place where they had arranged to rendezvous every time.

"Okay Stoner there he is over there," Ray said pointing the direction of Declan.

Stoner drove to the top of the town and cut through a gap in the central reservation and started to drive back the way he had come, towards the park.

"I hope he has found something out for us," Ray remarked worried.

"We should know something, because after all, his brother is one of the top Provies and if he doesn't know what's going on, who does?"

They lost sight of Declan for a short while, but as they cruised along Ray spied him walking towards the Park gates, "Ahh! There he is again he's going down towards the swimming pool, better put the boot down Stoner I don't want him to think we're not coming."

Stoner speeded up in the car and drove out along the Moira Road where he drove in through the Park gates.

"Where are we heading in here?" He asked.

"Take a drive in the direction of the cricket pavilion we should meet up with him around there somewhere."

As they travelled along the road that went around the back of the pavilion they both saw Declan walking towards them, as the police car reached nearly the middle of the back of the building Ray told Stoner to stop the car.

"Just wait here for a minute while I have a little word

with him," Ray said as he got out of the car and started walking to meet Declan.

As they reached each other, Ray was the first one to speak, "Well Declan what do you have to tell me? And I hope it's good news."

"I think you'll be pleased or at least I hope you will."

"So what's coming down?"

"From what I have managed to find, there are a few weapons being hidden in a hayshed out in the Tandragee direction opposite the Legahory estate."

"Do you know what sort of weapons they are?"

"I haven't got a bloody clue Ray, I only know that they are being hidden there ."

"What are they going to be used for?"

"As far as I know they are going to be used in a post office robbery, apparently the bigwigs of the IRA are needing some cash to buy some more weapons and so they thought that the boys here in Lurgan can get it for them."

"I don't suppose you know which Post Office?"

"As far as I have been able to find out apparently they are going to try to do one out in the Richill area, exactly which one I'm not sure."

"Are you sure about that? because we have heard a different story?"

"I'm positive Ray honest."

"So you won't have heard the rumour that there is to be an attack carried out on the police in the town?"

"I know nothing about that," Declan said looking puzzled.

"Well that is what we have heard and I wouldn't like to think that some of my colleagues might be murdered because you have given me a load of shit."

"Honestly Ray I'm telling the truth."

"You're not telling me that something will be happening in the Richill area just so that we all concentrate in that

direction and let our guard drop here in Lurgan are you?"
"What do I have to do to prove it to you that I am telling the truth and that's all I know, honest to God?"
The moment Declan said "Honest to God", Ray became suspicious as on previous occasions when he had been dealing with people who used those words they were usually lieing.
"Hmm that's a good one I'll just have to take your word for it I only hope for your sake that you are not wrong or you could find yourself talking to an IRA security squad."
The squad Ray was referring to was a group of IRA men who were responsible for the security of the IRA to make sure that nothing that the IRA were going to do was leaked to the Security Forces.
If they found any informants the poor person would suffer a very tortuous death.
This little threat made Declan swallow hard and Ray could see that he was thinking hard about what he had said. "What do you mean by that Ray?"
"I mean sunbeam that if I tell my superiors that there will be a post office hold up somewhere in the Richill patch and instead some of my mates are killed then I'll drop your name around the streets letting it be known that you are an informer."
This caused Declan to do little bit more thinking and after a short while he said, "Alright Ray there is going to be an attack on the police in the town it is going to be at the security barriers, as far as I know it will be while they are checking the traffic."
"Why didn't you tell me that in the first place?"
"Because I am scared of what my brother and Clooney were talking about last night."
"And what were they talking about that has you so worried?"
"After what happened at the roundabout a suspicion has come about that there is an informer somewhere."

"What do they intend to do about it?"

"My brother told Clooney to try and find out who it might be as he would rather he dealt with it himself rather than get the security team in."

"So rather than possibly give yourself away you would get some of my friends murdered, is that right?" Ray snarled.

"Well what do you think?"

"I think you're messing with the wrong cookie because if you start telling me lies, you'll find that I can be a lot worse than the security team so don't push your luck."

"You wouldn't hurt me would you Ray."

"Wouldn't I?" Ray said raising his eyebrows.

"Yeah I think you would," Declan replied noticing his look.

"Right then, when is the attack supposed to be taking place?"

"I am not sure of the exact date but I think it will be happening within the next two weeks."

"Well that's not much help I need to know roughly when."

"I'm sorry Ray but that is all I know, mind you it's definitely going to happen."

"Okay then, who and how many are going to be involved in it?"

"As far as I know there will be four, I think two of them are coming from out-of-town, and also two guys from Lurgan."

"I don't suppose you know their names?"

"I think that the two from Lurgan are Magoo and Biff the other two are coming in from Belfast I don't know their names."

"Would you happen to know where the two from Belfast will be staying when they get up here? Or when they might be likely to arrive?"

"I think they will be staying at one of the houses in

Taghnevan it is one of the safe houses."

"I would imagine that they would have to be up here at least two days before the job so that they can get the lay of the land, so now as soon as you get to know that they have arrived you let me know."

"Okay Ray that shouldn't be any problem, so I'll go now and see you some other time."

"Remember before you go Declan if you don't keep me properly informed of what is going on, you will not be a very happy chappie do you understand?" Ray reminded him.

"I know, I know, you don't have to keep reminding me, I'll see you later," Declan said as he walked away.

Ray turned around and made his way back to the police car, once he had got into it he said to Stoner "Okay let's go back to the station quickly, I have some very good news for Steve this'll make his day."

"That's good because he has been walking around recently like a bear with a sore head, I heard him giving off to one of the SB boys yesterday."

"Well when I tell him what I have just heard he'll be over the moon, he'll probably be buying coffees all round."

"Shall I put the two tone horns and lights on? Then we can really fly back to the station." Stoner said smiling.

They drove away from the back of the pavilion and made their way back to the Park gates, as they drove towards the boating lake Ray saw Clooney walking along the edge of it.

"Well, look who we have here its Mr Clooney pull over beside him Bobby while I have a wee chat with him to see what he is up to."

"You won't get anywhere with him Ray he's a right ignorant bastard, he won't say a word to you."

"I hope he didn't see me and Declan talking otherwise Declan could end up a dead man."

"Well at least then we won't ever have to worry about

Declan again, and you'll save yourself quite a bit of money."

"To be honest I don't really mind paying Declan at least I know the information he gives me is real."

"Yeah but one day he might just decide to set you up for a bullet, as much as you might trust him, I don't trust him as far as I can spit."

"Okay we'll leave Clooney for now he'll come another day just carry on back to the station."

It didn't take long before they were driving through the Station gates Stoner drove down to the back of the building and parked up while Ray went in search of Steve.

When he went to Steve's office he found him talking to two other men, one was the Superintendent of the HMSU and the other Ray recognised as being from Gough barracks interrogation centre.

"Ah! Ray what news do you have for me," Steve asked.

"Well I have just been speaking to my tout and I am about to make you're day, he told me where the weapons are being stored."

"Great did he tell you who's gonna be picking them up and using them?"

"Yes he told me that there would be two men from Lurgan and two from Belfast doing a job, he said that there will be an attack on the police on the town barriers."

"I don't suppose he told you when this will be taking place?"

"Apparently it's gonna be happening within the next two weeks, he'll tell me when the two gunmen come up from Belfast."

"Did he happen to mention who the two men from Lurgan might be?"

"Yes it's going to be Magoo and Biff, when the boys come up from Belfast they will be staying in a safe house in Taghnevan."

"I wonder who the two boys from Belfast can be?" The Superintendent of the HMSU pondered.

"Well we'll just have to get in touch with the SB in Belfast and see who might be missing for a couple of days," Steve answered him.

"Hmm that is easier said than done, we would have to keep surveillance on all of them and I don't think the authorities would sanction all the overtime for the men to carry out the job," the Superintendent say's.

"We'll just have to wait till they arrive up here, then we should have at least two day's notice before they carry out the hit," Ray remarked.

"Why do you think two days Ray?" Steve asked.

"Because I think it will take them at least two days to familiarise themselves with the area, so that they can learn the lay of the land and get to know where the escape routes are just in case things go wrong for them."

"Hmm and what if they don't come up two days before, we'll never get to know who they are."

"If that's the case Sir then we are no better off than what we are now, so it'll be just a waiting game won't it," Ray said.

"I see what you mean we'll just have to take the chance and tell the men on the barriers to be extra vigilant and watch out for any strange faces in town, with a bit of luck we might be able to catch them."

"Now that I have left you with that little problem is there anything else you want me for? before I go back out on patrol," Ray wanted to know as he started to make his way towards the office door.

"We will probably be wanting to see you a bit later on, we have some thinking to do before some poor cop loses his life and I think you might also be helping us with this job as well," the Superintendent told him.

"That's fine by me Sir, I could do with the extra overtime," Ray said as he left the office.

The fact that there was actually going to be an attack on the police at the town barriers did not really come as a surprise to Ray, because he knew that a lot of the Policemen carrying out the duties became bored after about an hour and a half.

So once the boredom had set in the men seemed to drop their guard because they got fed up with stopping cars and asking the same old questions like, can I see your driving license please? And where are you coming from? also where are you heading?

Unless it was somebody who was a known terrorist or sympathiser in the car things became rather mundane.

If the person or persons in the car were suspect then the car was pulled over to one side of the road and all the people in the car were taken out of it and their names and addresses were noted prior to the car being given a thorough searching.

This was for weapons or anything likely to be used in the commission of a terrorist act.

However the IRA were aware that any vehicle with a known terrorist or sympathiser in it would be stopped and searched, so to get around this problem they would have items like the weapons or explosives hidden in a car that would be driven by someone who they knew was not suspected by the police.

The vehicle would be driven either two or three cars in front of the IRA suspect's car, or the same distance behind it, causing the Police to direct their attention to the suspect's car thus ignoring any other vehicles.

CHAPTER – 16 – THE HAYSHED

Now that the authorities knew where the weapons were being hidden it was decided to put a surveillance unit into operation on the hayshed, being as the surrounding area to the hayshed was mostly open field this would not be easy.

Mainly because if any police vehicles were used they would be seen in the area, this would draw a lot of suspicion from the public.

After a good reconnoitre of the area by some of the members of the T C G. it was thought that the best way to get over this problem would be to put a listening device inside of the building.

Once the authority had been given to do this it was just a matter for a team from the HMSU to plant the devices, this would be done during the hours of darkness and would mean that the team would have to approach the shed by coming across country on foot.

Even though there was a road running alongside of the field it would have been unwise to drop them on the road for fear of being seen.

However the team did manage to get the devices into the shed, they managed to put two towards the back of the building, one to the left and the one on the right they also managed to install another just inside of the entrance of the building.

These devices were very sensitive and could pick up even the slightest sound or any movement inside.

Once they had finished planting the devices the team set about trying to find any place outside of the building that would afford any good cover for at least two teams from the HMSU to take up hiding so that whoever came to pick up the weapons they could be arrested.

Two days after Ray had made his report re the location of the weapons to Steve he was told to report to the HMSU offices in Mahon Road, as he entered them he noted quite a number of senior police officers were there.

"Ah! Ray there you are, welcome back to our little den," said the Superintendent.

"How do you do Sir, this place is beginning to seem like a second home to me," Ray said smiling while shaking the Superintendents offered hand.

"Well I thought you just might like to be in on our next little venture at the hayshed."

"To be quite honest with you Sir I didn't really expect that I would be needed on this, I would have thought that the HMSU would have done this without any outsiders?"

"That is true but I thought that you just might like to see the finality of all your hard work."

"Well I thank you for that Sir but with my being seen to come here to this unit so often I am becoming the talk of Lurgan station, and it is certainly not doing my cover any good, remember I am supposed to be just an ordinary cop."

"Yes I see your point, I'll tell you what we'll make this the last time we use you for any of the jobs, is that alright?"

"That would be great Sir as to be quite truthful all this is beginning to hold me back from finding out about other things that will be happening, I am not really getting the chance to meet with my other informants from South Armagh."

"You're not still seeing informants from down there are you?"

"As a matter of fact I am and I have just learned that the IRA have moved a sniper into the area to carry out some hits on the Army and police down there."

"Do you have a name for him?"

"Apparently he is an ex Green Beret from America and he is supposed to be very good at his job I haven't managed to get his name yet."

"And that's all we need is a sodding Rambo running around the place," one of the other men remarked.

"As of yet as far as we know he hasn't done any shootings, I only hope that doesn't start before we have finished this operation," Ray replied.

"Well let's forget about him for now we have a bit of planning to do here," the Superintendent interrupted.

"Sorry Sir," Ray apologised.

"Right first off Ray, you'll be assigned to one of the team's, the one I am putting you with one of the team's you will be with Bronze 2."

"Where will I find them?"

"They are most probably getting all their equipment together, you'll find them a bit further along the corridor that way," the Superintendent told him pointing where Ray should go.

"Who is in charge of them? do I know him?"

"I think you do Ray his name is Alex."

"Ah! Yes I do we worked together in South Armagh, I didn't know he was now with the HMSU this'll be like a reunion, okay I'll see you later Sir," Ray said as he made his way along the corridor.

As he walked he heard a noise in the distance, it was a noise of men talking and laughing it wasn't long before he reached the source of it and he saw his old friend Alex sitting in a chair laughing with a group of men whom Ray automatically took to be the members of Bronze 2.

As he approached, Alex got up from the chair and walked towards him putting out his hand to be shaken.

"Hello Ray you old Buzzard how the heck are you? long time no see what have you been getting up to?"

"Well they moved me from Newry to Lurgan because I became the IRA's flavour of the month and they put a contract out on me."

"So what do you think of being in Lurgan?"

"I hate the bloody place, you're in more danger inside of the station than you are out on the streets, back stabbing is an art form there."

"You could always apply to come here."

"No thanks I am quite happy with section work and being an ordinary cop, I've done my time creeping around in hedgerows and ditches."

"Starting to feel your age now are you Ray?" Alex laughed.

"Well I feel it's time that you young fellows did your little bit, you can't expect us old guys to do everything for you," Ray retorted.

"Anyway Ray I think it is time I introduced you to the rest of the team, they are, Bruce, Mark, Davie and last but not least Tony," Alex said indicating to them individually.

"You were stationed in Crossmaglen weren't you?" Mark asked Ray.

"Yes I was there only for a short while."

"Well it is an honour to be able to actually meet in person the famous Ray Rutherford, you are well known in Crossmaglen the locals there still talk about you," Mark said.

"I hope it's only good things they say about me," Ray smiled.

"I don't know about that, but they threw a lot of doubt on your parentage."

This caused quite a few laughs from the others.

"Well you can't please everybody in this job can you?" Ray said shrugging.

"I don't care what they say down there in Crossmaglen, all I can say is thank God you are on our side Ray," Alex said.

"Well it's nice to be appreciated," Ray smiled.

"Anyway Ray this is getting us nowhere is there any

equipment you need that we can fix you up with?"

"All I have with me is my Ruger."

"Would you like to borrow something bigger?" Alex asked.

"What do you have in the cupboard?"

"Well now let's see, there is an M1 Carbine, a Browning pump action shot gun, a
Heckler and Koch MP 5, or a good old Sterling machine gun I am afraid that is all there is left."

"Well if it's all right with you I'll take the MP 5, that's providing nobody else wants it."

"Okay Ray here you are," Alex say's handing the weapon and three magazines of rounds to him.

"So what time are we leaving here?"

"We'll be going as soon as it starts to get dark, we will be dropped off by vehicle just here," Alex said pointing to a spot on a map of the area.

"So how are we getting from there to the hayshed, which route are we taking," Ray wanted to know.

"We will be going across country through the field's, it shouldn't take too long the fields are fairly dry and clear of any real obstacles."

"And what time do you think we will be back? as I am back on duty in Lurgan to start at 07. 45."

"I thought you were to be with us all night, I think it will be best if you went to the Superintendent and asked him."

"Okay I'll go and see what he says, I'll not be long," Ray says leaving Alex and making his way back to the Superintendent.

When Ray had managed to find him he said to him
"Excuse me Sir I don't suppose you can tell me how long this will take or how long I will be out tonight?"

"You'll be with us all night Ray, why?"

"The thing is I am back on duty in Lurgan on the early shift tomorrow."

"I don't think you will be, didn't anybody tell you that you have been seconded to us for the duration of this operation?"

"No Sir this is the first I have heard, I thought I was only coming here in an advisory capacity."

"Well I'm sorry to disappoint you Ray but that is how it is," the Superintendent informed him.

"Well now that I know, is it Okay with you if I go to my home and get some of my equipment?"

"What sort of equipment?"

"It is a set of camouflage trousers and jacket, and also a sniper's rifle with a night sight that I have in storage there."

"I didn't know you had all this equipment, how long have you been keeping it?"

"I have had it since I left the Army, I keep it in the attic."

"What does the wife say about you keeping it there?"

"She doesn't know, she also doesn't know what my true purpose is over here or what my real job is."

"I see, well what do you think she will say when you go home and start to get all this stuff out of the attic?"

"She won't be there she's visiting her mother."

"I suppose you'd better go and get it all then, but you haven't got long we'll see you back here a bit later then."

"Right then Sir I'll not be long," Ray said leaving him and going out of the building to his car.

He quickly drove to his house in Richill where he picked up the equipment luckily for him Pauline was staying at her mother's for the night.

Ray made his way back to Mahon Road, on pulling up outside of the HMSU buildings he proceeded to take his equipment out of the boot of his car.

As he did so one of the UDR. men who was passing saw him taking his snipers rifle which was in a gun carrying bag from the back seat of the car.

"Hi there, looking at the size of that gun bag you must be going on safari," the soldier commented.

"I suppose you could say that, however the thing we are hunting is not an animal."

"I gathered that, just do me a favour and don't miss," the soldier said as he carried on his way.

Ray continued on his way into the building and went straight down to the room where he had left Alex and the others, as he walked into it the other men looked at him in surprise when they saw the gun bag.

"What the hell have you got in the bag, is it a Bazooka?" Alex enquired.

"No it's an Army snipers rifle, with this thing I can blow the balls off a fly at about 800 yards with no problem," Ray said taking the rifle out of the bag.

"I see you also have night sights on it as well, can I have a look at it?" One of the other policemen wanted to know.

"Yeah sure here you are, be careful and try not to drop it those sights are set just perfect and take a lot of time and bullets to get them right," Ray said as he handed the rifle to him.

"While he is looking at your rifle you had better start getting yourself ready Ray we'll be leaving here shortly," Alex said.

"Okay no problem it shouldn't take me along," Ray replied as he opened his hold all.

Ray took out his combat kit and got changed after he had finished getting dressed he covered his face and the back of his hands with camouflage cream, his combat kit had lots of pieces of sacking of different shades of Greens, Blacks and Browns sewn all over it like a Gillie suit.

"Your tailor isn't up to much he has done a bad job on your combat kit," Alex laughed.

"I know you just can't get the staff these days," Ray smiled.

It wasn't long before they were putting their kit into the back of a Ford transit van and were leaving the camp heading in the direction of the village of Tandragee, about two miles away from their objective they all disembarked from the vehicle.

As they all gathered their equipment and prepared to move out it was just starting to get dark, the route they had chosen to take to the hayshed would mean that it would be completely dark by the time they had got there.

So as not to give any passers-by any idea of the direction they were headed the group started out on a parallel course across the fields.

Once they had sufficient distance from the road where they were dropped off, the route was changed to bring them into the pre-determined places of where each member of the group would go into hiding.

As they made their way across the fields they each in turn tested their radio equipment checking the volume coming through their earpiece's and making sure that their throat microphones were fitted properly.

It wasn't long before they had all settled into position and the waiting began.

On this particular night it was to be in vain as not even so much as a mouse moved, just before dawn the relief group came and took over from them.

 Once this group had taken up position Ray's group made it's away to a different pick up point from where they had been dropped the night before.

It wasn't long before they were pulling up outside of the HMSU buildings, after everything had been unloaded from the vehicle they made their way to the briefing room to be debriefed.

The debriefing took roughly half an hour after which all

of them were told that they would be back out on the surveillance of the hayshed at the same time later in the day.

After a shower and a change of clothes and locking all of his equipment into a locker Ray made his way back to his car to start his journey home to Richhill where on his arrival after a cup of tea and some toast he climbed into his bed for a good sleep.

He didn't waken till about 4.30 in the afternoon then after getting a wash and making himself a cup of tea he sat and watched the television.

At around 5.30 he heard Pauline's car pull up outside of the house, as she came in through the front door he heard her stop and then the rustle of paper before she appeared in the doorway of the sitting room.

"Hello Darling how are you?" She asked.

"I'm fine thanks, they have got me doing night shift tonight," he lied as he moved towards her giving her a kiss.

"Why's that?" She wanted to know.

"Apparently they are a little short some of the guys are sick."

"So are you working tonight?"

"Yeah, it looks like I won't see you till the morning, I'm sorry sweetheart," Ray said sounding down.

"Well at least we have until you go to work at 11 tonight," Pauline said.

"I don't think so, because of the shortage we are starting at 8,"

"I see well would you like something to eat before you go?"

"No thanks sweetheart, I'll get something at work, I'll eat on the hoof," Ray smiled.

"Are you sure? I can always make something quick."

"Like I said love, I can eat on the hoof," Ray told her as he kissed her lightly on the forehead.

"I just didn't want you telling my mum that I never feed you," Pauline laughed.

"You have no worry of me ever saying that, anyway I must start getting ready," Ray said as he walked towards the kitchen.

After he had put his cup into the kitchen sink Ray went upstairs and got ready for work, it wasn't long till he was in his car and driving to Mahon Road.

On entering into the HMSU building he made his way to the briefing room where he found Alex and the others waiting for him.

Once the briefing was over they set about getting their kit ready for the night, Ray checked his snipers rifle and bullets before putting on his combat kit.

Just as it was becoming dusk they all made their way out to the van; Alex made the driver aware of the new drop off point before getting into the back with Ray and the others.

This time they were dropped off a little further away from the hayshed, it would be a good 2-½ miles of walking across the fields before they would reach it.

A couple of the men were not too happy about this even though Ray had done this sort of thing many times in his life he wasn't too happy about it either, as the terrain was mostly marsh and it was not long before he was wet up to his crotch.

"Who was the daft twat who thought this route up?" Ray asked as he closed up on Alex who was leading them.

"I did with the help of the collator he told me that it would be okay."

"Well either he or you can't read a map, because I am sure it must show this marsh on it or at least it should have given you a clue?"

"I must agree Ray my map reading is not exactly brilliant." Alex informed him.

"You can say that again remind me when we get back to

give you a few lessons."

Shortly after this they reached the hayshed and it didn't take long for them to get back into the same positions they were in the previous night.

Just as the other group were about to leave a message came over their radios, it was telling the other team that they were to stay in position as word had been received from the Special Branch that someone could be coming to the shed a bit later in the night.

This got everybody excited as now they would get their chance to tackle their enemy which was a thing that rarely happened as the IRA were cowardly and would rather bomb and shoot people in the back than stand and fight.

"I hope it happens tonight," Ray heard coming through his earpiece.

"Whoever it was who said that, belt up, there is radio silence," Ray heard Alex say.

The groups had been in hiding for nearly three hours when one of the other men reported on the radio that he had heard a noise coming towards the shed.

"Can you see anything?" Alex asked.

"Not yet but it sounds like at least two or three people," the man replied.

"Which direction are they coming from?"

"They are coming from along the side of the road."

Ray immediately raised his rifle to look through his night sight, when he did he saw four young lads walking in their direction.

"It's only four youngsters I would say they are about 17 years old," Ray said to inform Alex.

"Do you think they are coming this way to the shed?"

"I'm not exactly sure yet they might just walk on past."

"Keep an eye on them Ray and let me know what they are up to."

"Okay no problem I'll watch them."

Ray continued to train his sights on the boys, as they reached a gate to the field they all climbed over it and started to walk towards the hayshed.

"They're on their way towards you," Ray informed Alex. Alex broke radio silence and reported to the HMSU control room about the four boys just to let them know that it was only young lads going into the building.

"Mike Romeo from Bronze 2 over," he said.

"Mike Romeo send over," came the reply.

"Roger Mike Romeo, no doubt you can hear on your receiver that there is someone in the shed, for your information it is four youths I don't think they are the people we are expecting, over."

"Bronze 2 keep an eye on them and make sure they don't remove any of the weapons from the premises, over."

"Mike Romeo from Bronze 2, we are at a disadvantage here as we cannot hear what is going on inside of the building so we will be dependent on your say so, over," Alex told the radio operator back in Mahon Road.

"Roger we will keep you informed as to what is going on, over."

"Roger and out," Alex said ending the transmissions. All of the men in the two groups heard what had been said.

Roughly five minutes later the voice of the operator could be heard coming over the radios again.

"Bronze 2, from Mike Romeo we are picking up their voices and it appears that they have taken possession of the weapons, over."

"Mike Romeo, they are still in the premises, shall we arrest? Over."

"Bronze 2, if they try to take the weapons from the hayshed, then challenge and apprehend, over."

"Roger Mike Romeo, wilco out."

The tension in the air was electric most of the policemen

readied themselves in case the youths came out of the hayshed shooting or trying to make a run for it.

As they all sat watching the shed the operator's voice again came over the radio.

"Bronze 2 from Mike Romeo, we can hear the cocking of weapons, over."

"Mike Romeo, do you think there is any chance of them using these weapons on us? Over."

"Bronze 2, I don't think they are aware of your presence as of yet, however I will seek further instructions from the operations Commander so wait out, over."

"Mike Romeo, Roger to that could you make it fast in case these youths decide to move out, over."

Just a few minutes went by when a different voice was heard coming over the radio, everybody knew it was the Superintendent.

"Bronze 2 from Mike Romeo, if any of those youths try to make a run for it you have permission to shoot, over."

Ray couldn't believe what he had just heard and was surprised that a senior officer would give the group instructions to shoot.

He pressed his transmit button on his radio for the chat net.

"Alex, did I hear right there what the Super has just directed?" he asked.

"I'm as shocked as you are Ray, surely he must know that those men in there are only young lads?"

"Hmm, I would ask him again to clarify things just in case he doesn't," Ray advised.

"I think I will, hold on a minute," Alex said ending the chat.

Then Ray heard Alex's voice over the radio.

"Mike Romeo from Bronze 2, have you been made aware of the age of the men in the shed? Over."

"Bronze 2, yes I have and I have it on higher authority that if they try to escape they are to be shot, over."

"Mike Romeo, Roger understood however if they don't try to run do we just carry out the normal arrest procedure? Over."

"Roger wait out and I will just check, over." Came from the Superintendent.

While he was not on the radio Alex went back onto the chat net to speak to Ray.

"Are you hearing what I am hearing Ray?"

"Yes I got all of that, I wonder who he is checking with, or better still who is pulling his strings?"

"I haven't got a clue, but to me it seems a bit fishy."

"To be quite honest with you Alex it sounds as if these youths are going to be made an example of."

"Well I don't really feel that we should, we could easily arrest these boys they would probably shit themselves if we challenged them."

"I know just how you feel….."

Just then the Superintendent came back on the radio.

"Bronze 2 from Mike Romeo, over."

"Mike Romeo send, over," Alex replied.

"Roger Bronze 2, the directions I gave you have been confirmed by a very senior rank in this force, so now it is up to you to carry out your orders, over."

"Roger to that, however I still feel that an arrest is possible at this stage, over." Alex said hoping that the orders would be rescinded.

"Bronze 2, I have that senior rank standing beside me and from him, he says that should you feel you are not up to the job, a replacement for you in this unit can be found, over."

All of the men in the group knew what this meant, it would mean that Alex would be relieved of his rank and sent back to ordinary police duties as a Constable, and probably end up in a police Station in the back end of nowhere.

"Roger Mike Romeo, your message understood, over and

out." Alex replied ending the contact.

Now all the group knew what their future would be if these orders were not carried out and being as they had all worked so hard to get into the unit to start with it would be a shame to throw it all away.

Roughly ten minutes after the last transmission from Mike Romeo the operator came back on the radio.

"Bronze 2 from Mike Romeo, over."

"Mike Romeo send," Alex replied.

"Roger Bronze 2, from what we can make of the conversations in the hayshed these youths are about to leave with the weapons, over."

"Roger Mike Romeo, we will be ready, over."

No sooner had Alex said this than one of the boys came out of the shed with a rifle in his hands, he took up a firing position as if he had seen something and was going to shoot it.

This was the youth's downfall because the direction that he pointed it was straight at two of the police officers that were in hiding watching the front of the hayshed.

All hell was let loose and the two officers shouted for him to drop the rifle but the lad was either too frightened or shocked and continued to keep the rifle at his shoulder in the firing position.

Obviously thinking that they were going to be shot the two police officers opened fire hitting the youth in the chest.

As he went down the other two youths inside the shed came running out through the doorway to see what had happened.

However their misfortune was that they had forgotten to drop the weapons that they both had that they had undoubtedly been playing around with inside the shed.

Of course the policemen seeing this thought that these lads were about to try and shoot their way out and so more shots were fired by the police killing them also.

When all of the shooting had stopped and the three boys lay dead Alex and the policeman that was with him in hiding approached the bodies to check that they were dead, all the others stayed where they were.

After checking Alex called Mike Romeo to keep them informed as to what had taken place.

"Mike Romeo from Bronze 2, over."

"Bronze 2 send, over."

"Mike Romeo, that task is complete request extraction and notification of all relevant agencies, over."

"Roger Bronze 2, we will notify the local police to seal off the area, on their arrival with you move to the designated pick up point, Mike Romeo out."

With his report made Alex told everyone to stay in their positions and out of sight until the local police arrived, whilst they waited he walked over to talk to Ray.

"So Ray what do you think of tonight's little farce, and the way things have turned out?"

"I'm pleased to see that none of our guys were hurt, however I'm not exactly impressed with the targets I honestly think they should have been arrested."

"I was only carrying out orders, it was that or lose everything I had spent years working for."Alex told him.

"I know you were put on the spot it's very unfair'" Ray sympathised with him.

"Well, tell me what would you have done if you were me?"

"I would most probably have done exactly as you did, you know what my feelings are on terrorism."

"Do you think they were terrorists?" Alex asked him.

"Let's just say that they could well have been junior IRA members, and most probably had been told to go and collect the weapons."

"I see what you mean, so the big boys might have got wind of the stake out and sent them in just to see if it was true, so that they won't get caught."

"Now you're getting the idea, it's a dirty bloody war this ain't it, Alex."

"And no doubt when the media get to hear about this they'll have a field day, well I hope the Bosses don't back out on us?" Alex says.

"They probably will you know what they are like all protecting their own arses, mind you I have a very funny feeling that we shan't hear the last of this."

"What do you mean Ray?"

"Well by the time the IRA and Sinn Fein have finished Oh! And of course the Southern Government I wouldn't be surprised if there isn't a big enquiry into the activities of the Police in this area." Ray replied.

"I know what you men, it makes me laugh the way the IRA and Sinn Fein always want an enquiry into every shooting the Police are involved in and one of their members is killed, yet they never want one when they are quite happily murdering people."

"My opinion for what it's worth is that I will never show mercy to any of them and if I ever get one in a position that I can kill him I will, if you live by the sword expect to die by the sword, is my motto." Ray offered.

Just then the headlights of a Landrover could be seen coming slowly along the road in their direction.

"Okay here come the county mounties, stay where you are you guys and when I tell you to move cover yourselves up and make your way to the top of the field, I'll meet you there, then we can go to the pickup point," Alex said into his radio.

Ray moved away from him and went into cover the last thing he wanted was to be seen by any of the Craigavon cops as word that he was on this little venture would soon get around Lurgan.

Roughly ten minutes after the Landrover had pulled up and Alex had shown the Duty Inspector the bodies he told the group to move out to the pickup point, it wasn't long before they were getting out of the van at Mahon Road.

As they filed in through the HMSU building door they were met by the Superintendent and other senior ranks one of which was an (ACC) Assistant Chief Constable.

"Well done boys, that's three we won't have to worry about anymore," one of the Chief Inspectors commented.

"We could have arrested them rather than bloody shoot them," Alex said in reply as he walked past the man.

"What did you say Sergeant?" the ACC said in a loud tone.

Alex stopped and turned to look at him, "With all due respect to your rank Sir, I said we could just have easily arrested them."

"I think we had better have a little chat Sergeant, come with me please," the ACC says walking towards the Superintendent's office.

Alex handed his equipment to Ray, "Put that in my locker please Ray I've got a feeling I'm in for a right chewing here."

"I'll still be here when you've finished so I'll see you in the room after," Ray told him.

While all the men were getting out of their uniforms and putting their kit away a loud voice could be heard down the corridor saying "All you men when you've finished getting changed report to the briefing room for a debrief."

Nearly Thirty minutes later they all assembled in the briefing room and stood about smoking and talking.

Then the Superintendent appeared "Right gentlemen please be seated, we have a few things to discuss."

When they were all seated he began, "Now I know a few of you were probably not too happy about tonight's outcome, however let me tell you that what you done saved a few lives."

"It also took a few," was heard to come from the back of the room.

"Who said that?" the Superintendent asked.

Nobody would own up so the Superintendent continued, "Now I know these guys were only young lads and you thought that it would have been better to arrest them, but let me assure you, had they moved those guns and the people who were expecting them got them, then there would be quite a few people murdered by them."

One of the other policemen in the group put his hand up to speak, "Yes Belka what would you like to say?" the Superintendent invited him.

"That still does not answer why we didn't arrest them Sir."

"To be quite truthful with you Belka, they were not part of the overall plan which I can assure you is a lot more intense than this little episode that happened here tonight."

He went on, "Now the things that were going to be happening in this area by the IRA have now been set back and unbeknown to you all, you have saved quite a few innocent people from being murdered. Not only that the IRA in this area will think twice before they try anything."

With this speech finished all of the men were told to remain where they were until they had recorded a statement of what they had done and what part they had played in the shootings also how many rounds of ammunition they had fired.

When they had all finished they were allowed to leave to go to their rooms or to their homes.

Ray didn't really remember the drive home instead of concentrating on his driving he kept mulling over the events of the shootings in his mind.

He kept thinking about what the Superintendent said about the overall plan, if there was one how was it he knew nothing about it? Admittedly he was only a Constable so therefore he shouldn't know but on the other hand he had attended many of the tactical briefings but no one had mentioned anything.

He felt that he should have at least been made aware that something was happening or was it just a Police thing? And the military were not to know about it, he made a mental note to mention it to HQNI later that day.

When he reached his house he silently went in through the front door being careful not to waken Pauline.

He went into the kitchen and made himself a cup of tea and as he returned to the sitting room he stopped at the drinks cabinet to pour just a little drop of whiskey into the cup.

When he switched on the television he turned it to the 24-hour news channel, as he sat sipping his tea a report of the shootings came on.

Ray just sat and drank his cup of tea watching the report as if he had nothing to do with it, he tried to put it out of his mind.

He found it useless as it kept emerging so when he had finished his tea he topped up his mug with more Whiskey hoping that he could drink the incident out of his head.

It wasn't long before he had nearly finished a full bottle and he was very drunk, so putting what remained of the Whisky back in the cabinet he went up the stairs to bed and snuggled in beside Pauline she stirred slightly and moaned a little before going back to sleep.

He lay in bed for nearly 20 minutes, however he did not sleep so he went back downstairs to get himself another cup of tea.

As he sat drinking his tea he heard Pauline get out of bed and start to come down the stairs, it wasn't long before she entered the sitting room.

"Can't you sleep, what's wrong?" she asked him.

"Nothing for you to worry about," Ray told her.

As Pauline looked around the room she noticed that the Whisky bottle was nearly empty.

"Have you been drinking? Are you drunk?"

"Let's just say I've had a wee night-cap."

"A wee one, I'd say a bloody big one, there's hardly any left," she pointed out.

"I just fancied getting drunk, is there a law against it?" Ray snapped.

This shocked Pauline, as Ray had never even so much as disagreed with her on anything let alone snap.

She had never before heard him raise his voice as a matter of fact if ever she got mad at him he would just sit and smile at her then when she had finished he would walk over and kiss her.

"No there's no law against it, it's just that you never drink, I'm not used to it."

"Well just you go back up to bed I have things to think about." Ray told her.

Pauline was just going out through the door when a news reporter came on saying, "We now have more on the shootings just outside of Portadown in Northern Ireland."

Pauline stopped in her tracks and turned to watch it, when the report had finished she looked at Ray.

"Do you know anything about that?" she asked.

"Oh! Just a little."

"How much is a little?"

"Look you don't need to know, I don't want to talk about it okay?"

"So that is why you're drinking, trying to put it out of your mind eh!"

"I thought you were going back to bed?"

"Well if you don't want to talk about it then I'm going," Pauline said angrily as she stormed off back up the stairs.

A few minutes later Ray took out his copy of the statement that had been made for him about the incident and started to read it.

The following afternoon after trying to get some sleep he reported back for duty at Lurgan, as soon as he went into the briefing room the Inspector told him to go straight to his office as he wanted a chat with him.

On reaching the office Ray waited outside of it for the Inspector, while he stood there Steve came along the corridor.

"Well Ray how the heck are you? You lot done a great job last night I'm proud of you all, let me shake your hand," he said holding out his.

"You may think it was a good job as no doubt so did the rest of the senior ranks, but to be honest most of us thought it was a shit job," Ray replied limply shaking hands.

"Why do you think that?"

"We could have arrested those boys last night there was no need to kill them, fuck sake they had hardly lived."

"I know what you are saying but believe me those boys last night were junior IRA who no doubt in time would be shooting and planting bombs."

"If we had arrested them then they wouldn't be doing it for a while as they would have been inside the jail wouldn't they?"

"Yes I understand that Ray but the thing is they would probably have only got a few years and then would have been back out to carry on, whereas by what happened last night they won't get the chance to do it again will they?"

"You never know a spell in jail might have made them see the light, then they would know that they were fighting a losing battle."

"Yes but would they?" Steve asked.

"We'll never know the answer to that now, will we?"

"I know you are a bit pissed off about it Ray but sure it's all part of the overall plan."

"That's the second time I've heard that, tell me what the fuck this overall plan is about? I have never heard anything about it."

"If you must know it is about how we are going to try and put a stop to the terrorist incidents in the town by eliminating the IRA cell here."

"If you do that another cell will always be built up you seem to forget that the IRA have strong backing in this town." Ray informed him.

"All I can say is that as they appear we will take them out of the equation," Steve answered.

"I honestly think that you'll never stand a chance here, if you get rid of all the IRA suspects or cells in this town they'll only bring teams in from out of town, then we'll not know who to bloody watch."

"Why are you standing here anyway?" Steve said changing the subject.

"The Inspector wants a word with me and told me to wait here for him."

"I think I know what that is about so I had better clear off, I'll see you later in the canteen we can have a coffee and a serious chat ok?" Steve said walking away.

"What does he want me for? If you know tell me." Ray shouted after him.

"It's none of my business we'll talk later," Steve said carrying on walking away.

No sooner had he gone than Ray heard footsteps coming from around the corner to where he stood, shortly after, the Inspector came into sight.

"Right Ray come in and take a seat," the Inspector says opening the office door and going in.

When he had settled the Inspector started to speak.

"I suppose you are wondering what I want to talk to you about?"

"To be honest Sir I was taken back a little I thought it would just be a matter of getting briefed and going out on patrol," Ray answered.

"The thing is Ray I have been approached by the Superintendent of the HMSU and he has asked me to try and persuade you to join the unit as he feels you would be better employed with them than just doing ordinary police duties here."

"I'm sorry Sir but I joined this force to be a cop, a mister plod, the policeman if I had wanted to do the sort of things the HMSU do then I would have stayed in the Army."

"I just thought that you might have wanted their sort of life, of course you know that if they wanted to the authorities could just transfer you into the HMSU and there would not be a lot you could do about it."

Warning bells started to ring in Ray's ear he wasn't exactly sure if the Inspector had in fact spoken with the HMSU Superintendent or whether he was just trying his luck hoping that Ray would want to move.

"Can I ask you when this conversation between you and the HMSU Super. took place Sir?"

"I was speaking to him this morning Ray why?"

Ray knew that the Inspector was telling lies, as he was aware that the HMSU Superintendent was at a high level meeting all day at HQNI and he wouldn't have had the chance to speak to the Inspector.

"I take it that he must have phoned you at home then Sir, because if he had phoned here during the day he wouldn't have been able to get you, as you like me have only just started work this afternoon."

"As a matter of fact he did because he is that keen to have you join them," the Inspector said with his head down looking at a piece of paper on his desk.

Ray noticed this and decided to take the bull by the horns and clear something off his chest that had been niggling at him for some time.

"Tell you what Sir instead of playing little games with each other let's both put our cards on the table," he said.

"What do you mean by that?"

"I mean that I know you don't want me in your section and would move heaven and earth to be rid of me, the thing is, I have no intention of ever applying to join the HMSU and the minute they try to transfer me I'll make moves to get it stopped."

"You forget Ray you don't have that sort of power, you're only a Constable in this outfit."

"Well when I see your cards I'll let you into something that you don't know about."

"Right then I'll show my cards, you are right I don't want you in my section and yes I would do anything to get rid of you. If you won't voluntarily ask for a move then I will try my utmost to get you moved so now you

know the lay of the land," the Inspector says looking up at him.

"Now I know where we stand I have something to show you can I just take five minutes to get something from my locker Sir?"

"Providing you are not too long, you can."

"I'll be about five minutes Sir," Ray said as he made his way out of the office and walked towards the locker room.

When he got to his locker he put his hand under a pile of papers and an assortment of other things and pulled out the tape recording that he made on his Dictaphone when he and the Inspector first met.

After playing the recording back to make sure it was the correct tape he returned to the Inspectors office.

"Right what do you have to show me?" the Inspector asked as Ray entered.

"You have obviously seen one of these before," Ray replied showing him the Dictaphone

"Of course I have, what sort of a fool do you think I am?"

"Well can I refresh your memory about our little welcome to Lurgan meeting we had when I first arrived here and you told me not to make waves with the local terrorists."

"What do you mean?"

"The thing is, unbeknown to you I recorded that conversation just for such a day as this and I'm glad I had the foresight to do so, would you like to hear it Inspector?"

Not knowing whether Ray had in fact taped it or was just bluffing the Inspector agreed he sat in silence and could not believe his ears when he heard his own voice.

"What do you mean by taping our conversations?" he raged at the end of it.

"It is what is known in this job as covering your arse, now I'm sure that a lot of very senior ranks in this job would love to hear it," Ray smiled.

"Are you blackmailing me?"

"No, no, no, I wouldn't do that Sir, to do that is against the law and with me being a good cop I wouldn't want to break it would I?" Ray smiled.

"You think you're so fucking smart don't you?" the Inspector said going red in the face with temper.

"No I don't think I'm smart, I just know how twisted bastards like you perform, I have come across a few like you in my time and have learnt to fight fire with fire," Ray told him.

"So now that we have aired our differences where do we go from here?"

"Okay I told you that I would let you into a little secret so I'll tell you, after I have you'll know exactly how much power I actually have if I want to use it."

"Right I'm listening carry on," the inspector said leaning back in his chair.

Ray went on to explain to him what his true role was in the province and that if the Inspector ever let it out of the bag he could be facing very serious disciplinary action, the Inspector sat awe-struck.

"So there you have it and if you think I'm giving you bullshit then I'll get an ACC down here to tell you," Ray informed him.

"I never knew that this sort of thing was going on, my God why was I not told?"

"Obviously it is a need to know basis and the higher ups thought that you don't need to know, however you must remember what I have just told you must never get out, if it does, it's your balls in the noose not mine, oh! And by the way I'll let the ACC know that I have told you."

"You can be assured I won't be telling anyone, I just wish I had known earlier."

"I take it then that I am free to go now?"

"Yes Ray no problems, but as you go past the Sergeants office would you tell him I would like to see him?"

"Okay Sir and thank you," Ray said saluting before he left.

Just as he was approaching the Sergeants office on his way back to his locker to put the tape away, Ray saw the Sergeant just coming out of it with Steve.

"The Inspector has just told me to ask you to go and see him in his office Skipper."

"Okay thanks Ray, I'll see you later Steve and we can finish what we were talking about then," the Sergeant says quickly making his way to the Inspectors office.

"So Ray what did he want to see you about?" Steve said pointing at the Inspectors office.

"We just had a little peace pipe smoking and aired a few differences."

"Why? What was he saying?"

"Let's just say he told me how much he didn't love me and how he felt it would be best for me to transfer to the HMSU."

"What did you tell him?"

"As a matter of fact I told him all about me and what my real job was over here."

"I bet that shocked him, now that he knows I had better go and have a word with him just to make sure he knows not to tell anyone, I'll catch you, say in about 20 minutes in the canteen alright?" Steve said walking towards the Inspectors office.

"That seems okay to me, but you're buying the coffee's," Ray replied before continuing on his way to his locker. Having put the items back and securing the locker he went up to the canteen for a bite of something to eat and a cup of tea.

CHAPTER - 17 – KERRI-ANN

A short while after this little incident Pauline had to go to the hospital to give birth to their baby daughter, they had decided to call her Kerri-Ann.

Ray stood in the delivery room watching as Kerri-Ann came into the world, she had no trouble at all in letting the staff in the delivery room know that she had arrived after a bit of a splutter she cried with all her might.

Ray was standing beside Pauline and bent over to kiss her on the forehead.

"She is a little cracker, she will break a lot of hearts when she gets older," Ray told her.

Just as he said this one of the nurses handed the baby to Pauline for her to hold.

"Oh! But she is lovely I can't wait for my mum and dad to see her," Pauline said as she moved Kerri-Ann's head up in order that she could give her a little kiss on the cheek.

"I'll tell you what, I'll go and give them a call and let them know I won't be long the phone is just outside," Ray said squeezing her hand.

"They won't be up, they both have to work in the morning," Pauline informed him.

"I'll call them anyway I don't think they will mind, as a matter of fact I think they will be quite pleased," Ray says heading towards the door to the delivery room.

On closing the delivery room door behind him Ray went to the telephone and made the call once he had done this you went back into the room to be with Pauline and Kerri Ann.

By this time the staff in the delivery room had placed Kerri Ann in a crib with a little pink bracelet on her wrist and were about to take her to the nursery, they were also preparing Pauline to move her to the postnatal ward.

When they arrived at the postnatal ward Ray pulled up a

chair in order that he could sit beside Pauline where they talked for quite a while about their future and Kerri Ann. As they talked unbeknown to Pauline, Ray was really starting to worry about the safety of her and Kerri Ann. From the latest reports that had been received, an attack on him and his family and home was fairly imminent, and the last thing that Ray ever wanted to have was to have his family injured or killed.

On quite a few occasions he had been called into the Special Branch offices and had been made aware by Steve of the latest intelligence they had on any possible attack that might take place.

Ray sat with Pauline most of the night and after a while they both became very tired so Ray left the hospital and headed home.

On his arrival at home he telephoned the police station to let them know that he was now a father and he would like to avail of compassionate leave.

With his leave being granted Ray went to the hospital every day to see Pauline and Kerri Ann he was so proud to be a father and every time he saw his daughter he loved her even more.

One day prior to going to the hospital he received a telephone call from Steve.

"Ray I have some bad news for you, don't go to the hospital to visit your wife today, we have good information that there will be an attempt made on you today."

"But I'm going to pick Pauline up today to bring both of them home," Ray told him.

"Look Ray I'm only telling you this so you don't go and get your bloody head blown off, those bastards are waiting for you," Steve said sounding peeved.

"Well surely there is something you can do?" Ray asked.

"What do you suggest?" Steve asked.

"Why don't you get in touch with the local police and

have them get a mobile patrol to drive around the hospital car park," Ray put to him.

"But what if they are inside?"

"Then all you have to do is have two plainclothes police officers in the entrance to the hospital, and if we let them know roughly what time I'll be there they can be a position." Ray said.

"Okay I'll do that I'll give them a ring now, one thing though Ray be on your guard because I certainly wouldn't like to lose you," Steve told him hanging up the phone.

With this warning and even though he knew that the local police would be in the area Ray was still worried, he certainly did not want anyone taking a shot at him while he was walking out of the hospital with his wife and daughter.

Roughly 20 min before he left his house for the hospital Ray telephoned the police station to let them know that he was on his way.

On reaching the car park for the hospital he slowly drove around it looking into all of the parked cars to make sure that nobody was sitting in them, he also gave a little wave to the police vehicle as he drove past them before parking up his own.

As he got out of his car he immediately began to scan the surrounding area, he pulled down the zipper on his jacket in order that he would have easy access to his weapon which was in a shoulder holster under his arm.

On walking into the hospital foyer he spied one of the police officers in plainclothes and after a quick nod of his head to him he looked around for the other one, Ray spotted him standing by one of the wall mounted phones.

Now that he knew where they both were he proceeded on his way to the postnatal ward to pick up Pauline and Kerri Ann.

"Hello Darling I'm sorry that I'm a little late but I had a few things to do," Ray told her.

"You're not late we have only just finished signing my release papers," Pauline replied.

"So all the paperwork is done is it?" Ray asked.

"Yes she is now all ours, quick let's run while we still have her and before they change their minds," Pauline joked.

"Right I'm ready when you are, let's go," Ray said.

As Ray picked up Pauline's overnight bag one of the nurses stopped them, "where are you going Mrs Gray?"

"I've signed all my paperwork and we were just leaving," Pauline informed her.

"I'm sorry but it's hospital policy for all patients to be transported by wheelchair to the doors, so if you hang on a minute I'll just get one," the nurse said as she turned around to go and get one.

"I hope she isn't too long," Ray said to Pauline.

"Why's that? Are you in a hurry or something," Pauline asked him.

Not wanting to let her know what was going on Ray told her, "I just want to get you both home so we can all be together, I miss not having you around the house," Ray answered.

It wasn't long before the nurse returned with a wheelchair, Pauline was helped into it and she held Kerri Ann in her arms.

On reaching the hospital doors Ray told her to wait a minute while he went and got the car to drive it up to the doorway.

Once Pauline and Kerri Ann were comfortable in the backseat of the car Ray started the engine and was about to pull away when Pauline said, "Did you see those two men in the foyer of the hospital? they looked like police."

"I didn't really notice them," Ray lied.

"And look, there's a police car over there," Pauline said pointing at the car.

"Perhaps somebody is in hospital and they are guarding them," Ray suggested.

"You could be right there, I just hope somebody in the Security Forces hasn't been hurt," Pauline agreed.

"Maybe there is something on the radio," Ray said leaning forward and turning on the car radio.

"Hopefully if there is, it's nothing serious," Pauline remarked.

It wasn't long before they were turning off the Portadown Road and heading towards their house in Richhill on their arrival Ray quickly got out of the car and opened the front door of the house in order that Pauline could get into some warmth with Kerri-Ann while he retrieved her bags from the car.

Once they had both settled down and Kerri Ann was laid down in a carrycot to sleep Ray made a cup of tea for them both and as they sat drinking it he decided it was time to tell Pauline about what was going on.

"Can I tell you something Darling?" He started.

"Providing it's good I don't mind," She replied.

"Well to be quite honest it isn't, the Special Branch have received information that the IRA are targeting me."

"I don't believe you, you're pulling my leg," Pauline said in disbelief.

"It's true Darling if you want you can ring them," Ray suggested to her.

"Well how fresh is this information?" She asked.

"It's hot off the press and those two men in the hospital foyer were there for my protection, so was the police vehicle in the car park."

"Why all of a sudden have they taken an interest in you?" Pauline wanted to know.

"I really don't know," Ray replied knowing the real reason.

"You'll have to be really careful now because I know that those bastards won't give up until they get you, you realise that don't you?" Pauline says unhappily.

"Hopefully things will die down or the Special Branch will get more information on who is going to carry it out and can put a stop to it," Ray replies.

"I hope they can, we have only just got our daughter and the last thing I want is for her to be growing up without a dad," Pauline told him.

Later that day Ray received a telephone call from Steve asking him to come to the police station as he wanted to have a chat with him.

When he got there Ray went straight to Steve's office to see what he had to say.

"Hi Boss what's new?" Ray asked him.

"We have to have a serious chat and the Superintendent will be involved as well, it's pretty serious Ray."

They both left Steve's office and made their way to the SDC's office whereupon knocking on his door they entered it closing the door behind them.

"Sir" Steve began, "I've got Ray in for you to talk to."

"First of all congratulations Ray on becoming a father, however things are looking a little bit bleak for you at the moment from what I have been informed you are under quite a big threat," the SDC said.

"It must be pretty bad if I have had to come here to hear from you," Ray replied.

"Believe me Ray it is very serious, so serious in fact we would like you to leave the country for a couple of weeks until we can get things sorted out what you think of that?"

"To be quite honest Sir I don't think a great deal of it my wife just had our baby and now I'm going to have to leave them and get out of the country all because a load of bastards are making threats," Ray told him unhappily.

"I'm sorry Ray I sympathise with you however you're

more good to me alive than dead and that is the last thing I want I have been to enough funerals in this job," the SDC told him.

"I realise that Sir, but what happens when I come back then I'll still be in the same boat won't I?"

"Well hopefully the Special Branch will have managed to sort things out by the time you get back."

"And what if they haven't?" Ray asked starting to get a little bit fed up because he knew that whether he liked it or not the decision had already been made that he was to leave the country.

"Let's put it like this, if they haven't managed to sort anything out we'll play it by ear as to what our next move will be how does that sound?" The SDC suggested.

"So where do you want me to go?" Ray needed to know.

"Do you have family in England? You can go and see them for two weeks but just don't tell them what's going on," Steve put in.

"I haven't been to see my family for years I don't even keep contact with them and to be quite honest I don't know where they live."

"Well is there anybody else you can stay with, relatives like an auntie or uncle?" The SDC asked.

"To be very honest with you Sir, I have nothing to do with any of my family however I have friends who live in Scotland in a little place called Ardersier just outside of Inverness I suppose I could always give them a call and see if they let me stay with them for a couple of weeks," Ray told him.

"Good idea, now what I want you to do is go straight home and arrange things, and don't worry about the tickets we will pay for them and we can also take you to the airport." Steve agreed.

"I don't know what flights there are but I'll let you know as soon as possible," Ray informed him.

"I'll leave it in your hands then, as far as I am concerned

you are on leave as from today but as soon as you get the information on your flights let me know so that we can arrange to have a car take you to the airport, I'm sorry Ray but that is the way it has to be, I'll see you when you get back off leave," the SDC said standing up and shaking Ray's hand.

On leaving the SDC Steve and Ray went back to the Special Branch office, on reaching it Steve pointed towards a telephone, "If you want you can check for your flights here before you go," he suggested.

"No thanks I'll do it at home, and anyway I will have to explain this to my wife and I can tell you she will not be very pleased."

Ray left the police station and drove back to his home as he walked through his house front door Pauline was waiting for him luckily Kerri Ann was sleeping.

"So what did they want you for?" Pauline asked him.

"I think you had better sit down I've something to tell you."

Once Pauline had sat down Ray informed her of what had taken place at the police station, when he told her that he had to leave the country for a couple of weeks tears came to her eyes.

"Things must be really bad then, it's all we need, we have only just got the baby home and now you have to leave the country, it really makes me mad I'm really fed up with what is happening over here, mind you at least my mom can help me with the baby, damn but life is so unfair," she tearfully said.

"How do you think I feel? Never knowing when or where it's going to happen, it's not exactly pleasing knowing that one day I could be walking up the street shopping and low and behold some arsehole tries to waste me," Ray sympathised with her.

"I know I'm sorry Darling it's just that everything seems to come at once," Pauline sniffled.

"I had better give my friends in Scotland a ring and see if they will let me come over for a couple weeks."

"Are you going to tell them about what is happening?" Pauline asked.

"I'll play it by ear, I won't tell them just yet but if they ask while I am over there I'll tell them, I just hope they will let me come over," Ray said sounding optimistic.

At this time Kerri Ann woke up and started to cry and as Pauline picked her up Ray went to use the telephone. Shortly after telephoning his friends he went back into the living room where Pauline sat feeding Kerri Ann,

"They told me that I could come over any time I liked and they would be pleased for me to stay with them, they asked me if you add Kerri Ann were coming as well," Ray told her.

"What did you say when they asked that?" Pauline wanted to know.

"I just told them that you were very busy and that I would be coming on my own and they seemed to be quite happy with that, mind you I think they would have loved it and we could all of gone over."

"Maybe some other time we can I would like to go and see them as we have never met."

"It would be lovely, it is really nice over there the countryside is beautiful," Ray said.

"So what do you have to to do now?" Pauline enquired.

"Now it is just a matter of booking my flight to Glasgow and letting this station know the date and time, then they can come and take me to the airport, as a matter of fact I could call the airport now to book my flight," Ray says picking up the telephone book and looking for the number.

It wasn't long before he was talking to one of the booking clerks at the airport and he had made reservations for a flight two days later.

The two days were not long in passing and after being

driven to the airport Ray was on his flight to Glasgow, at Glasgow we had to change flights to get another one to Inverness.

His two weeks leave seemed to pass very quickly and the day after arriving back in Northern Ireland he reported back to the Police station where he went straight to the Special Branch office to get an update what had taken place in regards to the threat made against him.

On knocking on the office door it was answered by Pete, "It's good to see you back Ray how was your holiday?"

"It was pretty good however I miss my wife and daughter like crazy I wish to God I never had to go, on the other hand I would certainly be no good to them dead," Ray remarked.

Ray carried on into the main office and headed toward Steve, Steve got up to greet him.

"Hello Ray how're things?" He asked him.

"It all depends on what you have to tell me about this bloody threat, have you found out yet who's likely to be carrying it out?" Ray wanted to know.

"To be quite honest with you Ray things are not much different from what they were before you left, we have very little to go on apart from what the informant told us so all I can tell you is that you will have to be very careful in what you do, where you go, and just the general personal security stuff," Steve advised.

"So basically what you are telling me is that I wasted two weeks in Scotland when I could have stayed here with my wife and daughter, am I right?" Ray said sounding really pissed off.

"I suppose you are I have to agree with you there," Steve answered.

"Well at least I know thanks anyway, I'll probably see you round the station tomorrow as I start morning shift, by the way keep me informed as to what is happening and anything you might be able to find out, so I'll catch you later Steve," Ray said as he made his way towards the main office door.

Ray returned to his home where he told Pauline that things had not changed and went on to explain to her how big the threat was, he also made her aware of the risk that the whole family were under.

The whole episode weighed heavily on Ray's mind what really got to him was the fact that Pauline and Kerri Ann were also considered targets.

As time went by Ray found that he was not able to do his job to the best of his ability and arguments between him and Pauline were becoming more frequent due to the constant stress he was under because of the threats made against him.

So Ray decided that it would be best for him and Pauline to Part Company, not only because of the threats against him but mainly because of those that were being made towards his family.

So when Pauline was back on her feet after having Kerri Ann and was back to work, Ray decided to move away from the house and took up residence in the town of Banbridge in the County of Down where shortly after his moving he and Pauline were divorced.

Whenever he felt things were safe Ray would go over to Richhill and visit with Pauline and Kerri Ann, on some of the visits he would not only take her shopping in her pram but sometimes he drove over to the Armagh swimming pool with her where she loved to get in the water and splash around.

However due to work commitments the visits became less and less and on one visit Ray learned that Pauline had a new man in her life, Pauline informed him that the relationship was strong, so Ray felt that by still having contact with Kerri Ann it would only confuse her as to who in fact was her father.

He also thought that being as Kerri Ann was so young and that if Pauline's relationship led to her re marrying then Kerri Ann would probably think that Pauline's boyfriend would be her father.

CHAPTER – 18 – INVESTIGATION

During the years after the shooting incidents at the Hayshed and at the Roundabout a lot of media coverage on the incidents took place, a number of allegations were made about the police having a "Shoot to Kill" policy in force.

The IRA propaganda machine was working overtime and every time one of the IRA members were involved in any incident with the police in which that member was either injured or shot it would make headlines in th newspapers.

There were many television interviews made by the higher achy of the Sinn Fein political party who really if the truth be known were just the mouthpiece for the IRA murder squads.

The British Government in its infinite wisdom wanting to try and appease the Republican Catholic element of the community in a knee jerk reaction decided that the best way to try and keep face would be to hold an official investigation into the shootings.

Therefore a very senior English police officer would be sent to the Province with an administration team to investigate the killings.

Roughly a week before the man was due to arrive in Ulster to commence his investigation all the men involved in the shootings were called to a meeting at the HMSU HQ building for a briefing.

As Ray drove up to the building he saw a staff car of one of the top men in the RUC parked outside of it.

On getting out of his car he spied another one of the men who had been at the incidents as well, his name was Mark.

"This little get together must be quite serious if it got one of the big boys to come out of the woodwork," Ray said to him.

"I have a bit of a feeling that the shit has really hit the

fan this time, someone's balls must be in a noose and it must be tightening," Mark replied.

"Providing they're not mine I don't really give a toss, Mark." Ray told him.

"Nor do I, but I think someone sanctioned something he shouldn't have."

"Hmmm, I think you just might be right there, anyway let's get in to see what all the panic is about shall we?" Ray said unconcernedly heading towards the entrance doors.

As they went into the building they saw a chair with a blackboard on it and a big chalked arrow on it with the word Briefing written below showing the direction they had to take, it pointed along the corridor to the normal briefing room.

When they finally got to the room they found that nearly every member of the HMSU who had been at the shootings were sitting on one side of the room, while on the other there was a another group and amongst them was the Senior Officer.

Once Ray and Mark had settled in the Senior Officer got up to speak, "Right gentlemen you are all probably wondering why you have all been called together? Well for those of you who don't listen to the news let me enlighten you.

Next week one of the top police officers in England will be arriving here to carry out an investigation into the so-called "Shoot to Kill" policy in this force.

Now I surely don't have to tell you that his findings could do this force a great deal of harm should he be led to believe that there is such a thing going on.

No doubt that if he does suspect that you have a case to answer it could lead to some officers being dismissed from the force, I wouldn't like that to happen after all you were only carrying out your orders.

Things could get very sticky here, and there could be a

lot of ambiguity so to lessen it the Chief Superintendent of the CID has studied the statements that you had written re your part in the operations.

To make a few of them more readable he has had to make some slight alterations to them to just clarify a few things.

So therefore after this if you would all be so kind as to approach him and let him know who you are he can give you your new statement which I trust you'll re write in your own hand writing.

Now do any of you have any questions you'd like to ask? If you do, please raise your hand."

The man was quite taken aback by the amount of hands that went up and starting at the back of the group he pointed to a man.

"Yes you at the back on the left what would you like to ask?"

"You said that this investigation could cost a few men their jobs, but why should it because after all we were only carrying out the orders that we got from here and we all heard them over the radio."

"Yes we know that but like I said providing this man doesn't get wind off anything then he'll have nothing to go on will he?"

A lot of the hands went down after this so he pointed to another at the middle of the group.

"I see what you mean by that Sir but what if he manages to get hold of our taped radio messages, as you'll know all radio messages are taped and must be kept for up to 6 months should anything like this crop up?"

"Let me assure you gentlemen, our radio transmissions from that night have been destroyed because apparently someone forgot to change the tapes over and they were reused so everything was lost," he informed them.

With that question answered he pointed to another man

in at the back.

"How do we stand about the ballistics report Sir?"

"As you know there were obviously a number of bullets recovered from the bodies but I don't see any real problems in that direction, providing you all stick to what you have on your statements I can see no problems whatsoever."

"So basically what you are implying Sir' is All for one and one for all is it?" came from another man.

"If you want to put it like that yes or 'United we stand divided we fall' all we are trying to do here is what is more commonly known as damage limitation."

"Or cover your arse," was heard to come from the back of the room.

This caused a lot of sniggering and laughter, when it had all died down Alex put his hand up to ask a question.

"Yes Sergeant," the officer said.

"The one thing that is puzzling me is that we are all here because of the shootings and from what I can make out it seems that WE are the guilty parties. To be quite honest it appears that the only arse we are covering is that of the man who gave us the order to shoot, is that right?"

This seemed to flummox the officer and he was stuck for words, "I see what you mean Sergeant, and no doubt it would appear that way but I can assure you it isn't," was all he could say.

After hearing this Ray decided to ask a question and he put his hand up, "You have got us all together for this meeting and you have told us that we must all stick together, It's okay with us all doing that, but what I would like to know is, are the authorities going to stick with us or will there be a lot of back peddling so that we get hung out to dry?"

Before the officer could answer another man cut in, "Yeah cause' I have seen this sort of thing happen before where the authorities close ranks and are only bothered about their jobs rather than the men that have to do the dirty work."

"You will get the full backing of the police authority, there is no way that any of you will lose your job or be involved in any disciplinary action you can rest assured of that." Was the answer from the Officer.

Seeing no more hands up for questions the man ended the talk by telling all the men, "Now at this stage I strongly advise you all to study your statements well. Get to know where every word and where every full stop and comma is, it is in your own interest to know this, now I bid you good day, you may now go back to what you were doing before this meeting."

All the men stood up as the officer followed by his entourage left the room to let the men sit and discuss things.

The discussion that the men had between themselves took quite a long time and it was nearly finishing time before their ideas and suggestions were finalised, the statements that needed re written were done and Photostatted then handed in to the office clerk for forwarding to the CID.

Every minute Ray got before the arrival of the senior English police officer he looked at and studied his statement till in the end he could give it parrot fashion. The week was not long in passing and he was called to the HMSU HQ for interview, as he walked into the interview room the investigating officer cautioned him then proceeded his questioning.

"Well good morning Ray and how are you?"

Ray immediately heard warning bells sounding in his ears, what put him on his guard was that when a very senior police officer calls just an ordinary Constable by his Christian name it's time to watch out, as this was never done as normal practice.

"I'm fine thank you Sir."

"I see by your records that you're not actually from over here, in fact that you are English, well maybe you might be able to help me and throw a little light on what happened on the nights of the shootings?"

"Everything I have to say is in my statement Sir, I trust you have a copy of it with you?"

"Yes I have it here, is there anything you wish to correct, alter, or add to it?"

"No Sir."

"If I ask you any more questions about the nights in question will you be co-operative and answer them?"

"I feel Sir that what is written in my statement would be sufficient, so I see no reason to have to answer any further questions as it is a proper written account of my movements and actions that night."

"Is there anything you might have missed out?"

"No Sir."

"Would I be right in assuming that I would get the same sort of answer for everything I ask you?"

"As I have already told you I feel that what I have written and recorded in my statement I think is sufficient."

"I can see that I am wasting my time here, okay Constable you can go now, but I must warn you that you are not to speak to any of the others who have not yet been interviewed, is that understood?"

"Yes Sir," Ray replied getting up from the seat he was in and leaving the office.

The investigation went on for many weeks and at the end of it a court case was heard and no police officers were found to be guilty of any offence.

Because of the Nationalist's still wanting their pound of flesh it was decided by the Government that the whole unit should be disbanded and all of its members transferred to different stations away from the area.

It was deemed that no two police officers from the unit should work at the same station Ray for his part was transferred to the town of Banbridge which in itself was punishment enough, as about the most exciting thing that ever happened in this town was a bar fight.

The only good thing about being transferred there was that he had a lot more time to carry out his intelligence gathering.

Banbridge was the sort of place where they put most old cops out to grass, it was definitely the last place Ray wanted to be.

However he knew he would have to make the best of it his only problem would be that most of the other cops there knew of him as he had a bit of a reputation for being the sort of guy who would take no nonsense.

He had a great saying which went "I do not care if you are catholic or protestant, if you break the law you are mine"

Rays time was mostly spent dealing with the more general aspects of police work in the form of traffic accidents, shoplifters, drunk and disorderliness', thefts, and one of the main problems family disputes.

It was amazing how many husbands and their wives would get into arguments and low and behold it would nearly always end up in a physical confrontation, for the obvious reason which was the curse of the drinking of alcohol.

Ray always found that even though either the husband or wife were arrested for the assaults, every time the case was to be heard in court on the day of the court both parties would approach him saying that they had reconciled and wished to drop charges.

As most police officers know it is very frustrating having to arrest either the husband or wife then take him or her to the police station and go through all the procedure of fingerprinting, documentation, statement recording, getting a Doctor to examine the injured party, then have to write up a prosecution file.

From the start to finish of the whole case it could take several weeks before the case would reach the court.

After having this happen a few times to him, Ray decided that enough was enough and thought that if he was going to have to spend that much time on a case he was not going to let things drop, and he would then get the person who had made the initial complaint sign a statement to the fact that they would like the charges dropped.

Once he had that he would then tell the complainant that he was then going to prosecute them for "Wasteful employment of Police time"

It was not long before word got around town that he would take no messing in regards to family disputes, and whenever he was sent to these disputes he would always inform both parties that should they decide to change their minds and drop charges he would definitely have one of them prosecuted.